HARDCASTLE'S RUNAWAY

Graham Ison

This first world edition published 2017
in Great Britain and the USA by
SEVERN HOUSE PUBLISHERS LTD of
Eardley House, 4 Uxbridge Street, London W8 7SY.
Trade paperback edition first published
in Great Britain and the USA 2018 by
SEVERN HOUSE PUBLISHERS LTD.

Copyright © 2017 by Graham Ison.

British Library Cataloguing in Publication Data
A CIP catalogue record for this title is available from the British Library.

ISBN-13: 978-0-7278-8701-6 (cased)
ISBN-13: 978-1-84751-804-0 (trade paper)
ISBN-13: 978-1-78010-868-1 (e-book)

Typeset by Palimpsest Book Production Ltd.,
Falkirk, Stirlingshire, Scotland.

GLOSSARY

'A' FROM A BULL'S FOOT, to know: to know nothing.
APM: assistant provost marshal (a lieutenant colonel attached to the military police).

BAILEY, the: Central Criminal Court, Old Bailey, London.
BAILIWICK: area of responsibility.
BEF: British Expeditionary Force in France and Flanders.
BLACK ANNIE: a police or prison van.
BLADE: a dashing young man.
BLIGHTY ONE: a wound suffered in battle that necessitated repatriation to the United Kingdom.
BLIGHTY: the United Kingdom (*ex* Hindi *Bilayati*: far away).
BOB: a shilling (now 5p).
BOCHE: derogatory term for Germans, particularly soldiers.

CAGMAG: unwholesome meat; offal.
CAT'S PAW: a dupe.
CID: Criminal Investigation Department.
CLOBBER: clothing.
CLYDE (*as in* D'YOU THINK I CAME UP THE CLYDE ON A BICYCLE?): to suggest that the speaker is a fool.
COCK-AND-BULL STORY: an idle, silly or incredible story.
COMMISSIONER'S OFFICE: official title of New Scotland Yard, headquarters of the Metropolitan Police.
COPPER: a policeman.
CULLY: alternative to calling a man 'mate'.

DAPM: deputy assistant provost marshal.
DARTMOOR: a remote prison on Dartmoor in Devon.
DDI: divisional detective inspector.
DERBY ACT or DERBY LAW: Military Service Act 1916, formulated by Lord Derby, that introduced conscription.

DING-DONG: a fight or argument.
DOOLALLY TAP: of unsound mind (*ex* Hindi).
DPP: Director of Public Prosecutions.

EARWIGGING: listening.

FORM: previous convictions.
FOURPENNY CANNON, a: a steak-and-kidney pie.
FROCK COAT: term adopted by the military in the Great War to describe politicians.
FRONT, The: theatre operations in France and Flanders during the Great War.

GANDER, to cop a: to take a look.
GILD THE LILY, to: to exaggerate.
GUV *or* **GUV'NOR:** informal alternative to 'sir'.

JIG-A-JIG: sexual intercourse.

KATE CARNEY: army (rhyming slang: from Kate Carney, a music-hall comedienne of the late nineteenth and early twentieth centuries).
KATE short for **KATE CARNEY:** see above.

LASH-UP, a: a mess.

MANOR: a police area.
MC: Military Cross.

NICK: a police station *or* prison *or* to arrest *or* to steal.

OCCURRENCE BOOK: handwritten record of *every* incident occurring at a police station.
OLD BAILEY: Central Criminal Court, in Old Bailey, London.

PEACH, to: to inform to the police.
PICCADILLY WINDOW: a monocle.

POT AND PAN, OLD: father (rhyming slang: old man).
PROVOST, the: military police.

QUID: £1 sterling.

RECEIVER, The: the senior Scotland Yard official respon-
sible for the finances of the Metropolitan Police.
RIC: The Royal Irish Constabulary.
RNVR: Royal Naval Volunteer Reserve.

SAM BROWNE: a military officer's belt with shoulder strap.
SAPPERS: the Corps of Royal Engineers (in the singular a
member of that corps).
SHILLING: now 5p.
SKIP or **SKIPPER:** an informal police alternative to station-
sergeant, clerk-sergeant and sergeant.
SMOKE, The: London.
STAGE-DOOR JOHNNIE: man who frequents theatres in
an attempt to make the acquaintance of actresses.
STANHOPE: (usually with a lower case 's') a two- or
four-wheeled horse-drawn carriage for one person.
SWADDY: a soldier. (*ex* Hindi).

TOPPING: a murder or hanging.
TURNIP WATCH: an old-fashioned, thick, silver pocket
watch.
TWO-AND-EIGHT, in a: in a state (rhyming slang).
TITFER: a hat (rhyming slang: tit for tat).
TUPPENNY-HA'PENNY: a contraction of twopence-
halfpenny, indicating something or someone of little worth.

UNDERGROUND, The: the London Underground railway
system.

WALLAH: someone employed in a specific office (*ex* Hindi).
WAX to be in a: to be in a rage.

ONE

The euphoria that had engulfed the nation with the signing of the Armistice in November 1918 did not last for very long. By March 1919 the full effects of the Great War were beginning to take their toll. Factories producing the shells that had rained down on the enemy were, at best, now equipping their workshops to cater for the demands of peace. Others stood idle, their employees made redundant. Mills that had manufactured huge quantities of army uniforms, and those plants producing food or other necessaries for the military were suddenly faced with the disappearance of those markets and the real possibility of bankruptcy. It meant that in many cases war workers were now without jobs, but as many of them were women, and returned to their pre-war life of domesticity, the impact was not as great as had been feared.

And there was another problem. Sir Robert Horne, the Minister of Labour, decided that skilled men, essential to post-war industry, would be released from the armed forces first. But as they were often the last to have been conscripted, the long-serving men were incensed; riots followed, and in some cases mutinies. To resolve this wave of discontent and disorder, Winston Churchill instituted the principle of 'first in, first out'.

Nevertheless, blind men and men with missing limbs thronged the streets in search of work that was not there, and many discharged officers were persuaded to invest their meagre savings in dubious ventures that inevitably failed. Rudyard Kipling's evocative poem *Tommy* sprang to mind when it became apparent that 'our brave boys', who had 'fought the good fight' were in many cases regarded as an embarrassment.

The Kaiser had fled to the Netherlands where that ambivalent nation – one that had remained stolidly neutral throughout the war – charitably afforded him asylum. Attempts to extradite him for war crimes were thwarted by Queen Wilhelmina. And in Versailles the victors raked over the ashes of war, argued about the terms of a seemingly elusive peace treaty and attempted to calculate how much a bankrupt Germany could be expected to pay in reparations. When it came to it, they paid very little. In the meantime, British soldiers were deployed in support of the White Russians, who were hoping vainly to turn the flood tide of Bolshevism.

These troubles were serious enough, but they were now in danger of being overshadowed by a threat far graver even than the Great War and its consequences. The death toll of the influenza pandemic looked set to exceed the total of fatalities that the world had inflicted upon itself during the 'war to end all wars'.

Divisional Detective Inspector Ernest Hardcastle, head of the CID for the A or Whitehall Division of the Metropolitan Police, had his office on the first floor of Cannon Row police station. He was fully aware of the impact that the depressing state of the nation was having on crime. Figures were already reflecting an increase in burglaries, larceny and in some cases even smash-and-grab raids, principally on jewellers' shops and other purveyors of high-value goods.

Pawnbrokers did not escape this onslaught of crime either. In many cases, pawned goods were unlikely to be redeemed, their owners getting deeper into debt as the weeks passed without work. Occasionally, though, those owners had other ideas, and the police strongly suspected that they were repossessing their goods and chattels by way of shop-breaking, it being the only way in which they could lay hands on them again.

However, none of this occupied Hardcastle's mind on the morning of Monday the third of March, 1919.

'Good morning, sir.' Detective Sergeant Charles Marriott stepped into the DDI's office. Marriott was the first-class sergeant who oversaw the work of the junior detectives in the Cannon Row subdivision. He was also the officer whom Hardcastle invariably chose as his assistant whenever he investigated a murder. At thirty-six years of age, the six-foot tall

Marriott had a youthful appearance and the sort of chiselled features that caused many women to afford him a second glance and a hopeful smile. But they hoped in vain; Marriott was happily married to Lorna, a striking blonde only an inch or two shorter than her husband. And he adored their two children.

'What is it, Marriott?' Hardcastle, hands in his pockets, had been staring down into Westminster Underground station, but turned from the window as his sergeant entered the room.

'Detective Superintendent Wensley's clerk telephoned, sir. You're to see Mr Wensley as soon as possible. His clerk stressed the urgency, sir.'

'He stressed the urgency, did he, Marriott? Prone to panic, is he, this clerk of Mr Wensley's, eh? Still a PC, is he? Or have they made him a sergeant?'

Marriott permitted himself a brief smile; his chief was clearly in a jocular mood this morning. 'I don't think so, sir. He's been Mr Wensley's clerk for some time.'

'That's the trouble with these tuppenny-ha'penny pen-pushers, Marriott; they've been in the job so long they think the trumpets are sounding for them as well. Time they were sent back to the streets to find out what real police work's like.'

'Yes, sir.' Marriott, sensing the onset of one of Hardcastle's tirades about those he called 'office-wallahs', decided that a monosyllabic reply was the safest form of response.

Hardcastle glanced at his chrome half-hunter, wound it briefly and dropped it back into his waistcoat pocket. 'Better see what he wants, I suppose.' Putting on his bowler hat and grabbing his umbrella, without either of which he would never be seen outside, he made his way across the narrow roadway between Cannon Row police station and Commissioner's Office, as policemen are wont to call New Scotland Yard.

When Hardcastle had joined the Metropolitan Police twenty-eight years ago, he had stared in awe at Norman Shaw's impressive building. Then but a year old and already being referred to colloquially as 'the Yard', it had been built of Dartmoor granite hewn by convicts from the prison situated on that bleak moorland. Dominating Victoria Embankment, the Yard towered over most of the nearby buildings. But

Hardcastle was no longer impressed by it; he had visited it too often.

'All correct, sir.' At the top of the flight of steps leading to the main entrance, a constable opened the heavy door and saluted.

Hardcastle grunted in reply; he was always irritated by the routine reports which uniformed officers were obliged to make, and which they made whether everything was all correct or not. But, perversely, he would be just as annoyed if a junior officer omitted so to report.

It was only a short walk along the stone-flagged corridor to Wensley's office. Removing his bowler hat and hooking his umbrella over one arm, Hardcastle knocked lightly and entered without awaiting a response.

Detective Superintendent Frederick Wensley was an imposing figure, always immaculately dressed in a dark suit, laundered white shirt with wing collar and a pearl tiepin. He had been dubbed 'Ace' by the popular newspapers on account of his detective prowess, but to the officers under his command he was known by the irreverent sobriquet of 'Elephant' – an acknowledgment of the size of his nose. When he had started his career in the CID he had been a teetotaller, but that changed when he found that informants would not trust a detective who refused to take a drink with them. Now fifty-four years of age, he had been a policeman for thirty-one years and was in charge of all the detectives in a quarter of the capital, including most of East London and Bow Street.

'Does the name Austen Musgrave mean anything to you, Ernie?' asked Wensley, having told Hardcastle to sit down.

'I can't say it does, sir.'

'He's a member of parliament and lives in Vincent Square on your manor.'

'Has he been murdered, sir?' Hardcastle was already formulating the severe reprimand he would deliver to Detective Inspector Alexander Neville, the officer in charge of the CID for the Rochester Row subdivision, for failing to report this murder to him, news of which had somehow reached Mr Wensley before Hardcastle had learned of it.

'No, he's very much alive, but Mr Musgrave is worried

about his seventeen-year-old daughter. Apparently she's a bit of a wayward girl and has been missing for three days now. He's asked for police assistance in tracing her.'

'But the Uniform Branch deals with missing persons, sir,' protested Hardcastle. 'It's hardly a job for—'

'I know, Ernie,' said Wensley, raising a staying hand, 'but Mr Musgrave happens to be a friend of the Commissioner and he telephoned him this morning asking for assistance. Sir Nevil sent for me and asked me to put my best detective on to the matter. And now, Ernie, you're about to meet him.'

'Mr Musgrave, sir?'

'Not immediately,' said Wensley. 'You're to see the Commissioner first.'

Walking further along the corridor from Wensley's office, the two detectives mounted the several flights of stairs that led to the Commissioner's turret office overlooking the River Thames.

'Go in, Mr Wensley,' said the Commissioner's secretary. 'Sir Nevil is expecting you.'

Although Hardcastle had never met the man still referred to as the 'new' Commissioner, he knew something of his background. A professional soldier and now fifty-six years of age, General Sir Nevil Macready had spent the first two years of the Great War in France with the BEF, but in 1916 he had been appointed Adjutant-General to the Forces and transferred to the War Office in London. Unusually for a general, he was clean-shaven, but one of Macready's first acts in his new appointment was to rescind the order requiring all soldiers to have a moustache. Once that order was signed, Macready visited a barber and had his own 'unsightly bristles', as he termed them, shaved off.

'So you're Ernie Hardcastle.' After spending a few seconds appraising the A Division DDI's stocky figure and affording his bushy moustache an amused glance, Macready stood up and skirted his desk to shake hands with him. 'Mr Wensley says you're one of his best detectives.'

'Thank you, sir.' Hardcastle was stunned that the Commissioner had addressed him so informally. But that familiarity bore out what was already known throughout the

Force – that Macready was not averse to talking to constables and sergeants in order to better assess the morale of the rank and file. And in an attempt to discover whether there was likely to be a repeat of the abortive police strike that had taken place last year. Macready preferred to call it a mutiny and it had brought about his appointment following the resignation of the former commissioner, Sir Edward Henry.

'I imagine that Mr Wensley has told you that Austen Musgrave is a friend of mine.'

'Yes, sir.'

'Austen Musgrave made a great deal of money during the war manufacturing uniforms. He earned it honestly, which makes a refreshing change, and has contributed a substantial sum to soldiers' charities. But, like so many busy men, he had little time to devote to his only daughter and I gather, from what he's told me, that she's rather gone off the rails. Now, it seems, she's gone missing.'

'I see, sir.' Hardcastle was still overawed by the Commissioner's affable approach, which was unlike his predecessor's somewhat formal and starchy character, though Hardcastle had never met Henry. 'Am I to take it that Mrs Musgrave is deceased, sir?'

'Not as far as I know. I believe Marie Musgrave is estranged from her husband and lives somewhere in the shires but I'm not sure about that. Lily – she's the missing daughter – preferred to stay with her father, presumably because the location of his house affords easy access to the bright lights of London.'

'Is Mr Musgrave at home, sir? It being a Monday, sometimes the gentry aren't back from the country.' Hardcastle was struggling to formulate the right sentences with which to address the Commissioner.

Macready smiled. 'Yes, he telephoned me from Vincent Square this morning.'

'I'll go and see him immediately, sir.' Hardcastle paused. 'I usually take my best sergeant with me on enquiries, sir. I wonder if—'

Macready raised a hand. 'My dear fellow, you must do exactly as you see fit. I know very little about the police force, although I'm learning fast, and I know even less about the detective department. Mr Wensley trusts you and so, therefore, do I. Go about this case exactly as you would any other.'

'Would you want a daily report, sir?' asked Wensley of the Commissioner.

'Good heavens, no, Fred,' said Macready. 'I can't abide negative reports, and in any case I'm sure you'll keep an eye on things. Just let me know if there are any developments in the matter. And now, I'll not delay you gentlemen any further. Good day to you both.'

'Marriott!' Hardcastle shouted for his sergeant as he passed the open door of the detectives' office. 'Come in here, now.'

Quickly buttoning his waistcoat and donning his jacket, Marriott hurried across the passageway to the DDI's office. 'Sir?'

'We've got a missing-person enquiry to deal with, Marriott.' Hardcastle began filling his pipe with his favourite St Bruno tobacco.

'But—'

'Before you say anything else, Marriott, I've just seen the Commissioner and he's assigned me to this case. And when the Commissioner tells you to do something, you do it.'

'Yes, sir.' There was little else that Marriott could say in the face of the DDI's truism.

'Sit down, m'boy.' It was rare for Hardcastle to invite Marriott to sit down and equally rare for him to adopt a familiar approach. 'I've been in the Job for twenty-eight years,' he began reflectively, 'and this morning was the first time I've ever met a Commissioner, even though I've now served under three of them.' Lighting his pipe and blowing a plume of tobacco smoke towards the nicotine-stained ceiling of his office, the DDI told Marriott what he knew so far of the matter of the missing Lily Musgrave, which was precious little. 'And now we'll go to Mr Musgrave's house in Vincent Square and see what's what.'

When Hardcastle and Marriott alighted from their cab, the DDI paused and looked thoughtfully around Vincent Square.

'That's the back of Rochester Row nick, across there,
Marriott,' he said, pointing to a building on the far side of
the square, in the centre of which was Westminster School's
playing field. 'I wonder if the idle coppers who live in the
section house there saw anything.'

'I wouldn't think it would be anything useful, sir,' ventured
Marriott, not for the first time failing to follow his DDI's line
of reasoning. He doubted the girl had been abducted from
her own home and dragged out kicking and screaming to a
waiting motor car. But Hardcastle disliked any comment that
bordered on the sarcastic, although he was not above making
such comments himself.

Hardcastle turned and mounted the twelve steps leading to
the front door of Austen Musgrave's house, a three-storey
dwelling with a basement area. There was a railed balcony
on the first floor where the bedrooms were located.

'Good morning, sir.' The butler was a man of mature years
and, as befitted his profession, immaculately attired in tailcoat
and striped trousers.

'I'm Divisional Detective Inspector Hardcastle of the
Whitehall Division.'

'Quite so, sir. You are expected. If you'll follow me,
gentlemen, the master is in the morning room.' The butler
opened a door on the far side of the hall. 'The gentlemen
from the police, sir,' he announced.

Musgrave did not have the appearance Hardcastle was
expecting of a rich industrialist. Clean-shaven and probably
in his early fifties, his wavy, iron-grey hair was a little longer
than was fashionable. Although he was dressed in a dark suit,
he wore no waistcoat, and to add to the DDI's amazement he
had a soft-collared shirt and a rather flamboyant tie.

'I'm Divisional Detective Inspector Hardcastle, sir, and this
is Detective Sergeant Marriott.'

Austen Musgrave crossed the room and shook hands with
each of the detectives. 'Make yourselves comfortable, Mr
Hardcastle and Mr Marriott.' He indicated armchairs with a
wave of his hand. 'I'm about to have some coffee. I'm sure
you'd like to join me.'

'Very kind, sir,' murmured Hardcastle.

'I must say that I didn't really expect any preferential treatment when I telephoned Nevil this morning about Lily, but he said he'd put his best detectives on the case.'

'I hope we can live up to the Commissioner's expectations, sir,' said Hardcastle.

Having instructed Crabb to arrange the coffee, Musgrave turned to the matter in hand. 'Now then, what d'you want from me, Mr Hardcastle?'

'When did you last see your daughter?' The DDI signalled to Marriott to take notes.

'Last Thursday,' said Musgrave promptly. 'That would've been the . . .' He paused, calculating.

'The twenty-seventh of February, sir,' said Marriott, glancing up from his note-taking.

'Yes, that would be it,' said Musgrave. 'She left the house at about half-past seven, I suppose.'

'Did she say where she was going, sir?' Hardcastle asked.

'Not precisely, Inspector, no. She said she was going up to the West End to meet an old school friend. When I asked who this friend was, she refused to say and she also declined to say where exactly in the West End she was making for. But I suspect she was meeting a man.'

'What makes you say that?' asked the DDI.

'She'd taken special care with her cosmetics.'

Hardcastle had doubts about Musgrave's last statement. His own two daughters, Kitty and Maud, always took great care with their appearance regardless of who they were meeting. And that prompted Hardcastle to pose a question about the girl's mother, but he was forestalled by Austen Musgrave.

'The real problem, Inspector, is that Lily's mother no longer lives with me. And that means the girl is lacking the occasional stern word of maternal caution about her conduct.' Musgrave did not enlarge upon the reason behind his separation from his wife.

'Do you have a photograph of Miss Musgrave, sir?' asked Marriott.

'Yes, I do. Ah, the coffee. Put it down over there, Crabb, if you please, and perhaps you'd fetch the photograph of Miss Lily that's in my study.'

'Very good, sir.'

The photograph that Crabb handed to Musgrave proved to be useless in terms of identifying the missing seventeen-year-old. It showed a demure young woman attired in a full-length dress with her hair worn long and a face devoid of make-up.

'I'm afraid she looked nothing like that when she left here on Thursday, Mr Hardcastle.' Musgrave sighed and passed the framed photograph to the DDI. 'She'd had her beautiful hair cut quite short and was wearing an unbelievably short dress with a long string of beads that reached almost to her waist. And she had one of those ridiculous bandeaus around her forehead with a feather in it. As for her face, well, Inspector, I've not seen the like of it: eyes surrounded by kohl or something similar that made her look as though she'd received two black eyes in a fight.'

Hardcastle nodded sagely. 'I'm afraid that's the way young women are starting to dress these days, sir.' That said, he was fairly sure that his wife, Alice, would do her best to prevent their daughters Kitty and Maud leaving the house dressed in such a fashion. But he had to admit, if only to himself, that Kitty was a strong-willed twenty-three-year-old who had spent most of the war years as a conductorette with the London General Omnibus Company. As for Maud, she would be out of her parents' control in less than three weeks' time, when she married her army officer fiancé.

'How did Miss Musgrave travel to the West End, sir?' asked Marriott.

'I offered her the car and my chauffeur to take her, Mr Marriott, but she declined. Further proof that she didn't want me to know where she was going, I suppose. I sent Crabb out to find a taxicab.'

'I'll need to speak to Crabb, sir,' said Hardcastle.

'Of course.' Musgrave stood and made towards the bell-pull.

'I'd rather speak to him in his pantry, sir, if you don't mind. It would save taking up your time.' Hardcastle knew from experience that domestic servants were more forthcoming when their employer was not listening to what they had to say.

'If you're quite sure, Mr Hardcastle.'

'Quite definitely, sir.' The DDI stood up. 'But before I do so, I'd be obliged if you'd get someone to show me Miss Musgrave's room.'

'Why on earth would you want to see her room, Inspector?' Musgrave raised an eyebrow of curiosity rather than of censure.

'You'd be surprised what it might tell us, sir,' said Hardcastle mysteriously.

'I must say that the dark art of detection is unfamiliar to me, Inspector, although I have read *The Woman in White*.' Musgrave laughed. 'I'll show you up there myself.'

TWO

Lily Musgrave's room was similar to that of many young women of her age, something of which Hardcastle, having two daughters of his own, was well aware, but glancing around he immediately sensed a difference between his girls and the Musgraves' daughter. The decor and ornaments in Lily's room indicated to Hardcastle that not only was she spoilt, but was still very much a child. By comparison, his own eldest daughter, Kitty, was worldly and strong-willed, and Maud, although only a few years older than the missing Lily, had been matured by the harrowing task of nursing wounded officers during the war, one of whom she was about to marry.

A double bed adorned with a colourful bedspread stood in the centre of the wall opposite the window, its black and brass bedstead topped with large brass bed knobs. A rather worn and forlorn teddy bear was seated on one of the pillows. An oak wardrobe with an inset mirror stood against another wall alongside a chest of drawers, upon which were several baby dolls. To Hardcastle's discerning eye the Turkey carpet must have cost at least fifty pounds.

Musgrave picked up a copy of *Horner's Penny Stories* from

a bedside table and tossed it into a wastepaper basket. 'I've
told her time and time again not to read those trashy maga-
zines, Inspector, but she won't listen to anything I say these
days.' He sighed deeply.

'Maybe so, sir,' said Hardcastle, 'but I'd rather you didn't
disturb anything until my sergeant's had a look round.'

'Oh, of course. I do apologize.' Musgrave paused. 'But a
magazine of that sort is not what you'd call a clue, is it?'

'I've no way of knowing until I've examined it,' said
Hardcastle, a little tersely. 'But it might be evidence.'

'Evidence?' Musgrave sounded a little alarmed at the DDI's
use of the word.

'Evidence of where Miss Musgrave might've gone, sir. She
may have made notes in it. Young girls are inclined to do
unpredictable things like that.'

'Yes, I suppose so.' Musgrave reflected on what Hardcastle
had said. 'It would probably be better if I left you gentlemen
to get on with your work, but perhaps you'd come and see
me again before you leave. I shall be in the morning room.'

Once Musgrave had departed, Hardcastle and Marriott
began a meticulous examination of the room. It was not, of
course, the scene of a crime, but rather somewhere that may
yield an indication of where the missing Lily had gone.

'This might be interesting, sir,' said Marriott, holding up
a leather-bound book secured by a small brass lock designed
to keep the contents from prying eyes.

Hardcastle took hold of the book and examined the lock.
'You should be able to open that easily enough, Marriott. See
what you can do.'

It took Marriott no more than a few seconds to break the
flimsy lock and he thumbed through the pages of the book.

'What's it about, Marriott? A diary, is it?'

'Not as such, sir, although it looks like a day-to-day account
of what she's been doing. I can't see anything useful in it.'

'Bring it with you, though. I'll examine it later.'

'D'you think we ought to get Mr Musgrave's permission, sir?'

'No, I don't, Marriott. I'll just tell him I've seized it,' said
Hardcastle firmly. 'Anything else?'

'Nothing that will assist, sir. Plenty of frocks and fancy

underwear and jewellery; all expensive stuff by the looks of it. There's some make-up on the dressing table that's got labels on it that I don't recognize. It looks expensive, too.'

'Would be,' muttered Hardcastle. 'I'm coming to the conclusion that Lily Musgrave is an empty-headed, spoiled young woman, Marriott,' he said, giving voice to the thoughts he had entertained the moment he set foot in Lily's bedroom. 'I daresay her father will give her anything she asks for.' He was already tiring of the ostentatious way in which the obvious wealth of the Musgrave family was displayed. Furthermore, he was a little piqued that Musgrave should have used his influence with the Commissioner that resulted in Hardcastle doing a job that should have been dealt with by a Uniform Branch inspector at best. 'Might be a gift from some fancy man. From what Musgrave was saying, I rather think that his precious Lily has been seeing someone. Probably a bit of jig-n-jig an' all. Whenever a young woman starts acting all secretive there's usually a beau at the end of it. What's more, it usually ends in tears. Something you'll have to keep an eye on when your young lass is of an age.'

'Yes, sir, I certainly will,' said a somewhat mystified Marriott. He didn't foresee any problems with his daughter, Doreen, but she was only eight years of age and his wife Lorna didn't stand for any nonsense, even at that age.

'You didn't come across any letters, I suppose. Nothing like that?'

'Nothing, sir.'

'In that case we'll go down and see if Crabb can shed any light on this young lady. In my experience, Marriott, butlers are the only people in a household what know everything that's going on.'

'Yes, sir.' Marriott received that little homily on every occasion that he and the DDI had occasion to talk to domestic staff.

It was spartan and gloomy below stairs in Austen Musgrave's house, brought more into contrast by the luxury of the upstairs rooms. It was, however, no different from the other great houses that Hardcastle and Marriott had visited.

In common with most of those houses, there was a kitchen,

a scullery and a servants' hall with stone-flagged flooring throughout that lent a cold feeling to the entire area. One wall in the kitchen bore a collection of copper saucepans while against another was a huge range that doubtless was kept alight permanently.

The moment the two detectives appeared in the doorway of the servants' hall, a buxom, grey-haired woman put down her knitting on the long, scrubbed table where the staff took their meals and stood up. Her expression was one of surprise coupled with a measure of apprehension at the arrival of two strangers who were not members of the family and clearly not tradesmen.

'Can I help you, sir? I'm Mrs Briggs, the cook. And do mind your step, sir: the skivvy's only just washed the floor. We weren't expecting nobody to come down from upstairs, you see, sir.'

'We're police officers, Mrs Briggs,' said Hardcastle. 'We're looking for Crabb the butler.'

'You'll find Mr Crabb in his pantry, sir. Over there,' said the cook, pointing to a door on the far side of the room. She wiped her hands on her apron – an automatic gesture when she was a little nervous and she was nervous now, her apprehension justified. She wondered why the police wanted to talk to the butler and was immediately alarmed that her petty pilfering from the household provisions had come to notice, particularly as they had become bolder since the departure of Mrs Musgrave. She was afraid that Crabb had called the police to report the matter. It was the sort of thing – in her view, anyway – that he would have done; the butler had never disguised his dislike of the cook with whom he had had several 'fallings out'. What Mrs Briggs did not know, however, was that Crabb was perpetrating his own frauds, most of which were to do with the wine cellar.

'Thank you, Mrs Briggs.' Hardcastle and Marriott avoided the damp patches on the floor and the DDI tapped on the butler's pantry door.

'Ah, Mr Hardcastle, sir.' Crabb put down a copy of yesterday's *Daily Mirror*, took off his spectacles and rose hurriedly to his feet. 'How can I help you, sir?' he asked, smarmily solicitous. 'And please take a seat, gentlemen.'

'I'm told by Mr Musgrave that you called a cab for Miss Musgrave last Thursday, Mr Crabb,' said Hardcastle once he and Marriott were seated and Crabb had resumed his seat.

'That's not quite correct, sir. I sent Dobbs, the second footman. It ain't no job for a butler going out looking for cabs, if you take my meaning, sir.'

'Quite right and proper, Mr Crabb. What time was this?'

'Dobbs came back with the cab at a quarter past seven, sir, and Miss Lily left the house at a minute or two after half past the hour.'

'I assume you opened the door for her when she left. Did you hear where she asked to be taken?'

'No, sir. She must have told the driver once she was inside but she always was a bit secretive, even as a child.'

'Where did your man Dobbs find this cab?'

'The cab shelter in Vauxhall Bridge Road, sir.'

'Excellent,' exclaimed Hardcastle.

'D'you think you'll be able to find him, sir? I mean, should you wish to do so.' Crabb raised his bushy eyebrows. Personally he would not have any idea how to go about finding one of London's four thousand or so cabmen.

'Find him?' scoffed Hardcastle. 'When I put out the word, Mr Crabb, that cabbie will be knocking on my office door before you can say Jack the Ripper.'

'Ah, I suppose so.' Crabb was duly impressed but did not understand why Hardcastle had mentioned the infamous East End murderer in the same breath. He was not, however, the most intelligent of men.

'Now, Mr Crabb, I'm going to seek your advice, knowing as I do that butlers are the fount of all knowledge.'

'Oh, very kind of you to say so, sir, I'm sure.' Crabb paused to pull his watch from his waistcoat pocket. 'I daresay you gentlemen wouldn't be averse to a glass of sherry.' Again he raised his eyebrows. 'Or perhaps something a little stronger. The master keeps a very good malt whisky.'

'Now you're talking my language,' said Hardcastle warmly. He was not much impressed by the sycophantic Crabb. In common with many of his calling, the butler tried to be all things to all people and certainly failed in the DDI's view. But Hardcastle

wanted the sort of information that he knew Crabb would possess.
Or, more to the point, would be prepared to impart.

Without moving from his chair, Crabb reached across to a
cupboard near his right hand and took out three crystal whisky
tumblers and a bottle of Laphroaig. Hardcastle just restrained
himself from licking his lips. It was his favourite malt, but
at nigh on seven shillings a bottle it was something he was
only ever able to afford once a year, usually at Christmas.

'Now, Mr Crabb,' Hardcastle began once the whisky had
been poured, 'I'd like you to be frank with me.'

'If there's anything I can do to assist you gentlemen just
say the word, sir.'

'What sort of girl is this Lily Musgrave?'

Crabb glanced at the pantry door to make certain it was
firmly closed and then leaned closer to the DDI. 'In my
opinion, Mr Hardcastle,' he said, lowering his voice, 'she's
what you might call a flighty young baggage. Anything Miss
Lily wants, Miss Lily gets. Not to put too fine a point on it,
sir, she has the master twisted round her little finger.'

Hardcastle nodded as though having his opinion confirmed.
'When did she start behaving like that?'

'The moment the mistress upped sticks and left, sir. Mind
you,' continued Crabb, moderating his voice even more, 'that
one ain't no better than she ought to be. You see, sir, she was
on the stage when the master married her,' he added, as though
mention of that profession was sufficient to define a loose
woman.

'D'you know where Mrs Musgrave went when she left
here, Mr Crabb?' asked Marriott.

'Last I heard she was kicking her legs in the air in some sort
of theatrical production at the Brighton Hippodrome. Marie Faye
she's called on the stage.' Crabb emitted a sniff of derision.

'How old is she, then?' Marriott knew that Austen Musgrave
must be at least fifty years of age.

The butler gave the question some thought before
answering. 'I'd say about thirty-six, sir. I did hear tell she
was only seventeen when Miss Lily came along, or even a
bit younger, I wouldn't be surprised.' He sniffed as if to
emphasize his scepticism. 'A bit of a mistake by all accounts,

so they say. And the cook's not sure that the master was the girl's father either. Cooks know about these things.'

'Have you any idea why Mrs Musgrave left, Mr Crabb?'

'Well, sir,' began Crabb, his voice becoming even more conspiratorial, 'her lady's maid did let slip as how the mistress was seeing another man what she'd got to know from her theatre days, but I don't know whether there was anything in it. Mind you, Mrs Musgrave's a good-looking woman and I wouldn't blame any man for taking a fancy to her. But I can tell you that Forbes – he's the first footman – did hear the master and Mrs Musgrave having a right ding-dong about an hour before she swept out of the house. She sent for her things the very next day and we haven't seen hair nor hide of her since.'

'When was this?'

'About six months ago,' said Crabb promptly.

'D'you know if Lily was seeing a man?' asked Hardcastle.

'Wouldn't surprise me, sir, not that I know for sure, of course. Mind you, like mother like daughter is what I always say, and the mistress wasn't above waggling her bum at any man she liked the look of. There again, the master's got a roving eye and all. There's an American lady called Sarah Gillard who stays here from time to time, says she's an actress. In fact, she's here now. Them stagey types seem to appeal to the master. I did hear he met up with her when he was in America, up to some dodgy business, so they say.'

'Thank you, Mr Crabb,' said Hardcastle, finishing his whisky and standing up. It was clear to him that the conversation had reached the point where speculation had replaced fact, not that there had been much of that either. 'You've been very helpful.'

'A pleasure, sir. Any time you're passing do call in.'

'I reckon Crabb will say anything to stay on the right side of the law,' said Hardcastle as he and Marriott mounted the stairs. 'Mind you, every butler I've met is like that and I'd lay odds he's fiddling Musgrave's wine account.'

'He didn't have much to say about Lily, sir.'

'No, he didn't, but I'm interested in the Musgraves. I'm wondering what Crabb meant when he mentioned dodgy business. And Lily's mother might be able to shed a bit of light on

her runaway daughter. I think we'll have a ride down to Brighton
when we've got a moment and have a word with Marie Faye,
as Mrs Musgrave is known now,' said Hardcastle as he pushed
open the door of the morning room. Austen Musgrave, reclining
in an armchair, was awaiting the detectives' return.

'Did you learn anything from Crabb that might be of
assistance, Mr Hardcastle?'

'Unfortunately, no, sir. Very tactful is your butler, disinclined
to breach a confidence, if you take my meaning.'

'Yes, he's a very trustworthy fellow. I'm lucky to have
found him.'

'Indeed you were, sir.' Hardcastle's face was impassive.
'There is just one thing, though. There was some make-up in
Miss Musgrave's room that I didn't recognize. I wondered if
it had been given to her by a man friend. Having daughters
of my own, I can usually put a name to face powder and
rouge and that sort of stuff that young girls put on their faces
these days, but not the pots in Miss Musgrave's room.'

Musgrave laughed openly. 'I can see that I was very lucky
that Nevil assigned you to search for Lily, Inspector. You obviously know what you're about. Yes, I was in America not long
before the end of the war. I'm thinking of going into business
with a textile firm that supplies costumes for the moving pictures
that are all the rage. The cinema is the coming thing and it will
soon replace the theatre. In Hollywood they're even experi-
menting with putting sound on the movies, but it will still be a
while yet before pictures with speech on them become a reality.'

'I find that hard to believe, sir,' muttered Hardcastle.

Musgrave laughed. 'If you've got any cash to spare,
Inspector, you should buy shares in the moving pictures. You
could be a rich man in a few years.'

'You seem quite taken with America, sir,' said Hardcastle,
who had no spare cash, especially as his daughter's wedding
was looming.

'There's no doubt, Mr Hardcastle, that America is the
future.' There was an almost dream-like expression on
Musgrave's face. 'It really is a go-ahead nation. It's definitely
the place to be. This suit I'm wearing is American and, as
you can see, waistcoats are becoming a thing of the past over

there, as are stiff collars. I'm angling to import some of this American clothing if I can manage to wangle my way around the import tariffs, but I've got a few friends who might be able to pull strings. You'd be amazed what can be achieved if you grease a few palms and cut a few corners.'

'That's all very interesting, sir, but the make-up?'

'Oh, yes, I'm sorry. I tend to get carried away whenever I start talking about the home of the movies. There's a man called Max Factor in Hollywood who has cornered the market in cosmetics for film stars because the old theatrical slapstick is unsuitable for cinematography. They say it looks awful on film. He gave me some of the stuff to give to Marie and Lily. That's what you saw in her room.'

'Who is Marie, sir? Is she another daughter?' Hardcastle pretended innocence well, knowing that the Commissioner had told him that Lily was an only daughter.

'No, Inspector. She's my wife but she's run away with another man.'

'I see, sir,' said Hardcastle, surprised that Musgrave was so open about his wayward wife, but assumed that it was something to do with his experience of the people involved in what he called 'the movies'. 'We'll be on our way now, sir. I'll keep you informed of any developments.'

'I'm very grateful for the trouble you're taking, Mr Hardcastle,' said Musgrave, shaking hands with each of the detectives.

'Not at all, sir.' Hardcastle forbore from saying that he had no option.

When the two detectives were once more outside in Vincent Square, Hardcastle let fly. 'I don't really know what to make of that lot, Marriott,' he said, looking around for a cab. 'I wouldn't trust Crabb the butler as far as I could throw a grand piano. And as for Austen Musgrave, he strikes me as an unreliable sort of man.' He paused as a cab drew into the kerb. 'I don't think the Commissioner knows what sort of individual Musgrave is, but I wouldn't want to claim him as a friend. In fact, I'll have a word with Mr Wensley about him. I think he should tell Sir Nevil Macready what we've found out.'

* * *

Back in his office at Cannon Row police station, Hardcastle immediately sent for Henry Catto. Within seconds the good-looking, slender figure of the detective constable tapped apprehensively on the DDI's door. A confident officer under all other circumstances and who cut a dash with the ladies, he became nervous and indecisive in Hardcastle's presence.

'You, er, wanted me, sir.'

'Yes, Catto, that's why I sent for you. And for God's sake come in, man, instead of hovering in the doorway.'

'Yes, sir.' Catto edged into the room.

'Last Thursday evening at a quarter past seven, a footman called Dobbs went to the cab shelter in Vauxhall Bridge Road and brought a cab from there back to Vincent Square.'

'Sir?' Catto was already mystified by this piece of information and was about to ask why the DDI had told him when Hardcastle appeared to have solved the problem.

'I want that driver here in my office by three o'clock this afternoon, Catto. If he argues the toss remind him that the Commissioner licences cab drivers and can just as easily take those licences away. Go!'

'Yes, sir.' Catto fled, thankful that Detective Sergeant Marriott had taught him how to go about such a task.

Catto pushed open the door of the green wooden structure in Vauxhall Bridge Road to be greeted by a wall of tobacco smoke and an overwhelming smell of frying bacon.

The cabmen inside the shelter knew immediately that the smartly-dressed man with the curly-brimmed bowler hat was not a cab driver. In fact, they knew instinctively what he was.

'Can we help you, guv'nor?' asked one driver.

'My divisional detective inspector . . .' began Catto.

'That'd bc Mr 'Ardcastle, wouldn't it, guv'nor?' asked one driver, his woollen muffler still wrapped around his neck despite the oppressive heat that prevailed inside the shelter.

'I can see you're sharper than you look,' said Catto, 'in which case you'll know what he wants.'

'We're always willing to help the law,' put in one sycophant.

'In that case, you're just the man to assist me right now,' said Catto, taking immediate advantage of the offer. 'A driver from this shelter was hired by a footman from Vincent Square last Thursday evening at just before a quarter after seven. Tell that cabbie to be in Mr Hardcastle's office at three o'clock prompt this afternoon.'

'But he might have a fare,' wailed the sycophant, regretting his offer of assistance.

'Well, he'll have to explain that to Mr Hardcastle an' you might have to an' all,' said Catto, 'but I wouldn't like to be in his boots – or yours – if he's late.' And with that parting shot, he left, slamming the door behind him.

THREE

Once Catto had been despatched to interrogate the cab drivers at their shelter in Vauxhall Bridge Road, Hardcastle and Marriott made their way to the down-stairs bar of the Red Lion in Derby Gate. Situated immediately outside New Scotland Yard, this particular pub was a favourite with the detectives both at the Yard and at Cannon Row police station, and Albert, the landlord, knew them all by name.

'Good morning to you, Mr Hardcastle, Mr Marriott.' Regardless of the time, Albert always greeted his customers with a 'good morning' until he had had his dinner, as he called it, after the pub closed at half past two. He gave the spotless top of his bar a cursory wipe with a cloth and then, unbidden, poured a pint of bitter for each of them.

'Good afternoon, Albert.' Hardcastle took the head off his beer but made no attempt to pay. Even if he had done so, his money would have been refused; Albert was at pains to keep on the right side of the head of the CID for the police station he referred to as his local nick. Not that Albert had any fears on that score; he was a law-abiding licensee and ran an orderly public house. As he often said to his wife, he would be a fool to do otherwise with that many policemen right on the doorstep.

'Busy, Mr Hardcastle, or has it eased off a bit since the

Armistice?' Albert scratched his rather long nose and inclined his head to one side.

Hardcastle scoffed and wiped his moustache with the back of his hand. 'Eased off? It's got worse, Albert. We've now got a whole load of ex-soldiers milling about the place. And don't forget they've spent the last four years killing and plundering. If you think about it, they're difficult habits to shake off.'

'Yes, I suppose so,' said Albert and, not wishing to get involved in a lengthy discussion, moved along the bar to serve another customer.

'What d'you make of this business with Lily Musgrave, Marriott?' Hardcastle drained his glass and pushed it across the bar. 'Two more pints when you've a moment, Albert,' he said as he caught the landlord's eye, 'and a couple of fourpenny cannons.'

'Coming right up, Mr H.' Albert opened the hatch between the bar and the kitchen and repeated the order for two steak-and-kidney pies to his wife who, as Hardcastle frequently said, made the best fourpenny cannons in London.

'I think Austen Musgrave is the sort of man who makes friends with anyone he thinks might do him some good, sir.' Marriott was surprised that Hardcastle had sought his opinion; it did not often happen. 'I'm not sure the Commissioner knows what sort of friend he's got there. Personally I wouldn't trust him an inch.'

'Yes, well, I said as much earlier, and that's why I'm seeing Mr Wensley this afternoon, Marriott. Of course, when Sir Nevil described Musgrave as a friend, he might well have meant that he was an acquaintance. There's a great deal of difference, you know,' Hardcastle added philosophically. 'I suppose when you're the Commissioner all sorts of people toady up to you, just to be on the safe side.'

Inspector Eric Crozier was the officer in charge of the Palace of Westminster police and it was said that he knew everything that went on in both Houses of Parliament. But those who knew him had quickly discovered that this apparent omniscience was one of Crozier's boasts rather that a view shared by others. Shortly after being appointed to his present post, he had deemed it necessary to take elocution lessons in order to impress the peers and members of the Commons with whom he dealt on an almost daily basis. It is fair to say, however, that members of the Lords and the Commons were far too busy to notice any change. In fact, they hardly noticed Crozier at all, but the inspector's subordinates thought this newly acquired affectation to be rather amusing. As a consequence, this self-important, red-faced and overweight man had become something of a figure of fun as he strode pompously around the Palace of Westminster. Hardcastle dismissed him as being full of piss and importance, from which it may be deduced that he was a little piqued that Hardcastle should have sent for him, but Hardcastle, as a DDI, was a class-two inspector whereas Crozier was a class three.

'You *sent* for me, sir.' Crozier positively oozed resentment as he entered Hardcastle's office and saluted punctiliously before removing his cap.

'It was good of you to come so quickly, Mr Crozier,' said Hardcastle with a heavy sarcasm that went unnoticed by Crozier. 'Do take a seat.'

'I do have pressing duties to perform, sir.' Crozier glanced at the clock in the DDI's office and spoke as though his own responsibilities were so onerous as to outweigh those of mere detectives.

'But not as important as the matter I have to discuss with you now, Mr Crozier.' Hardcastle was rapidly tiring of this inspector's pretentiousness. 'I saw the Commissioner this morning and Sir Nevil gave me a special task to undertake. I wouldn't want to tell him that I didn't get any help from you.'

'Oh, indeed not, sir,' said Crozier, becoming positively sycophantic at the mention of Sir Nevil Macready and impressed that Hardcastle had actually spoken to him. 'We at the Palace of Westminster are only too willing to assist, as you know, sir.'

'What d'you know of Austen Musgrave, Mr Crozier?' Hardcastle took his half-smoked pipe from the ashtray and, having lit it, leaned back to await the inspector's reply.

'A very pleasant and cultured gentleman, sir.'

'Don't give me all that parliamentary claptrap, Mr Crozier,' exploded Hardcastle testily. 'What's the real story? From what I've heard, he's bent.' The DDI had only slender evidence to support that allegation but Crozier did not know that.

The Palace of Westminster inspector blinked and emitted a nervous cough. 'Er, well, I 'ave 'eard rumours about 'is dealings during the war, sir, but I can't specify as 'ow what they might be, so to speak.' Unnerved by Hardcastle's straight talking and hectoring tone, Crozier's elocution lessons were forgotten and he regressed to the idiom of the Hoxton where he had been born and raised. Nevertheless, he tried to maintain the sort of gentility of accent usually found in seaside boarding-house landladies.

'That's more like it. What else d'you know? And this better be kosher, Mr Crozier, because I don't want to find that you've been misleading the Commissioner.'

Hardcastle's neat shift of responsibility from himself to Crozier further unnerved the inspector. 'I did 'ear that some of the uniforms what he was turning out in his factories was substandard, but they was still sent off and it wasn't until they got to the Front that it was found out how bad they was. But they was too busy fighting the war that they never 'ad time to do nothing about it and it all got forgotten.'

'And now?' demanded Hardcastle.

'Now, sir?' Crozier was starting to perspire a little, despite it being quite a cold day, and Hardcastle's office was not overheated.

'Yes, Mr Crozier, now. What are they saying about Musgrave now?'

'Well, I did 'ear that Mr Musgrave is pulling a few strings to try and get round the tariff restrictions so's 'e can export some fancy clobber to America for them new-fangled talking pictures they're gettin' all excited about.' Crozier ran a finger around the inside of his stiff tunic collar which suddenly felt too tight.

'Where did you hear that?'

For a moment it seemed that Crozier would refuse, but then he relented in the face of Hardcastle's frown. 'You gets to 'ear all sorts of scuttlebutt just by standing in the Central Lobby, sir. You'd be surprised at 'ow indiscreet some members of the 'ouse can be.'

'I'm not at all surprised,' said Hardcastle dismissively. 'Thank you, Mr Crozier. That'll be all. If you hear anything else to Musgrave's detriment, you'll let me know immediately. Is that understood?'

'Yes, sir.' A relieved Crozier stood up but paused in the doorway. 'There's one other thing, sir: it's common knowledge round the Central Lobby that Mr Musgrave's after a Cabinet job, but that might just be more scuttlebutt.'

'I reckon our political rulers have got bugger-all else to do but stand around gossiping,' commented Hardcastle. But the comment was lost on Inspector Crozier, who had left as fast as he could.

'Excuse me, sir, but there's a Joshua Fairbrass downstairs asking to see you.' A uniformed constable hovered in the doorway of the DDI's office.

'Are you going to let me into the secret, lad, or do I have to guess?' enquired Hardcastle sarcastically. He always called constables 'lad' regardless of their age and he was in a worse mood than usual after his encounter with the servile Crozier.

'Er, the secret, sir?' The PC's face screwed itself into an expression of perplexity.

'Yes, lad. Who the bloody hell is Joshua Fairbrass?'

'Oh, yes, sir, I see, sir. He's a cab driver and he reckons he was told to come here by Detective Constable Catto, sir.'

'Well, don't stand there – bring the bloody man up here.'

A minute or two later the stooped and dishevelled figure of the cab driver edged nervously round the door of the DDI's office. He had a moustache and a full, unkempt beard. His brown overcoat reached almost to his ankles and, judging by the frayed state of the lapels, it had clearly seen better days. He held a bowler hat in his mittened hands, constantly revolving it between his fingers. The hat was now so old that it was shiny in places and most of the brim had lost its original braiding.

'Begging your pardon, sir. Joshua Fairbrass at your service.' The voice was deep and throaty.

'You were hired to take a young lady from a house in

Vincent Square at about half past seven on the evening of
Thursday the twenty-seventh of February, Fairbrass. Where
did you take her?'

'Er, I don't rightly remember, sir.' Fairbrass looked hungrily
at Hardcastle's tobacco pouch as the DDI began to fill his
pipe.

Hardcastle placed his pipe on his desk and leaned menac-
ingly towards Fairbrass. 'Well, my lad, there's no reward for
giving information to the police but you'd be well advised to
start remembering if you want to hang on to your hackney
carriage driver's licence.'

'Ah, yes,' said Fairbrass rapidly, 'it's coming back to me
now, sir.'

'I thought it might,' said Hardcastle as he picked up his
pipe and applied a match to it. 'Well?' He expelled a plume
of smoke towards the ceiling.

'Rupert Street, sir.'

'Where in Rupert Street?'

'Ah, now, let me think.' Fairbrass tugged at his beard.

Hardcastle stood up and slapped the top of his desk with
the flat of his hand so violently that the cab driver took a
step back, doubtless fearing he was about to be attacked. 'I
don't have any time to waste on you, Fairbrass,' he said, 'but
I could certainly find the time to cancel your licence, after
which you'll have plenty of spare time to think where you
took her.'

'It was the VanDoo Club, guv'nor,' said Fairbrass hurriedly.
'They calls it that on account of it being at number twenty-
two, see.'

'I'd more or less worked that out,' said Hardcastle drily.
'Is that the only time you took that young lady there?'

'As far as I know, sir. To tell you the truth, all these young
flappers look the same to me.'

'They might all look the same but what was this young
lady wearing?'

'She had on one of them short black dresses what hardly
covered her knees. I tell you, guv'nor, if my Daisy come
down the stairs looking like that my Mabel would have a few
sharp words to say to her.'

'I daresay, Fairbrass, but what else d'you remember about your fare?'

'She had a sort of black band thing round her head an' all with a feather stuck in it and a long string of beads what must've come down to her belly button. Oh, and she had black eyes. If you want my opinion she looked like she'd been dragged through a hedge backwards.'

'What d'you mean, she had black eyes?'

'It was that make-up stuff. I dunno if it was that kohl what they puts on 'em but I've heard that these days they uses ash outta the fire grate mixed up with Vaseline. But whatever it is, they put it all round their eyes. Gawd knows why, 'cos they looks bloody stupid.' The cab driver paused. 'In my opinion, o' course.'

'All right, Fairbrass, you can go.' Hardcastle waved a hand of dismissal. Donning his Chesterfield overcoat and seizing his bowler hat and umbrella, he crossed to the detectives' office on the other side of the corridor. As he pushed open the door, Marriott and the few detectives who were there rose to their feet.

'Sir?' Seeing that the DDI was about to go out, Marriott grabbed his jacket from the back of his chair.

'We're going to twenty-two Rupert Street, Marriott. That cab driver that Catto turned up took Lily Musgrave there last Thursday evening.'

'May I remind you that you were going to see Mr Wensley with your suspicions about Austen Musgrave, sir?'

'I haven't forgotten, but I've decided to gather a bit more information about Musgrave before I worry the superintendent. I don't want to pass on any information that ain't strictly true, so to speak.'

'Very good, sir.' Quickly buttoning his waistcoat and grabbing his bowler hat and overcoat, Marriott raced after the DDI as he descended the stairs.

Hardcastle swept through the front office so fast that the station officer hardly had time to leap to his feet and report that all was correct.

In Whitehall, the DDI hailed a passing cab. 'Vine Street police station, driver,' he ordered once he and Marriott had

taken their seats in the passenger compartment. 'And make
sure you take the most direct route.'

'Of course, guv'nor.' The driver recognized Hardcastle as
the policeman who had a reputation among cabbies for his
encyclopaedic knowledge of the quickest route to almost
anywhere in central London. Rather than go round Piccadilly
Circus, the driver was careful to cut through Jermyn Street
to get to Piccadilly, and then into Swallow Street to Vine
Street. After all, he did not want to lose his licence and
there were plenty of returning soldiers who would jump
at the chance of becoming a cab driver. At least, that's what
he'd been told by Hardcastle on a previous occasion, but the
truth was that very few serviceable cabs were for sale and
those that were on the market proved to be too expensive for
ex-soldiers with little money.

'I thought we were going to Rupert Street, sir,' said Marriott,
once again bemused by one of Hardcastle's mercurial changes
of plan.

'I've decided to speak to Mr Sullivan first.'

Divisional Detective Inspector William Sullivan, head of
the CID for the C or St James's Division, possessed all the
qualities that Hardcastle detested. He was vain and self-
opinionated, confirmed by the fact that when Sullivan stepped
out of Vine Street police station he always wore a curly-
brimmed bowler and carried a rattan cane. Furthermore, he
sported a monocle and that, together with his well-cut suits,
was the reason villains called him 'Posh Bill with the Piccadilly
window'. It had also been discovered that he had a small
mirror fixed inside his hat so that he could check the tidiness
of his hair whenever he entered a building.

However, despite Hardcastle's dislike of Sullivan, he attempted
to hide his animosity for the sake of the essential cooperation
that arose when his enquiries strayed over the divisional border
into Sullivan's manor which, as now, they frequently did. He
could not, however, resist the occasional derisory remark.

'I'm surprised you're still here, Bill.' Hardcastle took out
his half-hunter and stared at it. 'I thought you might have
gone home by now. It's damn near five o'clock.'

'Unlike your little patch, old boy, crime never stands still in my bailiwick. The West End is a hotbed of criminality.' Sullivan opened the bottom drawer of his desk and took out a bottle of malt whisky. 'You'll take a glass, Ernie? And you too, Skipper?' he added, addressing Marriott.

'You must be going up in the world, Bill,' said Hardcastle, glancing at the label. He knew that Begg's Lochnagar Special Reserve malt whisky retailed at about seven shillings a bottle and was too expensive for the wallet of a DDI.

'Gift from a friend,' said Sullivan with a wave of his hand.

'Really?' Hardcastle wondered what particular offence Sullivan had overlooked in order to benefit from gifts of expensive bottles of Scotch. 'What d'you know about the VanDoo Club in Rupert Street, Bill?'

'The VanDoo?' Sullivan savoured the name and then laughed. 'Not thinking of joining, are you, Ernie?'

Hardcastle did not rise to Sullivan's jocular question. 'I'm trying to trace a missing girl,' he said.

'My word! Is that all you've got to do in Westminster, Ernie?'

'I was sent for by the Commissioner this morning and given the job,' said Hardcastle mildly.

'Oh!' Sullivan was suitably impressed. 'What can I do to help, then, Ernie?'

'For a start, you can tell me who runs the place and what you know about him.'

'Station Sergeant Goddard is the best man to answer that, Ernie. He's responsible for overseeing the licensing regulations for the clubs on my manor. What he doesn't know about the West End isn't worth knowing.' Sullivan crossed his office and opened the door. 'Get George Goddard in here!' he shouted.

The man who entered Sullivan's office a few moments later was dressed in a suit of good quality, a shirt with a conventional stiff collar but a rather flamboyant cravat with a pearl tiepin. Hardcastle thought he looked something of a dandy but, given Sullivan's own appearance, C Division's DDI was unlikely to reprove any of his subordinates for aping him.

'This is DDI Hardcastle of A, Skipper,' said Sullivan. 'Tell him what you know about the VanDoo Club.'

'Ah, yes, the VanDoo. We've carried out raids there from time to time, sir, more for the sake of appearances than anything else, but there ain't never been any trouble. The owner is a man called Max Quilter. He was a major during the war but spent most of his time at the base camp in Boulogne, so I'm told by my informants. The VanDoo's a fashionable club, very popular with society toffs, and there's a rumour doing the rounds as how minor royalty gets in there from time to time but I ain't seen any on the odd occasions I've taken a quick gander.'

'Thank you, Skip,' said Hardcastle.

'Was you thinking of paying them a visit, sir?' asked Goddard.

'I don't think that'll be necessary.' Hardcastle turned to Sullivan. 'Thanks for the Scotch, Bill,' he said. 'Me and Marriott will be on our way.'

FOUR

Staring up at the facade of the VanDoo Club in Rupert Street, it was obvious to Hardcastle that the building, in the heart of London's Soho, had once been a dwelling house. But now, in common with most of the properties in this and the surrounding narrow streets, it had been converted to cater for people who flocked to the West End in search of glitzy shops and restaurants with international cuisine. And even mildly risqué entertainment.

'Good evening, sir.' The dinner-jacketed man who opened the door of the VanDoo Club examined Hardcastle and Marriott closely. One glance was enough for him to decide that they were not the class of people whose presence would enhance the establishment's reputation and should therefore not be admitted free of charge. 'It's twenty shillings each, if you please, gentlemen.'

'I'm Divisional Detective Inspector Hardcastle of the

Whitehall Division and you can show me to the manager's office a bit *tout de suite.*'

'Yes, sir. Certainly, sir. I'll just get someone to show you the way.'

'And you needn't press that,' said Hardcastle as the doorkeeper made for a bell-push sited near the entrance. 'It's not a police raid.' He paused. 'Not yet.'

The doorkeeper gave a nervous laugh and made a brief call from a nearby telephone. A few moments later a waiter appeared and led Hardcastle and Marriott through the bar area, past champagne drinkers seated at tables and across to a staircase in the far corner. Mounting the stairs, the trio passed a swirling mass of humanity gyrating their way around the room to the ragtime music of a small jazz band. Without exception the men were attired in evening dress, most in white tie and tails, but some had opted for the more comfortable and increasingly popular dinner jacket. The women wore a variety of colourful frocks but fashion was already dictating that most were short. Ostrich feathers in bandeaux and long strings of beads were much in evidence. It seemed to Hardcastle that the end of the war had brought with it an end to the conventions of dress and behaviour that he had always regarded as the norm.

The waiter edged his way around the dance floor and stopped at a door at the very back of the room. 'This is Major Quilter's office, sir,' he said.

Without bothering to knock, Hardcastle pushed open the door and entered.

'Inspector Hardcastle? I'm Max Quilter. I'm the owner of this establishment.' The speaker was a tall, slim man of youthful appearance. Hardcastle thought that he was probably no more than thirty years of age, if that. He wore an immaculately cut dinner jacket, open to reveal a scarlet cummerbund. 'Don't look so surprised, Inspector. Sergeant Goddard telephoned me to say you might pay a visit. He's the vice squad chap at Vine Street.'

'I know who he is,' snapped Hardcastle. He was furious that a mere station sergeant should have tipped off Quilter to his impending arrival, even though he had told Goddard that it was not necessary for him to visit the VanDoo Club. He would certainly have a few sharp words to say to DDI Sullivan about it. He might even suggest to him that it could be worth finding out what benefit Goddard derived from telling Quilter that Hardcastle was taking an interest in the VanDoo Club.

'Yes, I suppose so,' drawled Quilter. 'Nothing wrong, I trust?'

'That remains to be seen,' said Hardcastle, who had taken an instant dislike to the suave owner of the nightclub. He despised hostilities-only officers who continued to use their rank once they had left the army.

'Please take a seat, gentlemen, and tell me how I may assist you.' Quilter indicated a comfortable settee adjacent to a rather fine oak desk. 'May I offer you a drink?' he asked as his hand hovered over a side table upon which were decanters and glasses.

'No, thank you, Major,' replied Hardcastle tersely. 'I'll not waste too much of your time but I'm seeking the whereabouts of a young woman called Lily Musgrave.'

'Austen Musgrave's girl, you mean?'

'You know her, then?'

'Oh, yes. I think it's fair to say that probably everyone knows her,' said Quilter with a lascivious laugh. 'Well, our male patrons, that is.'

'What exactly d'you mean by that?'

'Oh, she has something of a reputation for . . .' Quilter paused. 'There's no delicate way of putting it really, Inspector, but Lily has a reputation for being a young lady of easy virtue. She probably spent a wicked weekend in the country somewhere with a young blade. I daresay she'll roll up at home looking slightly the worse for wear.'

'Do you recall seeing her in here on Thursday evening, Major Quilter?'

'I think I did catch a glimpse of her but Thursday is always our busiest night. Most of our guests are the sort of landed gentry who disappear to the shires on a Friday. So Thursday night's the best night for a young fellow to find a filly for a naughty weekend in the country.'

'Is Miss Musgrave here this evening?'

'Haven't seen her.'

'Do you happen to know whether she *did* get taken off to the country?' Hardcastle was becoming increasingly annoyed with the languid and offhand Major Quilter.

'Couldn't say, I'm afraid.'

'Do you encourage meetings of that sort being arranged in your club, Major?' asked Marriott quietly. 'People meeting for the sole purpose of arranging a "naughty weekend" was how I think you described it.'

Quilter suddenly detected a warning signal. 'Good heavens, no! I can't be responsible for what my clients do, Sergeant. They are adults, after all, and I certainly wouldn't brook that sort of behaviour in the club. I mean, it's only tittle-tattle that I'm repeating. If I was aware of such goings on I'd clamp down on it immediately.' He knew enough of the law to understand that there was a thin line between the legal definition of a brothel and a nightclub where liberal behaviour was acceptable.

'Perhaps you'd make some discreet enquiries among your, er, guests, Major,' said Hardcastle. 'See if anyone knows whether Miss Musgrave left with anyone last Thursday evening.'

'I can hardly go about questioning my guests, Inspector.' Quilter chuckled and brushed his moustache.

'I suppose not,' said Hardcastle thoughtfully. 'It looks as though I'll have to do it myself. Of course, I'd have to bring in a few more policemen to help me.'

'Ah! Probably be better if you left it me, eh what?' Quilter's smile vanished along with his supercilious attitude. The thought of a crowd of uniformed policemen interrogating his guests would sound the death knell to his business. It was not as if his was the only club in the West End; competition in the immediate post-war months was exceptionally keen, if not cut-throat. In some cases, literally so.

'Yes, I thought so. If this young woman should reappear in the meantime, Major Quilter, I'd be obliged if you'd let me know straight away. You'll find me at Cannon Row police station, immediately opposite Scotland Yard.' Hardcastle and Marriott stood up.

'Yes, of course, Inspector. Are you sure you won't stay for a drink?' asked Quilter.

'Have you ever spent the weekend with Lily Musgrave yourself?' demanded Marriott suddenly. 'To take advantage of her "easy virtue", as you described it.'

'Good God, no, Sergeant.' Quilter conjured up an expression of injured innocence.

'In that case, we'll bid you good evening,' said Hardcastle.

'D'you reckon he'll come up with any information, sir?' asked Marriott once the two detectives were in the street.

'I wouldn't be surprised, Marriott. I don't think the galloping major would want a bunch of coppers swarming all over his establishment, and the slightest hint to the licensing authorities that all is not well at the VanDoo Club would shut him down a bit *tout de suite*.' Hardcastle hailed a cab. 'Scotland Yard, cabbie.' In an aside to Marriott, he added, 'Tell 'em Cannon Row and half the time you'll finish up at Cannon Street in the City of London, you mark my words.'

'Yes, sir,' replied Marriott, attempting to keep the weariness out of his voice. It was a piece of advice that the DDI offered on almost every occasion the two of them took a cab back to the police station.

'How old d'you think Quilter is, Marriott?'

'I'd say about twenty-six or twenty-seven, sir.'

'Yes, that's what I thought. He was very quick to tell us that Lily Musgrave was a young lady of "easy virtue". And he's a bit of a suave bugger – a man for the ladies, I'd have thought. Despite his quick denial, I wouldn't put it past him to have had a bit of jig-a-jig with her himself. Otherwise, how would he know she was easy, Marriott?'

Taken aback by the DDI's uncharacteristically naive comment, Marriott chose to remain silent.

Ernest and Alice Hardcastle had lived at 27 Kennington Road ever since their marriage in 1893. There was nothing to distinguish this particular road from others in that part of south-east London save that Charlie Chaplin had once lived at number 287. But this piece of inconsequential information had no impact on Hardcastle for he had other things on his mind this

morning: he was still thinking about the task he had been set
by no less an officer than the Commissioner himself and how
he was to resolve it.

As was his custom, Hardcastle was up at just after
six o'clock on the morning after his interview with Sir
Nevil Macready and was ready to sit down for breakfast by
seven.

'There's not much butter left, Ernie,' said Alice. 'We're
almost at the end of the week's ration. You wouldn't have
thought we'd won the war. We're still short of food and if
we go on at this rate we'll finish up eating cagmag.'

'We haven't won the war yet, Alice,' responded Hardcastle,
glancing up from that morning's edition of the *Daily Mail*.
'Not according to that bunch of politicians who are still
arguing the toss in Versailles. That's the trouble when you
get frock coats sitting down at a table: they go on forever.
They should've taken a leaf out of Queen Victoria's book.
She always made the Privy Council stand up for meetings so
they wouldn't go on too long. And another thing,' he continued,
stabbing a forefinger at an article in the newspaper, 'coal's
gone up to sixpence for two hundredweights. That'll be the
Welsh miners wanting more money, and on top of that they're
demanding a six-hour day. But Lloyd George will let them
get away with it, what with him being Welsh as well.
Scandalous, I call it.'

'Really, dear?' Realizing that she had inadvertently set her
husband off on another of his diatribes about the effects of
the war, and not wishing to encourage him further, Alice
confined herself to a non-committal response. Nevertheless,
despite the shortages that still obtained, she managed to
produce two fried eggs, a couple of rashers of bacon, two
pieces of fried bread and a sausage for her husband's breakfast, without which he claimed he could not face a day's
work. This substantial first course was completed by two
slices of toast and marmalade, and washed down with
three cups of tea, each of which contained two spoonfuls of
sugar.

On more than one occasion, Hardcastle had thought that
Alice was able to provide such a sumptuous repast because

her husband was a senior police officer and received a few favours from the grocer in Lambeth Road. But he did not care to enquire too deeply into the matter.

At half past seven he donned his overcoat and bowler hat, picked up his umbrella and kissed his wife.

'Take care of yourself, Ernie,' cautioned Alice. It was something she said every morning when her husband was leaving for work.

Closing his front door firmly, Hardcastle made off down Kennington Road towards Westminster Bridge Road with the intention of catching his usual tram.

'Morning, guv'nor.' The Hardcastles' milkman gave a cheery wave. 'I hope you ain't thinking of getting a tram this morning 'cos they're all out on strike.'

Hardcastle stopped. 'Are you sure about that?'

'Positive, guv'nor,' said the milkman. 'Just like your lot was last year.' And with that sarcastic comment he directed a derisory cackle at the DDI.

Hardcastle confined himself to glaring at the milkman. It still rankled with him that some twelve thousand police officers had mutinied the previous August, albeit for only a couple of days. More to the point, Hardcastle was now faced with a walk to work of nearly two miles. Hardly a prospect to put him in a good mood.

But fortune was with him. As he passed Kennington Road police station a despatch van emerged from the station yard. A small wagon with a box at the back, it was drawn by a single horse and driven by a constable in uniform. This officer must have been approaching sixty years of age, sported a beard and was clearly overweight.

'Oi, you, lad!' shouted Hardcastle, waving his umbrella. 'Hold on.'

'Whoa, girl!' The constable brought the conveyance to a standstill and, leaning down from his high seat, pointed his whip at Hardcastle. 'Who the 'ell d'you think you're talking to, cock?' he demanded. 'I'm not a bleedin' cab, yer know.'

'I'm DDI Hardcastle of A. Are you taking that thing to Commissioner's Office?'

'Oh, begging your pardon, sir, yes, I am.'

'Good,' said Hardcastle. 'Then you can give me a lift. All the trams are on strike, so I'm told.'

'Yes, they are, sir, and you're welcome to climb up here and take a seat alongside of me, but I warn you, sir, this contraption ain't got no springs.'

'Any port in a storm,' muttered the DDI as, somewhat unceremoniously, he clambered aboard the despatch van, almost losing his bowler hat in the process.

Having been shaken about and obliged to hold on for dear life as the despatch van sped over the uneven roads, Hardcastle was not in the best of moods when he arrived at New Scotland Yard. It was a mood not improved by the fact that the PC on duty in the courtyard recognized him and afforded him a textbook salute, followed by the routine, 'All correct, sir.' Hardcastle was convinced he detected a smirk on the constable's face.

'Stop chewing your bloody chinstrap, lad,' Hardcastle responded and, alighting thankfully from the despatch van, made his way into the police station and upstairs to his office. The moment he settled behind his desk and began to fill his pipe, Detective Sergeant Marriott knocked and entered.

'How did you manage to get here so early, Marriott? All the trams are on strike.'

'Doesn't make any difference to me, sir,' said Marriott. 'I always come in on my bicycle. It's no distance at all from my quarter in Regency Street. I even walk it sometimes. You ought to get a bike, sir. Save you coming in on the M Division despatch van,' he added, risking a reproof.

'Not something I make a habit of, Marriott.' Discovering that his sergeant was aware of how he had arrived at work that day, Hardcastle knew that the story – in all probability suitably embellished – would be all around the division by lunchtime. 'But are you seriously suggesting that a DDI ought to come to work on a bicycle, Marriott? Anyway, I couldn't afford one.'

'Mine only cost three pounds at Gamages, sir. Mind you, that was before the war.'

'How could you afford that on a sergeant's pay?' the DDI demanded. He knew that there were corrupt policemen

in the Force but had never suspected Marriott of being one
of them.

'Hire purchase, sir. A bob a week.' Marriott decided that
the discussion about bicycles and a pointed enquiry about his
finances had gone far enough. 'Major Quilter telephoned just
before you arrived, sir. He'd like to see you at the club.
Apparently he's got some important information for you.'

'Oh, he has, has he? And who the hell does Major Quilter
think he is, sending for me as if I was some swaddy? He
ought to realize that he's not in the Kate Carney any more.'
Hardcastle lit his pipe. 'I suppose we'd better get round there,
Marriott,' he continued, softening his irascibility slightly. 'He
might have something useful to tell us. If he ain't, I'll likely
get a warrant and give the place a thorough going over. Missing
persons,' he muttered. 'It's a job for the Uniform Branch.'

'Yes, sir.' Marriott came to the conclusion that the DDI
was in a worse mood than usual and, like Alice Hardcastle,
decided that it would be unwise to provoke him any further.

The front door of the VanDoo Club in Rupert Street was wide
open when Hardcastle and Marriott arrived.

Inside the club, the bar area had the tawdry look of the
morning after the night before. The tables, now without their
tablecloths, were seen to be cheap wooden affairs, and the air
was heavy with an excess of stale cigar and cigarette smoke,
a result of poor ventilation. In the harsh daylight it was hard
to believe that by evening the club would be converted into
a form of respectability by discreet lighting, plush curtaining
and attentive waiters in evening dress.

'Can I 'elp you, gents?' A scruffy and unshaven individual,
clearly a scullion of some sort, leaned on his broom and
peered at Hardcastle and Marriott through finger-marked
spectacles.

'Where's Major Quilter?' asked Marriott.

'Up here,' shouted a voice from the top of the stairs leading
to the dancing area. 'Is that you, Inspector?'

'It is,' replied Hardcastle and, followed by Marriott,
mounted the stairs.

FIVE

Max Quilter was as immaculately attired as he had been the previous evening, but this morning he was wearing a grey flannel suit of a style much favoured by the Prince of Wales.

'Come and have a cup of coffee, Inspector,' said Quilter as the two detectives mounted the staircase. He led them across the dance floor and past the tiny platform where last evening a lively band had been playing ragtime. But now, in the harsh reality of daylight, the whole area looked like a tatty storeroom.

No sooner had the three men sat down in Quilter's office than a waiter appeared with a tray of coffee.

Somewhat pointedly, Hardcastle pulled out his watch and examined it. 'I am extremely busy, Major Quilter,' he said, briefly winding the watch before replacing it in his waistcoat pocket. 'I understand from my sergeant that you have some important information for me. Can we get on with it?'

'Last night, Inspector, you asked me if I knew who Lily Musgrave had left with on Thursday.'

'And do you?'

'As you suggested, I asked around, and eventually someone said they thought young Lily had gone off with Oscar Lucas in his Lagonda.'

'When was this?' asked Hardcastle.

'Around five o'clock, I suppose,' said Quilter.

'D'you know this man Lucas yourself, Major?' asked Marriott, noting the name in his pocketbook.

'Only in passing. I'm told he was a captain during the war and I believe he was in the Connaught Rangers.' Quilter pulled a wry face as though there was some stigma attached to a regiment raised in the west of Ireland. 'I'm told he was somewhere in Mespot – that's what the army called Mesopotamia, Inspector – but his battalion was moved to the

Somme just in time for the infamous first day of the battle. It seems that Lucas copped a Blighty one in the first ten minutes but was back to duty in time for the triumphal march into Cologne just before last Christmas. Then, like the rest of us, he got chucked out when they didn't need him any more.'

There was an element of bitterness in Quilter's comment and Hardcastle was forced to agree that the army had been treated shabbily once the hostilities were over. Not that he was about to say so. Quilter appeared to have done rather better than a lot of ex-officers, many of whom had actually been reduced to begging, and he doubted that Oscar Lucas was obliged to solicit alms in the streets, given that he owned a Lagonda.

'How old is Lucas?' asked Marriott.

Quilter adopted a thoughtful expression and lit a cigarette while he was thinking about the answer. 'Around twenty-two, I should think,' he said eventually. 'Give or take a year or so.'

'And do you have a home address for him?' Marriott opened his pocketbook.

'Good Lord, no,' said Quilter airily. 'We don't bother too much about home addresses, and to be frank half these chaps are living in places they'd rather no one knew about.'

'Have you seen Lucas since Thursday?'

'No, I haven't, Sergeant.'

'If he comes in tonight, I want to know immediately,' said Hardcastle forcefully. 'You can contact me at Cannon Row police station. Sergeant Marriott will give you the telephone number. Is that understood?'

Quilter bridled at that. 'Now look here, Inspector, I've been as cooperative as I can but our member's activities are private. We don't tell just anybody what they get up to.'

'I'm not just anybody, Quilter, I'm a divisional detective inspector of the Metropolitan Police and right now I'm tempted to close this place down and seize the books. In my view it's beginning to look as though you've got something to hide, what with young women being picked up for the sole purpose of sexual intercourse. Come opening time tonight,

I'll have policemen crawling all over your precious club until I find what I'm looking for.'

'You don't have any reason to do that,' said Quilter arrogantly. 'I defy you to find any cause for closing me down.'

'Oh, don't you worry about that,' said Hardcastle mildly. 'I'll find something.'

'I shall complain about this,' spluttered Quilter, now red in the face. 'Your Commissioner will hear of your high-handed attitude. I'm not without influence, you know. As a matter of fact, I served under General Macready on the Western Front during the war and got to know him quite well.'

'When was that?' Hardcastle's question sounded as though it had only been posed out of interest.

'Oh, about 1917, I suppose.' Quilter waved a hand in the air.

'On the Western Front?'

'Yes, of course.'

'I assumed that you'd been at a base camp in Boulogne for most of the war,' said Hardcastle, with no justification for the comment save wishing to rile the major. Although Station Sergeant Goddard at Vine Street had suggested Boulogne, Hardcastle was ill-disposed to trust the man. 'But apart from that, it might interest you to know, Major Quilter,' said Hardcastle, 'that in 1917 General Macready was stationed at the War Office in London, and had been there since 1916. Furthermore, these enquiries are being made on his express orders and he instructed me in person yesterday morning. So I suggest you do as I ask, otherwise by this time tomorrow you won't have a club. And that is more likely to be General Macready's decision than mine.'

'Most ex-officers give their club as an address – if they've got one – so that they can be contacted if necessary,' said Quilter, rapidly yielding in the face of Hardcastle's threat and his knowledge of the Commissioner's military background. He did not know whether Macready had ordered Hardcastle to undertake his enquiries but was not prepared to take the chance of having his establishment closed down. 'I believe Oscar's a member of the In and Out.'

'The In and Out?' For a moment, Hardcastle wondered what the ex-major was talking about and could not immediately think why the owner of the VanDoo Club would want to contact one of his patrons anyway.

'The Naval and Military Club, Inspector. So-called because of the signs on the gates. It's in Piccadilly.'

'I know where it is, Major,' snapped Hardcastle. He swept out of Quilter's office and, followed by a hurrying Marriott, sped down the stairs.

'Ah, fresh air,' exclaimed Hardcastle. 'I've had quite enough of that jumped-up prig, Marriott, and I have to admit I was on the verge of losing my temper with him.'

'Yes, sir.' Although Marriott was accustomed to assessing the DDI's moods, he was at a loss to believe that Hardcastle was under the impression he had been restrained during his talk to Quilter. 'Where to now, sir?'

'The Naval and Military Club,' replied Hardcastle, waving his umbrella at a cab.

The cab pulled into the forecourt of the 'In and Out' and the detectives alighted. For a moment or two Hardcastle studied the three-storey building.

'Lord Palmerston used to live here, Marriott.'

'I didn't know they had living-in members, sir.'

Hardcastle afforded his sergeant a withering glance. 'He lived here *before* it was a club, Marriott. It was his London home.'

'He was prime minister, wasn't he, sir?' Marriott knew perfectly well who Palmerston was but he thought that Hardcastle's occasional flashes of historical facts were akin to someone who alighted from each station on the Underground railway system, familiarized himself with the immediate surrounding area and then professed to know London thoroughly. Nevertheless, he thought it advisable to flatter the DDI.

'Quite right, Marriott. He was prime minister in the eighteen-fifties. He had a great sense of humour, too. When William Palmer, the mass poisoner, was executed, the people of Rugeley, Palmer's home town, sought the prime minister's permission to change the town's name.' Hardcastle chuckled. 'Well, Palmerston was prime minister at the time and he suggested the town be named Palmerston. However, we mustn't stand here wasting our time by gossiping. Pay the cabbie, Marriott, and don't forget to take the plate number otherwise you won't get your money back from the Receiver's Office.'

'Of course, sir,' replied Marriott, attempting to keep the frustration from his voice; he had been reminded of this requirement by Hardcastle every time they had taken a cab.

'If that's anything to go by, I'd say that Lucas is here.' Hardcastle pointed his umbrella at a maroon Lagonda coupé parked in the courtyard.

Marriott forbore from suggesting that there was more than one Lagonda in London. He took a great interest in motor cars and hoped one day to be able to afford one, although he realized that he would need to rise by several more ranks before that ambition was achieved. 'That particular Lagonda model's a powerful car, sir,' he said as he admired the coupé's graceful lines. 'It's twelve horsepower and costs about three hundred and fifty pounds.'

Hardcastle stopped and turned. 'I sometimes think you spend too much time gathering trivia, Marriott, instead of concentrating on the job in hand.' But the real reason for his acerbic comment was that he hated the idea that a sergeant knew more than he did.

A club servant, immaculately attired in green livery, held open the door as Hardcastle and Marriott mounted the two steps to the entrance. 'May I be of assistance, sir?' He possessed the ability to recognize every member of the Naval and Military Club and knew the name of each; one glance was sufficient for him to know that the two detectives were not members.

'I'm a police officer,' announced Hardcastle, 'and I'd like a word with a Mr Oscar Lucas who I believe is a member of this here club.'

The servant lifted his head slightly, giving the appearance of looking down his nose at Hardcastle. 'If you'd care to take a seat in the reception room, gentlemen, I'll see if Captain Lucas is in the club.' He pointed towards a set of double doors, beyond which was a circular table set in the centre of a large carpet and several spindly-legged sofas that at first sight appeared to be rather uncomfortable and were later proved to be so.

'I'll put money on him being an ex-sergeant major, Marriott. From the Brigade of Guards, most likely.' Hardcastle glanced around the spacious room. 'They do all right for themselves, these here army and navy toffs, don't they?'

'I imagine it costs a lot to be a member of this club, sir.'

'I'm surprised you don't know just how much, Marriott.'

But before Marriott was able to reply to Hardcastle's barbed comment, a young man appeared in the doorway of the reception room and stared around. Although Hardcastle and Marriott were the only occupants of the room, it appeared to take the man some time for their presence to register.

'I'm Oscar Lucas,' drawled the young man eventually. 'Are you the police chappies who want to have a word with me?'

Lucas was about five foot nine in height, painfully thin and of pallid complexion. He appeared too young to have held the rank of captain, and without his guardee moustache would not have looked out of place in the prefects' common room at a public school. Hardcastle knew that young men had been promoted to ranks of life-and-death responsibility during a war that had seen a culling of great swathes of junior officers, many of the scions of the aristocracy among them. The life expectancy of a subaltern on the Western Front had been set at six weeks and had repeatedly been proved an accurate estimate. Oscar Lucas was one of the lucky ones to have survived, especially from the opening day of the Battle of the Somme. The first of July 1916 would be remembered as the worst day in the history of the British Army when it suffered over 50,000 casualties, of which 21,000 were dead before midday, mown down like scythes of corn.

'I'm Divisional Detective Inspector Hardcastle of the Whitehall Division, Captain Lucas. I'm looking into the disappearance of a young lady by the name of Lily Musgrave.'

'Disappearance?' Lucas settled himself in one of the sofas and Hardcastle and Marriott sat down in the one adjacent to it. 'I don't understand why you have come to talk to me. When did she disappear?' He raised his eyebrows as if the whole affair was a complete mystery to him.

'I have been told, Captain Lucas, that she left the VanDoo Club last Thursday evening in your Lagonda.'

'Yes, she did, but what's that got to do with the police?' Despite Lucas's spirited response, his face reddened and he looked away.

'Very simply, Captain Lucas,' said Marriott, entering into the conversation for the first time, 'because she hasn't been seen since.'

'But this is absolute nonsense, Inspector.'

'Perhaps you would tell me what exactly you mean by that.' Hardcastle leaned back against the rear of the sofa but, finding no comfort in the rigid framework, sat forward again. Taking out his pipe, he slowly filled the bowl with tobacco before looking at Lucas again. 'Where did you go after you and she left the VanDoo Club?' He applied a match to the pipe and glanced up at Lucas again.

'To my father's apartment in Albany.'

'So you stayed in London all weekend?'

'Yes. My father wouldn't approve of me taking a girl back to Epsom; he has an estate there along with a set of racing stables. He understands that all young men meet girls from time to time but emphasizes that such meetings must be discreet. My pater's a bit old-fashioned, you see. However, he does allow me to use his apartment in Piccadilly.'

'How did you spend the weekend, then?' asked Marriott. 'Did you stay in the apartment the whole time?'

'Most of the time, but we went out for luncheon and dinner, of course.'

'Where did you go for those meals?' asked Hardcastle.

Lucas stared at the wall above Hardcastle's head. 'Romanos, the Savoy, the Criterion, Kettner's, Rules, Bellini's.' He reeled off the names as though he was reciting a restaurant guide. 'And one or two others that I can't remember.'

'And did you return Miss Musgrave to her home after your weekend of jig-a-jig, Captain Lucas?' If Lily Musgrave's father was to be believed, the girl had not been home since last Thursday, but he was interested to hear young Lucas's version of events.

'Yesterday morning, Inspector.' Lucas spoke sharply, giving the impression that he was becoming irritated by the DDI's questioning. 'But I have to say that I don't much care for your insinuations. Miss Musgrave is a perfectly respectable young lady and any suggestion that she and I—'

'I don't care whether you like it or not, young man, but I'll ask whatever questions I like and make any insinuations I like. Now then, did you take her home to Vincent Square or didn't you?'

'I would suggest that you answer my inspector's questions, Captain Lucas,' said Marriott. 'Otherwise he might be tempted to arrest you on suspicion of abducting a minor.'

'A *minor*?' Lucas was clearly shocked by Marriott's statement, the more so as it was delivered in mild tones.

'She's only seventeen years of age.'

'Good God!' Lucas was obviously taken aback by this revelation. 'She told me she was twenty-one last Christmas Day. I remember that because we had a joke about her missing out on two sets of presents.'

'Did you deliver this young lady to her home, Captain Lucas?' Marriott asked patiently.

'No, I dropped her off at Harrods in Brompton Road,' volunteered Lucas hurriedly. 'It was where she asked me to leave her.'

'In Brompton Road itself?' Hardcastle asked.

'Of course in Brompton Road.' Lucas adopted a superior tone as though dealing with someone who was not of the financial standing to be able to patronize Harrods.

'There's an entrance in Basil Street as well,' said Hardcastle, 'although that tends to be used more by royalty and theatrical performers. It's to avoid the publicity, you see.'

'Oh!' Lucas was rapidly re-evaluating this rough detective. 'I didn't know that.'

'What time was it when you dropped her off at Harrods?'

'About half past ten, I suppose,' replied Lucas after hesitating for a moment or two.

'When did you see her again?'

'I haven't seen her since, Inspector.'

Hardcastle grunted and stood up. 'Very well,' he said, 'but I'll very likely have to see you again, Captain Lucas. Come, Marriott.' And leaving the somewhat bemused young ex-officer, he led the way out of the club and into Piccadilly.

'What d'you make of him, sir?' Marriott asked.

'A strange young man, Marriott, but I suppose being in the Battle of the Somme must have had an effect. Did you notice the way his hands was shaking? I s'pose that's what they call shell shock.'

'I'm sure you're right, sir.' Marriott's brother-in-law, Frank Dobson, had survived the entire war unscathed. In the latter months he had been commissioned and rapidly promoted to captain, and on Armistice Day had made formal application for a regular commission. Although reluctant to talk about his experience on the Western Front, refusing absolutely to discuss it with his sister, he did open up to Charles Marriott on occasions and talked of the dreadful effect of constant shelling. Although the generals were ill-disposed to recognize shell shock as a serious mental illness, preferring to think of those men as cowards, Frank Dobson and others who had witnessed it first-hand knew differently.

'I think I'll have a word with DDI Fowler of W Division, just to see if these here stables at Epsom are kosher.'

Marriott could not see the point of that but Hardcastle frequently embarked on an aspect of the investigation that Marriott thought unnecessary only to prove that it was the right course of action.

'Ah! At last,' exclaimed Hardcastle, spotting a cab.

'Where to, guv?' The cabbie wrenched down his flag as the two detectives clambered in.

'Brixton nick,' said Hardcastle, 'and by the most direct route, mind. I don't want a tour of London.'

The cabbie sniffed, but any criticism of a passenger he rightly guessed was a policeman remained unspoken.

'Well, well, well! And what brings you up to the sharp end, Ernie?' DDI Cornelius Fowler stood up from behind his desk and shook hands with Hardcastle.

'The sharp end!' scoffed Hardcastle. 'Don't tell me you've had a crime to solve out here in the leafy suburbs of Brixton. It's a good job you don't have to cope with my bailiwick, Connie. I've got the seat of government on my patch, along with Parliament, Buck House, Clarence House, Marlborough House and Westminster Abbey, to say nothing of Windsor Castle and the Palace of Holyrood House in Edinburgh.'

'Bloody hell, Ernie, you'd better have a drink.' It was what Fowler always said when the usual exchange of badinage took place between him and Hardcastle. Without further ado, he took a bottle of Scotch and three glasses from his bottom drawer.

'You know my skipper, Marriott, don't you, Connie?'

'Yes, of course. Your guv'nor not worn you out yet, then, Marriott?'

'Not yet, sir,' said Marriott.

'Well, Ernie, now we've got the mutual insults over and done with, what brings you to a working nick? Has the Elephant given you another job?'

'No, the Commissioner has.'

'The Commissioner? Well, he tells all of us what to do, in a manner of speaking, so you needn't try to impress me just because you belong to the Royal A.'

Hardcastle explained how he had been sent for by Sir Nevil Macready yesterday morning and what Sir Nevil had tasked him to undertake.

'Blimey! He really did send for you,' exclaimed Fowler. 'Sounds to me like a job that can make or break a career. But how d'you think W Division can help? Is there a suggestion the girl's somewhere on my patch?'

'No, not at all.' Hardcastle told Fowler about Captain Oscar Lucas and his father's racing stables at Epsom. 'I'd be obliged, Connie, if you could have someone check it out, seeing as how Epsom's on your manor. I think this youngster's straight up but I'd rather be certain as the Commissioner's involved.'

'I'm not worried about the Commissioner, Ernie, but seeing as it's you I'll put one of my best men on it.' Fowler poured another round of Scotch. 'I'll let you know as soon as I get a result.'

SIX

Hardcastle pulled out his watch, briefly wound it and dropped it back into his waistcoat pocket.

'Just time for another pint, I think, Marriott.'

'What are you proposing to do next, sir?' Marriott was surprised by the DDI's apparent hurry. In his experience, Hardcastle never rushed his lunchtime beer unless he had suddenly decided that there was something pressing he had to do.

'We shall go to Harrods,' Hardcastle announced. 'Albert!' Having caught the eye of the Red Lion's landlord, he made a circling motion around the two empty glasses.

'Coming right up, Mr H.' Albert pulled two pints in fresh glasses and stood them on the bar. 'Busy today, guv'nor?'

'Never stops, Albert,' said Hardcastle phlegmatically.

'D'you think we'll find out anything at Harrods, sir?' Once again, Marriott was surprised by Hardcastle's sudden decision to go to the prestigious establishment in Brompton Road. 'I know that's where Captain Lucas said he dropped Lily Musgrave on Monday morning but do you think anyone would have recognized her?'

'Lily Musgrave is ruined by her old pot an' pan, Marriott. I reckon she spends money whenever she feels like it and Austen Musgrave foots the bill. If she was in the store – and I've got doubts about that – someone will have remembered her, because she probably ran up a hefty bill.' Hardcastle downed his pint of beer and swept up the stairs to street level, leaving Marriott to rush his drink and hurry after him.

The cab delivered Hardcastle and Marriott to the main entrance to Harrods. The uniformed commissionaire saluted; it was almost a reflex action prompted by the fact that Hardcastle was wearing a bowler hat and possessed what the commissionaire would probably have described as a 'presence'.

'Whereabouts is the ladies' fashions department?' asked Hardcastle.

This question, coming as it did from a middle-aged man accompanied by another man, elicited no reaction of surprise, and the commissionaire gave Hardcastle the appropriate directions.

'D'you reckon that's where she was making for when Lucas dropped her off, sir?' Marriott asked as he followed Hardcastle through the vast store.

'Have you got a better suggestion?' The DDI snapped out his answer without breaking step.

Marriott decided to leave it at that. He had worked with Hardcastle long enough to know when the DDI was in one of his moods.

A woman, who by her demeanour clearly held a managerial post of some sort, stepped forward as the two detectives arrived in the fashions department. She was in her mid-forties, elegantly attired and her hair had been expensively coiffed, the Marcel waves lying flat on her head.

'May I help you, gentlemen?' The woman did not seem very happy at the arrival of two men in her essentially female department.

'I'm a police officer, madam. Divisional Detective Inspector Hardcastle of the Whitehall Division,' said the DDI as he raised his hat.

'Really?' said the woman doubtfully. 'How may I help you?' she asked again, but at once giving the impression that she was reluctant to do so.

'I'm trying to discover the whereabouts of a young woman by the name of Lily Musgrave, madam. I have reason to believe that she may have been in this store and possibly in this department, yesterday morning at about half past ten. It is likely that she made some purchases. Perhaps you could tell me if she was, in fact, here.'

'Miss Musgrave, you said?'

'That's correct.'

'One moment.' The woman disappeared behind a showcase and was gone for some minutes.

'Either she knows who Lily Musgrave's father is or she's

looking up her order book,' said Hardcastle, gazing around at the array of dresses. 'They look a bit on the pricey side, Marriott.'

'Yes, sir, but it's the sort of shop where, if you have to ask the price, you probably can't afford it anyway.' Marriott afforded himself a brief smile that amounted to little more than lifting the corners of his mouth.

'Where did you learn that?' demanded Hardcastle.

'It was something that Lorna said, sir.'

'Lorna?'

'My wife, sir.'

'Oh, that Lorna.' Hardcastle turned as a man approached him, followed by the assistant to whom the DDI had first spoken.

'I'm the chief security officer. My name is Crosby,' announced the man, doing his best to refrain from smiling. 'I understand that you told Miss Raynor you were police officers.'

'That is correct.' Hardcastle introduced himself once again and showed Crosby his warrant card.

Crosby laughed. 'I knew it was you the moment I set eyes on you, sir. You won't remember me but I was a PC at Vine Street when you were a detective sergeant there. I finished my time as a section sergeant at Gerald Road on B Division and got this billet when I retired from the Job, well, just after, really. I was deputy to start with, but when my boss retired I got his job.'

'Yes, I do remember you,' lied Hardcastle, aware that he needed this retired policeman's assistance. 'This is Marriott, my first-class sergeant.'

'Pleased to meet you, Skip,' said Crosby, and shook hands with each of the detectives. 'Now, sir, what can I do to help?'

Hardcastle explained about the missing Lily Musgrave and that Captain Lucas had claimed that he left her at Harrods' main door yesterday morning at about half past ten. 'I reckon that if she did come into the store she'd have come into the ladies' fashions department.'

Crosby turned to the department manageress. 'Would you be so kind as to check whether a Miss Lily Musgrave

purchased anything in this department sometime yesterday
morning, Miss Raynor?' He paused and turned to Hardcastle.
'Is it likely that Miss Musgrave is an account customer, sir?'

'Most likely it's her father's account, Mr Crosby. His name
is Austen Musgrave.'

'Oh, the MP!'

'That's the one.'

Miss Raynor disappeared again to busy herself with
checking the previous day's sales. When she returned a few
moments later, she was clutching an order book.

'I recall now that I did serve the young lady,' she announced.
'She purchased two silk georgette Charleston dresses, one in
emerald green and one in scarlet. They're a new line especially
imported from the United States of America and are proving
to be very popular with the younger ladies, particularly as
they retail at forty shillings.' As if to emphasize her sales
pitch, she waved an arm at a rack of dresses.

'They don't look long enough to be frocks,' said Hardcastle,
wondering if Miss Raynor was trying to sell him one. 'Are
you able to tell me the time she made this purchase, Miss
Raynor?' he asked.

'I think you said that Miss Musgrave arrived in the store at
about half past ten, Inspector. We don't record the time of a
sale but I would opine that it was somewhere between the time
you say she arrived and half past eleven, when I take my break.'

'Thank you for your help, Miss Raynor,' said Marriott.
He knew that Hardcastle was a trifle short on the social
graces but it did no harm to show gratitude for the woman's
assistance on the basis that the police may need her help
again one day.

'D'you want to check any of the other departments, sir?'
asked Crosby.

'No, thank you, Mr Crosby,' said Hardcastle. 'I've confirmed
that she actually came to the store yesterday morning, which
is all I needed. What I don't know is where she went from
here, but that's not your problem.'

'I don't know if it's important,' said Miss Raynor as the
detectives were on the point of leaving, 'but there was a
gentleman with Miss Musgrave.'

'What did he look like, Miss Raynor?' Hardcastle turned and took a step closer to the saleswoman.

The manageress adopted a pensive expression before eventually answering. 'He was about the same height as your companion,' she began, indicating Marriott, 'but much older than Miss Musgrave. I would imagine he was about thirty. He had a moustache and dark hair. He didn't say much, but when he did speak you could tell he was very well educated. Cultured, I'd say.'

'Thank you, Miss Raynor. That's most helpful,' said Marriott as he scribbled a few words in his pocketbook. Not that he thought the woman's brief description would be of any use in attempting to trace Lily Musgrave's latest escort. It certainly did not fit Oscar Lucas, and in any case he had stated that he dropped the girl off at Harrods' main entrance.

'I wonder who that was with Lily, Marriott. It wasn't anyone we've come across so far,' said Hardcastle as the two detectives made their way out of the store. 'Sounds like some ne'er-do-well with more money than sense, but I wonder what he gets in return.'

Marriott did not think Hardcastle's rhetorical question worthy of a reply; they were each cynical enough to think they knew the answer.

The commissionaire at the main door of Harrods blew his whistle and raised a finger of his gloved hand. A cab glided to a standstill in front of him within seconds. Crossing the pavement, he opened the door of the cab and touched his top hat.

'Much obliged,' said Hardcastle as he and Marriott got in, but did not offer the commissionaire a tip.

'Bloody skinflint!' muttered the commissionaire as the cab drew away.

Hardcastle tapped on the dividing window of the cab with the handle of his umbrella. 'Victoria Station,' he said when the cabbie responded.

'Where are we going now, sir?' asked Marriott, once again taken aback by another of Hardcastle's sudden inexplicable decisions.

'Brighton, Marriott. I've a shrewd suspicion that we might

find young Lily with her mother who, according to Crabb the
butler, is hoofing it on the stage of the Brighton Hippodrome.'

'Shouldn't we check first, sir?' Marriott was amazed that
Hardcastle should be undertaking the journey purely on speculation. 'Crabb might be wrong or Mrs Musgrave might've
moved on to another theatre.'

'You've got to have confidence, Marriott, otherwise you'll
never get the job done. Anyway, once you start making
enquiries someone would tell the lady in question and I don't
want her to know we're on our way to interview her.'
Hardcastle leaned back in his seat and looked out of the
window until they arrived at Victoria Station.

'Get two tickets, Marriott, and make sure they're second
class.' As a DDI, Hardcastle was entitled to second-class rail
travel, as was anyone of a lower rank travelling with him. 'And
I'll have a copy of the *Star* when you buy your own paper.'

'Very good, sir.' Marriott knew that he would never be
reimbursed for Hardcastle's newspaper.

The Brighton Hippodrome was in a narrow street a few
yards up from King's Road, the thoroughfare that ran along
the seafront.

'Don't look much like the sort of theatre we're used to in
London, Marriott.' For a moment or two, Hardcastle gazed up
at the façade of the theatre. 'I don't see Marie Faye's name
on the billboards.'

'Perhaps Crabb the butler got it wrong, sir.' Despite the
DDI's excuse for not making enquiries, Marriott still thought
they should have done so and taken the risk of the woman
finding out.

'Quite possibly, Marriott, quite possibly. I don't think he's
too reliable a witness, as you might say.' Hardcastle pushed
at one of the doors of the theatre but found it locked. 'What's
the time?'

'Just gone five o'clock, sir.' Marriott could never understand
why Hardcastle always asked him the time when he had a
watch of his own. On one occasion, Marriott jokingly
remarked to his wife Lorna that Hardcastle thought he might
wear out his watch if he looked at it too often.

'I wonder what time first house is.'

'Twenty minutes to seven, sir,' said Marriott, pointing at the billboard. 'And second house is at a quarter to nine.'

'Better see if we can find the stage door, then.' Hardcastle set off in search of a side entrance to the theatre. 'Ah, here we are.' Once inside, he approached a small glass-panelled cubicle and tapped on the window.

The aged stage doorkeeper, who had clearly been dozing, woke up with a start. After a few moments in which he attempted to recover himself, he opened the window. 'What's all the fuss about?' he demanded of no one in particular, and then focused on Hardcastle. 'If you're after one of them chorus girls, they don't turn up till about six o'clock. Which one of 'em is your bit of fluff, eh?' He gave the DDI the sort of look he reserved for lecherous old men who were up to no good with girls half their age.

'I'm not looking for a chorus girl, I'm a police officer,' snapped Hardcastle. 'And I suggest you get a new pair of glasses.'

'Oh, I do beg your pardon, guv'nor. I thought you was—'

'You haven't got the equipment for thinking, so don't try,' said Hardcastle. 'I'm looking for an artiste called Marie Faye who I'm told is appearing here.'

'Ah, our Marie. Yes, she's the goods, she is.'

'I'm not interested in your opinion of her; I just want to know where she is.'

'Go down them steps, guv'nor.' The doorkeeper emerged from his box in order to give directions and pointed a grubby finger. 'Her dressing room's the third door on the right. It's got her name on it.' He sniffed and wiped his unkempt moustache with the back of his hand. 'But you might find as how she's got a gent with her. She often has.'

Hardcastle and Marriott made their way down the steps and along a dank corridor. The DDI pushed open the door marked Marie Faye and entered. The woman was seated on a stool in front of a mirror and was vigorously brushing her long black hair. Reclining in an armchair, his feet pushed out straight in front of him, was a man attired in full evening dress. Overweight and at least fifty years of age, his rubicund complexion and heavily veined nose betrayed a martyrdom to gin.

'Don't you knock before entering a lady's dressing room?' Without turning, the woman addressed Hardcastle's reflection in the mirror.

'Are you Marie Faye?' Hardcastle answered the woman's question with one of his own.

'I think I must be,' she said, swinging round on her stool. The peignoir she was wearing fell open to reveal a scanty fur-edged red basque and shapely legs encased in tights. 'Anyway, that's the name on the door,' she added, placing her hands on her knees.

'I'm Divisional Detective Inspector Hardcastle of the Metropolitan Police and this is Detective Sergeant Marriott.'

'I don't think they're auditioning for policemen today.'

'Just listen to me,' snapped Hardcastle, fast losing patience with this rather foolish woman who seemed prone to making flippant remarks. 'I'm here because your daughter Lily has gone missing and my job is to find out what's happened to her.'

'Gone missing?' Marie Faye closed her legs and wrapped her peignoir more closely around herself as if covering her brief outfit would emphasize the seriousness of the situation. She glanced at the red-faced man. 'Bugger off, Percy.'

'Yes, rather, what?' Percy ferreted about on the floor to retrieve his walking cane and opera hat, and with some difficulty levered himself out of the chair in which he was sitting. 'How about a spot of supper after second house, Marie, darling?'

'Not tonight, Percy. And it's no good you calling round after the show because the answer will still be no.'

'Ah, yes, right. Perhaps tomorrow night, eh what, old girl?'

'Before you go, perhaps you'd give your name to my sergeant, sir,' said Hardcastle.

'I don't see that's any of your business, Inspector,' exclaimed Percy and turned towards the door of the dressing room, only to find that Marriott had taken up a position which blocked Percy's exit.

'I think my inspector asked for your name, sir,' said Marriott in what could only be construed as a menacing manner.

'Ah, yes. It's Percy Fortune.'

'And your address?' Marriott wrote the name in his pocketbook.

'I'm staying at the Grand Hotel on the seafront, don't you know.'

'Is that your permanent address?'

'Well, not exactly. I do have rooms in Knightsbridge, in the Brompton Road actually, but I'm not often there. Bit of a stage-door johnnie, you might say. Tend to follow the shows around, don't you know. Especially those starring the lovely Marie.' Fortune shot a hopeful glance in Marie Faye's direction but she ignored him.

'Were you in Harrods this morning?' Marriott wondered if he had been the man accompanying Lily Musgrave in the ladies' fashions department, despite his not fitting Miss Raynor's description.

'Good grief, no. Never go near the place. If I need anything I send my man or ring them up and they deliver it.'

'Thank you, Mr Fortune,' said Marriott and stood to one side to allow the man to leave, something he did somewhat hastily as though extracting himself from an unsavoury situation.

'Now, what's all this about my daughter going missing, Inspector?' Marie Faye seemed to have abandoned her flippancy now that Percy Fortune had left. She swung back to her dressing table and took a half bottle of gin from a drawer. She poured a substantial amount into a tumbler and added an equal amount of water from a carafe. 'Would you coppers care for a drink?' she asked.

'Your husband—' began Hardcastle, ignoring the woman's invitation.

'What about him?' said Marie.

'Yesterday morning, Mr Musgrave informed the police that his daughter had not been home since the previous Thursday evening when she left his house in Vincent Square. Mr Musgrave had no idea where she'd gone but our enquiries indicated that she spent the evening at the VanDoo Club in Rupert Street.' Hardcastle thought it unnecessary to tell Marie Faye that Austen Musgrave had reported the matter direct to the Commissioner.

'Good for her,' said Marie. 'And now, I suppose, you're going to tell me that she went off with some man.'

'She did, as a matter of fact,' said Hardcastle.

'Well, she is something of a free spirit, Inspector, and young women today are far more liberated than my generation were allowed to be.' Marie sighed. 'When I think of those dreadful long skirts and corsets with whalebone stays it makes me shudder, but now things are different, thank God. A lot of women did men's jobs in the war and they're not prepared to be put back in their little boxes now that it's over. And we've got the vote. Well, about forty per cent of us who are over thirty, but even that will change, you mark my words, Inspector.'

'Mrs Musgrave, I don't—'

'I prefer to be called Miss Faye or, better still, just Marie.'

'Miss Faye, I don't need a lecture on the emancipation of women.' Hardcastle's response was blunt to the point of rudeness. 'I'm concerned in finding out what happened to your daughter.'

'The fact that she left home on Thursday evening and probably spent the weekend with some young blade is not a cause for concern, Inspector. After all, Thursday evening to Monday morning isn't a lifetime.'

'Although she was seen in Harrods on Monday, she has still not returned home to Vincent Square.'

'Well, I don't see how I can help you.' Marie took another sip of her gin and water. 'Are you sure you won't join me in a drink, Inspector? I hate drinking alone.'

'No, thank you.' Hardcastle did not imagine that Marie Faye had too much of a problem drinking by herself or, for that matter, finding a drinking companion. 'When was the last time you saw Lily, Miss Faye?'

'Just after Christmas. I was appearing in *Cinderella* at Worthing. She stayed with me for a week but spent most of her time with the man playing Buttons.'

'What was his name?' asked Marriott.

'Sidney Preston,' said Marie without hesitation, 'and he was much older than Lily, not that it matters these days.'

'Where does he live?'

'Like the rest of us, Sergeant, wherever the job happens to take him. It's not all beer and skittles, this game, you know. It's one dreary set of theatrical lodgings after another.'

'Well, d'you know where he's appearing now?'

'No idea, but I do know he's not seeing Lily any more. Like the old song says, "his wife won't let him".'

'Let me know if you do see or hear from her again,' said Hardcastle in a manner that brooked no argument. 'My sergeant will give you the telephone number. By the way, that Mr Fortune who was here . . .'

'Percy's just a drunken sot who's trying to work his way into my bed, Inspector.' Marie laughed scornfully. 'There's no chance of that, of course, but as long as he keeps buying me slap-up meals, I'll keep him guessing.'

SEVEN

By Wednesday morning the tram strike had been settled and Hardcastle was at the police station by a quarter past eight. But Marriott was already there, waiting outside the detectives' room for the DDI's arrival.

'Good morning, sir.'

'What is it, Marriott?' As usual, Hardcastle did not return his sergeant's greeting but swept straight into his office.

'There's a Detective Sergeant Gandy in my office, sir. He says he has information for you.'

Hardcastle paused in lighting his pipe and frowned. 'He's not from Special Branch, is he?' The DDI had an intense dislike, almost to the point of paranoia, of what was known internally as the 'Political Branch'. On several occasions he had been unwillingly embroiled in their enquiries and always got the impression that the head of the branch, the fearsome Detective Superintendent Patrick Quinn, was never quite satisfied with what he had achieved. Fortunately, at least as far as Hardcastle was concerned, Quinn had retired on the first of January last.

'No, sir, he's from W. He's Mr Fowler's first-class sergeant.'

'Well, show him in, Marriott. Don't stand there shilly-shallying.'

The man who entered the DDI's office was at least six-foot-two-inches tall and well-built. He had a luxuriant moustache and a permanent frown that gave the impression of a stern personality with whom it would be unwise to argue. In fact, he was the sort of officer it would be useful to have on your side in a rough house rather than against you.

'DS Gandy, sir. Mr Fowler asked me to bring this report to you personally. He said it was important.' Gandy handed over a three-page document.

'Who prepared this, Gandy?' asked Hardcastle, fingering the report.

'I did, sir. Mr Fowler said as how he wasn't prepared to trust it to anyone else in the circumstances.'

'What circumstances were they, Gandy?'

'He never said, sir.'

'I'll read it later, but just tell me what you found out about these here racing stables belonging to Captain Lucas's father.'

'His father is Lord Slade, sir, and Captain the Honourable Oscar Lucas is his only son. He inherited the racing stables, by which I mean Lord Slade did, sir, from his late father. Incidentally, it's an Irish peerage, sir, and Lord Slade seems to spend most of his time in Ireland where he has interests in stables over there an' all, mainly from the point of view of buying stock, as you might say.'

'Where did you get this information from, Gandy?' asked Hardcastle.

'Most of it came from Lord Slade's head stable lad, sir. He's a man of about twenty-five – Padraig O'Reilly, he's called – but he's only been with His Lordship since the Armistice, on account of having served with the North Irish Horse during the war. Was in the fighting down near Cambrai, so he said. I also put myself about in Epsom town itself, mainly in the pubs, and just kept my ears open. The best place for a bit of earwigging was the Spread Eagle in the High Street. Very popular with the racing fraternity is the Spread Eagle. Once I'd casually mentioned Lord Slade's name, I just sat back and listened.'

'Did you ask this head stable lad whether he'd seen Captain Lucas and a young woman at the stables last weekend, sometime between Thursday night and Monday morning, Gandy?'

'Yes, sir. Mr Fowler said as how I should make such an enquiry and O'Reilly said there was a young filly there what come down with Captain Lucas.'

'When you say a young filly, Gandy, I suppose you mean a young woman,' suggested Hardcastle, who wanted to make sure that Lucas had not arrived with a horse.

'Oh, yes, sir.' Gandy did not take Hardcastle's comment as a rebuke but merely laughed. 'It's mixing with these racing chaps what does it, you see, sir.'

'Did you get a description of this young woman?'

'Yes, for what it's worth, sir. If it had been a horse I've no doubt O'Reilly would've been able to describe it from its ears right down to its back fetlocks, but the description he give me of the young lady was a bit sketchy. It's in the report, sir.' Gandy pointed at the document on Hardcastle's desk. 'It's right at the end, sir.'

Hardcastle turned to the page and read the brief description. 'That'd fit a hundred young flappers,' he said, tossing the report to one side. 'To save me another trip out to Brixton, ask Mr Fowler if you can keep in touch with this here stable lad, Gandy, and let me know if you hear any more about this mysterious young woman.' He categorically refused to use the telephone to speak to DDI Fowler, or anyone else for that matter. Although he disliked the telephone, and viewed it as a passing fad, he was slowly accepting that it could be quite useful, provided he did not have to use the instrument himself.

'Very good, sir.' Gandy ran his sleeve over his bowler hat as if grooming the nap, then turned to leave the office.

'On your way out, ask Marriott to come in.'

'Very good, sir.'

A few moments later, Charles Marriott appeared. 'Yes, sir?'

'Have a look at this report that Gandy brought up, Marriott, and tell me what you think.'

It took Marriott but a few minutes to scan DS Gandy's report. 'When we interviewed Lucas at the In and Out, he told us that he and Lily spent the weekend in London and stayed at Lord Slade's apartment in Albany,' he said, returning the report. 'Which means that Lucas is a liar, sir,' he added. 'Or the stable lad is, which I doubt.'

'Have you got that list of the restaurants Lucas said he and Lily dined at, Marriott?'

By way of a reply, Marriott opened his pocketbook at the relevant page and handed it to the DDI.

'We'll pick one of them for a start, Marriott.' Hardcastle ran his finger down the list of names. 'Bellini's will do.'

'A table for two, sir?' The tail-coated man who greeted Hardcastle and Marriott at the entrance to Bellini's in the Strand was the epitome of attentiveness.

'No,' said Hardcastle. 'We're police officers and I want to speak to whoever's in charge here.'

'Oh, I see. George Pickard, maître d'hôtel, at your service, sir.' He paused. 'No trouble, I hope.'

'Not at all, Mr Pickard,' said Hardcastle, introducing himself and Marriott. 'Just a little information if you have a moment.'

The maître d'hôtel glanced around and flicked his fingers at a passing waiter. 'Take over here for me, Luigi, while I have a word with these gentlemen.'

'Certainly, *signore*,' said Luigi, and picked up a few menus from the maître d'hôtel's station.

'Now, sir,' said Pickard, 'if you'd care to come with me, we'll go somewhere quiet where we can talk without being disturbed.' He led the way into a small office near the restaurant entrance. There was a desk and one or two upright chairs, and Pickard invited the detectives to sit down before seating himself behind the desk.

'Do you happen to know Miss Lily Musgrave by sight, Mr Pickard?' asked Hardcastle. 'She's Austen Musgrave's girl.'

'Indeed I do, sir. An attractive young lady.'

'Was she here at any time over the last weekend?'

Pickard appeared to give the question some considerable thought. 'No, sir,' he said eventually. 'But if memory serves me correctly, she was here the previous Saturday evening.'

'Can you describe the man she was with on that occasion?' Hardcastle knew that she would not have dined alone or with another woman, except perhaps for her mother. But Marie Faye was in Brighton, performing at the Hippodrome.

'I can do better than that, sir. She was with Major Quilter. He owns the VanDoo Club in Rupert Street.'

'Oh, does he?' said Hardcastle mildly, pretending that this was news to him.

'Did she and Major Quilter appear to be close, Mr Pickard?' asked Marriott.

'Very much so, sir. In fact, they were holding hands from time to time – discreetly, of course. Mind you, she always seems to be close to the gentlemen who entertain her here, if you take my meaning.'

'I notice that you didn't describe them as *young* gentlemen, Mr Pickard,' suggested Marriott.

'Ah, I can see you're a detective, sir,' said Pickard with a smile. 'And you're quite right: some of them were often quite mature gentlemen.'

'Do you happen to have the names of any of the men she dined with? Was she, for instance, ever in the company of a Captain Oscar Lucas?'

'Captain Lucas.' For a moment Pickard savoured the name. 'Oh, yes, Lord Slade's son and heir. Yes, he's been here with Miss Musgrave once or twice.' He paused. 'He's been here with other young ladies, of course.' He emitted a sigh. 'What it is to be young, eh, Mr Hardcastle? In part it's a result of the war, I suppose. These young blades that served count themselves lucky to be alive and they're taking full advantage of it. You can't really blame them, and they're entitled to a bit of fun after the Front.'

'Can you remember any of the other men who brought Miss Musgrave here, Mr Pickard?' prompted Hardcastle, steering the maître d'hôtel away from his philosophizing.

'If you care to wait a moment, Inspector, I'll fetch the reservations lists for the last couple of months.'

'So much for Quilter's statement that he never entertained Lily, sir,' said Marriott once Pickard had left the room.

'Don't come as no surprise, Marriott. He denied it a bit too quick to be convincing. And I wonder where Quilter took this young lady of "easy virtue" after he'd wined and dined

her. In my experience, men of Quilter's sort who buy dinner
for a flapper in a swish place like this expect something in
return.'

Pickard returned to the small office. 'She seems to have
been a regular visitor here, Inspector.' He was clutching a
sheaf of paper and now wore a pair of spectacles. 'Over the
last two months, she was here on four occasions, usually on
a Friday or Saturday evening, apart from once at lunchtime.
That was about six weeks ago.'

'Do you have the names of the men who made the reservations, Mr Pickard?'

'Indeed I do, sir. There was a Colonel Rendell, Mr Roland
Kelsey, Major Nigel Toland and a Mr Carl Frampton.' Pickard
paused for a moment. 'I seem to remember that Mr Frampton
was in the navy, sir. He had two rings on his cuff but they
were those wavy ones.'

'That's the Royal Naval Volunteer Reserve,' commented
Marriott, and received a frown from Hardcastle. 'I don't
suppose you have addresses for these gentlemen, do you, Mr
Pickard?'

'I'm afraid not, sir, and they usually pay in cash, although
one or two of our patrons pay by cheque. But they'll have
been banked by now, so I can't even tell you which banks
they were drawn on. There is one thing that might help,
though, sir, and you could be doing me a favour.' Pickard
opened one of the drawers of his desk and withdrew a gold
cigarette case. 'Colonel Rendell left this on his table when
he and the young lady left. I kept a hold of it in the hope
that he'd come in again, but he hasn't. I took it round to Bow
Street police station but the sergeant said he couldn't accept
it as it was mislaid on private premises.'

'Quite correct,' said Marriott. 'D'you happen to recall the
date Colonel Rendell left it here?'

'Yes, I did. Because it looked valuable, I noted it in my
daybook. It was Saturday the fifteenth of February last.'

'I'll take it and restore it to the colonel when we find him,
Mr Pickard,' said Hardcastle, making it sound as though he
was doing the maître d'hôtel a favour. But, in fact, he knew
that it would help him trace at least one of Lily Musgrave's

other beaux. 'My sergeant will give you a receipt.' He turned to Marriott. 'Show it as a yellow metal cigarette case, not a gold one, Marriott.'

'I know, sir,' said Marriott wearily. He tired of the DDI reminding him of basic police duty as though he were a probationer uniformed constable, and it was difficult at times to keep the frustration from his voice.

'Thank you for your assistance, Mr Pickard,' said Hardcastle. 'You've been most helpful.'

'As a matter of interest, Inspector,' Pickard began hesitantly, 'has something happened to this young lady?'

'We hope not, Mr Pickard, but she's gone missing and I've been given the job of finding out where she's gone.'

'I'm sorry to hear that, sir. Is there any way that I can assist?'

'Perhaps so. If she comes in here at any time in the future, I'd be obliged if you'd telephone my police station. Discreetly, of course. Sergeant Marriott will give you the number to ring.'

'Certainly, sir. I hope no harm's come to her. She's a pretty little lass and lively, too.'

Following their usual liquid lunch in the Red Lion in Derby Gate, Hardcastle and Marriott returned to the police station.

'What are you proposing to do next, sir?' asked Marriott once he and Hardcastle were in the DDI's office.

'I think we'll send for Captain the Honourable Oscar Lucas and find out what the hell he's playing at. We still have to consider the matter of him carrying a minor off somewhere for a dirty weekend, which might have been against the young lady's will. After all, why tell us he stayed in London when he took the young woman to Epsom?' The DDI smiled archly. 'I think we'll need to remind him about the Offences Against the Person Act. And at some time in the near future we'll have few words with Major Quilter. If he thinks he can have one over on Ernie Hardcastle, he's very much mistaken.'

Detective Constable Henry Catto burst into the DDI's office. 'Begging your pardon, sir,' he gasped.

'What the blue blazes are you all in a two-and-eight about, Catto? And how many times do I have to tell you to knock before you come into my office? If Sergeant Marriott can knock, I'm bloody sure you can afford me the privilege.'

'Sorry, sir, but I thought you'd want to know straight off as it's urgent.'

'Are you going to impart this urgent information, Catto, or is it so important that you're going to keep it a secret?'

'Yes, sir. I mean, no, sir. Mr Musgrave just telephoned the station officer to say that Miss Musgrave has returned home.'

'What time?'

'Last night at about eight o'clock, sir.'

'*What?*' exclaimed Hardcastle.

'Last night at about—'

'All right, Catto, I heard you the first time,' snapped Hardcastle. 'To think that man is a member of parliament, Marriott. He needs few lessons in manners. Who the hell does he think he is?' Hardcastle, red in the face, took out his pipe and began to fill it. But such was his anger with Austen Musgrave that he stuffed the tobacco in so tightly that it would not draw properly and he had to empty the bowl and start to fill it again. 'What are you waiting for, Catto? Get about your duties.'

'Yes, sir.' Relieved, Catto fled.

'That looks like the end of the enquiry, sir.'

'Far from it, Marriott, far from it.' Hardcastle lit his pipe and gazed thoughtfully at the wall above Marriott's head. 'I'll send for Lily Musgrave and see what that young minx has to say.'

'Do you intend to interview her on her own, sir? As you said, she is a minor.'

'I'll get Bertha Cartwright to sit in on the interview. That'll keep young Miss Musgrave from coming the artful. Bertha docsn't suffer scatter-brained little hussies like Lily Musgrave.' Hardcastle smiled. 'Fetch Catto back in here, Marriott.'

'Sir?' Catto hovered in the doorway a minute later.

'Come in, Catto. I'm not going to eat you.'

'Sir.' Catto moved closer to the DDI's desk, giving the impression that he was about to be reprimanded for some grave omission.

'D'you know where Vincent Square is, lad?'

'Yes, sir, it's where the nurses' homes are.'

Hardcastle nodded thoughtfully. 'It comes as no surprise that you know where they are, Catto. However, that's not where you're going. Take a cab and go to Mr Austen Musgrave's residence and bring Miss Musgrave back here *tout de suite*. Now, is that clear?'

'Yes, sir,' said Catto, astounded that the DDI had authorized the hiring of a cab by a detective constable.

'And watch yourself,' cautioned Hardcastle. 'Miss Musgrave is an attractive young woman and I don't want to hear of no hanky-panky between you and her in the back of that cab. And to make sure, you'll take Keeler with you. Go!'

'Marriott,' said Hardcastle once Catto had left the office, 'get on that telephone thing and tell Mr High-and-Mighty Musgrave that Catto's on his way, and tell him I don't want any obstruction from him. If he argues the toss about his precious daughter being brought to the police station, just mention the Commissioner's name and tell him you're acting on his orders.'

'But did the Commissioner say we were to fetch Lily Musgrave here, sir?' Marriott was disturbed by Hardcastle's high-handed attitude, but at once sensed that the DDI was extremely annoyed at having been involved in a missing person's enquiry – something that, quite rightly, should have been handled by the Uniform Branch.

Hardcastle glanced at his sergeant with a look of despair. 'Sir Nevil said we were to find Lily Musgrave, Marriott. He didn't specify how. Therefore, whatever I do, or for that matter tell you or anyone else to do, is on the Commissioner's orders.'

'Even so, sir, don't you think that I should have gone, rather than sending a detective constable?'

'Certainly not, Marriott. I don't send first-class sergeants on errands of that nature. In the meantime, I'm going across the road to see Mr Wensley. It's time the Commissioner was told what sort of questionable friend he's got in Austen Musgrave.'

EIGHT

When he was not in the presence of the DDI, Henry Catto was full of confidence and an extremely proficient detective. Basil Keeler, on the other hand, tended to be in a state of nervousness most of the time.

'How are we going to tackle this, Henry?' Keeler asked as the two detectives mounted the steps.

'*You* are not going to tackle anything, Baz. Just be there and don't say a word. I'll do the talking.'

'Yes? What is it?' The supercilious expression on the butler's face implied that the two police officers standing on the doorstep were itinerant salesmen, possibly hawking insurance.

'You must be Crabb the butler,' said Catto.

'Er, yes, I am.' Catto's refusal to be cowed by Crabb's attitude disconcerted the butler. 'And who might you be?' he added, recovering a little of the bombast he assumed when dealing with those he believed to be beneath his master's station in life, or even his own perceived standing.

'We're police officers and we need to see Mr Austen Musgrave. Now!'

'I'll enquire if the master is at home,' said Crabb loftily, employing the euphemism that implied an interview was by no means a foregone conclusion.

'Well, he'd better be, cully,' said Catto as he swept off his bowler hat and pushed past a shocked Crabb, followed by an equally shocked Keeler, 'because this is important, and we don't have time to waste.'

Crabb hurriedly showed Catto and Keeler into the drawing room and went in search of his master.

'Popinjay!' muttered Catto at the butler's retreating back.

'He might complain about you being rude to him like that, Henry,' said Keeler.

'Rude?' exclaimed Catto hotly, and began to examine the

pictures and ornaments, giving the impression that he was not overawed by the obvious wealth of their owner. 'You were witness to what I said and you'll testify to the fact that I wasn't at all rude.' He glanced over his shoulder, fixing Keeler with a steely gaze.

It was some twenty minutes later that Austen Musgrave entered the room. 'I'm most awfully sorry to have kept you waiting, gentlemen,' he said affably. 'I presume you're some of Mr Hardcastle's chaps?'

'We are, sir. I'm Detective Constable Catto and this is Detective Constable Keeler.'

To Catto's surprise, Musgrave shook hands with each of them. 'How can I help you, gentlemen? And please do take a seat.' He indicated a settee under the window.

'This won't take a moment, sir,' said Catto, declining to sit down. 'I understand from my inspector that Miss Musgrave returned home at about eight o'clock last night.'

'That's correct. I telephoned the police station earlier today to let Mr Hardcastle know.'

'My inspector would like to have a few words with the young lady, sir.' Catto refrained from mentioning that Hardcastle had flown into a towering rage at the belated and seemingly casual way in which the police had been informed of Lily's return. 'He's asked me to escort Miss Musgrave to the police station,' he said in such a way that brooked no refusal. 'I have a cab waiting, sir.'

But rather than demur, Musgrave greeted the request with enthusiasm. 'What an excellent idea,' he said. 'Perhaps Mr Hardcastle can talk a bit of sense into the girl. Between you and me, Mr Catto, she doesn't take a blind bit of notice of anything I say, and her mother, Marie Faye, the actress, has left home and is treading the boards somewhere on the south coast. Or was, the last time I heard from her.' He crossed the room and rang for the butler.

'Sir?' Crabb entered the room within seconds, almost as if he had been waiting for such a summons, possibly in the hope that he would be asked to eject the two policemen.

'Ask Miss Lily to come down, if you please, Crabb.'

As the butler left, a woman swept into the room making

what is best described as a grand entrance. She was tall and slender, probably in her late thirties. Barefooted, her long blonde hair was in disarray and she was wearing a peignoir. Despite her careless appearance, there was no doubt that she was an extremely handsome woman.

'Oh, I'm so sorry,' she said, affording the two detectives a fetching smile and raising her arms as if making an impassioned appeal to the gallery, 'but I didn't realize we had visitors. I'm Sarah Gillard.' The woman, who spoke with a noticeable American accent, was quite unembarrassed by her state of undress and was making a point of directing her remarks to Catto.

'Miss Gillard is an American theatre actress, gentlemen,' volunteered Musgrave hurriedly, as if that was sufficient to explain her attire, 'but she's appearing at the Theatre Royal Haymarket and is staying with me for the time being.'

'My dears, you would not believe how awful some theatrical diggings are,' said Sarah, continuing to address the two detectives. 'You're not in the profession by any chance, are you? Austen is a great patron of the arts, although he seems to think that this cinematograph business will be the death of the theatre once they've worked out how to put sound on to the film. Personally, I don't think it'll ever come to anything. There's nothing like live theatre.' She laughed, a gay, tinkling laugh. 'Can you imagine seeing Shakespeare's *Hamlet* at the Bioscope in Vauxhall Bridge Road? It's too laughable for words.'

'These gentlemen are detectives, Sarah,' said Musgrave, in an attempt to slow the woman's inane prattling. 'They've come to take Lily to the police station for an interview.'

'Oh, how delightfully thrilling, Austen my dear,' said Sarah, laughing gaily. 'Has young Lily been a naughty girl again?'

'Again, madam?' Catto did not miss the implication.

'Oh, she's a real little minx, isn't she, Austen?'

'In what way?' Catto wanted to know.

'Going off to nightclubs and that sort of thing,' said Sarah carelessly, 'but it's what young people do these days. The war has much to answer for, you know, Detective.'

Crabb appeared in the doorway. 'Miss Lily, sir,' he said, ushering the young woman into the room.

'The policeman who was assigned to find out where you were over the weekend wants to talk to you, Lily. He is Inspector Hardcastle.'

'I really don't know why you had to make such a fuss, Pops,' said Lily, pouting. 'It was silly to involve the police.'

'You really shouldn't talk to your father like that, Lily, dear,' said Sarah Gillard.

'It's nothing to do with you, Sarah,' said Lily haughtily, and turned back to her father. 'Why does this inspector want to see me, Pops?'

'I've no idea,' said Musgrave, 'but no doubt you'll find out soon enough. Now be a good girl and run along with these two nice policemen. They've a cab waiting outside. And don't be late back for dinner. You know how Sarah and I hate to be kept waiting, apart from the inconvenience to the staff, and especially Mrs Briggs.'

'I'll be out for dinner this evening so I can't spend too much time hanging around in police stations,' Lily announced. 'I'll just get my coat.' She shot a contrived coy smile at Catto and Keeler and swept from the room.

'We won't hold you up any longer, sir,' said Catto. 'We'll be outside with the cab when the young lady's ready.'

'Thank you, gentlemen. I'll send her straight out.'

The pair had reached the pavement before Keeler posed the question that had been nagging him ever since he had seen Sarah Gillard. 'What did you think of the actress who's staying with Mr Musgrave, Henry?' he asked. 'Very attractive, I thought.'

'Actress, my foot!' scoffed Catto. 'She might be an actress, Baz, but I reckon she'd just tumbled out of Musgrave's bed. Did you see the state of her? And did you notice how long it took Musgrave to come into the drawing room? I reckon he had to get dressed in a bit of a hurry once Crabb told him we were waiting.'

'I'm here, boys.' Lily Musgrave appeared at the top of the steps, struck a pose and blew a kiss at the waiting detectives. 'Ready when you are.' If it was an attempt at seduction it failed as far as Catto was concerned, and Keeler failed to recognize it as such.

* * *

'What is it, Marriott?'

'Catto and Keeler have arrived with Miss Musgrave, sir.'

'Send Catto in.'

Moments later, an apprehensive Henry Catto appeared in the door of the DDI's office.

'You wanted me, sir?'

'What have you to report? Any trouble from the Musgrave family?'

'No, sir. In fact, Mr Musgrave thought it was a good idea for you to give the girl a bit of a talking to, sir.'

'Did he indeed,' replied Hardcastle, chuckling.

'I reckon Lily Musgrave's a bit of a handful, sir,' continued Catto, now regaining some of the confidence he usually only displayed out of Hardcastle's presence, and went on to tell the DDI about Sarah Gillard's intervention and Lily's reaction. He described her little performance at the top of the steps. 'She's not above making eyes at any man who talks to her, neither, sir.'

'Is that so, Catto? Very well.'

'By the way, sir, she did say she'd got an appointment for dinner this evening.'

'Did she *really*?' said Hardcastle sarcastically. 'Well, Miss Musgrave will have to learn that a divisional detective inspector don't respond to the whims and fancies of a seventeen-year-old floozy. It won't hurt that young lady to cool her heels for a bit. She needn't think she can flick her fingers and get what she wants. It might work with her father but it don't work in here.' He began to fill his pipe slowly, as if deliberately wasting time. 'Ask Sergeant Marriott to enquire if Mrs Cartwright is free for half an hour or so. If she ain't too busy, that is. If she is, then La Belle Musgrave will have to sit and twiddle her thumbs for a bit.'

'You wanted to see me, sir?' said Bertha Cartwright as she and Charles Marriott entered Hardcastle's office a few minutes later.

'Come and sit down, Mrs Cartwright. I have a job for you, if you're willing to assist me and you're not too busy. You stay here as well, Marriott.' Hardcastle lit his pipe and watched the smoke spiral towards the nicotine-stained ceiling.

Bertha Cartwright, a state-registered nurse, was a buxom,

widowed woman of some fifty summers. For several years now she had been the matron at Cannon Row police station and, in Hardcastle's view, made the best cup of tea on the division. She may have appeared nervous when in the DDI's office, but it was in fact deference to Hardcastle, a man she greatly admired. However, anyone making the mistake of thinking that she could easily be intimidated was in for a surprise. In a murder case in which she was called as a prosecution witness, she gave evidence at the Old Bailey and had surprised even Hardcastle in the way she had countered Sir Rowland Storey's cross-examination. Storey, an eminent King's Counsel, was appearing for the defence and Bertha Cartwright had answered all his questions confidently and firmly. Realizing that she was not to be browbeaten, he gave up and sat down.

'How's your boy Jack getting on, Mrs Cartwright?'

Jack Cartwright was the apple of his mother's eye. While serving in the Royal Garrison Artillery he had been fortunate to survive the entire war without so much as a scratch. Within weeks of the hostilities beginning, Jack had been promoted to lance bombardier, an elevation that had delighted his mother more than the meagre promotion merited. Hardcastle had been kept informed of the boy's progress from time to time and, the last he had been told, Jack Cartwright was about to be promoted to regimental sergeant-major.

'He's been made a captain, sir.' Mrs Cartwright beamed with the obvious pride she had in her son's success as a soldier.

'That's a splendid achievement,' said Hardcastle, 'but no doubt he'll be pleased to get home and find a decent job somewhere.'

'Oh, no, not Jack, sir. You see, he had a bit of luck, although I shouldn't call it that in the circumstances. After he got made RSM, the colonel said he ought to be an officer. Well, sir, when he was a second lieutenant there was a terrible accident when a shell exploded in the breech of a Howitzer. It so happened that the brigade commander, the very colonel who'd recommended Jack for a commission, was standing nearby and was killed instantly, along with the battery captain. Well, these things happen in war and before he knew where he was,

Jack was a captain himself. Anyway, sir, to cut a long story short, Jack wants to stay on in the army and he's hoping to be given a regular commission.'

'That's good news, Mrs Cartwright. Give him my congratulations.' Although Hardcastle had never met Jack Cartwright, he felt that he knew him.

'Oh, I will, sir, and thank you kindly. But I didn't come here to talk about my boy Jack,' said Bertha Cartwright, despite having gone on at some length about him. 'You wanted me to do a job, you said.'

Hardcastle explained about the sort of life Lily Musgrave led and went on to relate what Catto had told him about the girl's behaviour in the presence of young men.

'She strikes me as a thoroughly spoiled young woman, Mrs Cartwright, but I have to satisfy myself that she was a willing party to spending a weekend with this ex-officer down at Epsom in some racing stables. Otherwise, the ex-officer concerned may be facing charges.'

'I think I know what sort of lass you're talking about, sir.'

'I'm about to question her in here, Mrs Cartwright, and I'd like you to be present because I don't want any silly behaviour from her.' In truth, Hardcastle did not wish to be the subject of any allegations of improper conduct. Police officers had discovered over the years that such allegations are easily made but difficult to disprove.

'Oh, I quite understand, sir,' said Bertha Cartwright, who was shrewd enough to have guessed the real reason. 'D'you want me to say anything?'

'If she gets a bit uppity I'll rely on you to put her in her place, Mrs Cartwright, and I don't care what you say to her. She's more likely to take notice of you.'

'Don't you worry, sir. I'll see she behaves herself.'

'I'm sure you will, Mrs Cartwright.' The DDI was under no illusion but that a word from the matron would put the fear of God into the girl. He had seen it happen before. 'Very well, Marriott, fetch her in here.'

The description of Lily Musgrave that Austen Musgrave had given Hardcastle did not prepare him for the young woman who entered his office. And the photograph that

Musgrave had produced could easily have been of an entirely different girl.

Her shapeless dress, a mixture of black and bronze silk, had a hemline that stopped just above the knee but a fringe continued for another four inches, doing nothing to lessen the effect. She had a string of beads that fell to below her waist and that, together with the bandeau and its accompanying feather, made the entire ensemble the epitome of modern fashion. At least, in Lily's view, and in the view of her peers. Hardcastle thought that the entire get-up looked rather ridiculous.

'I don't have very much time, you know.' Lily did not look directly at either Hardcastle or Bertha Cartwright, but instead gazed superciliously around the office.

'You'll have as much time as I decide, young lady,' said Hardcastle brusquely. 'Sit down.'

Lily was taken aback by the DDI's abrasive manner, if not a little scared. It was probably the first time that anyone had ever spoken to her like that and she promptly sat down on the hard, straight-backed chair that was in front of Hardcastle's desk. He had deliberately placed it at an angle so that the matron, from her place at the side of the desk, would be able to observe the young woman closely.

'For a start, you can tell me where you spent last weekend,' Hardcastle began.

'I don't see that it has anything to do with—' Lily said arrogantly.

'If you know what's good for you, girl, you'll just answer the inspector's question,' snapped Bertha Cartwright loudly.

There was a sharp intake of breath from Lily Musgrave to whom this office, and its hostile occupants, was an alien environment, and she was now unsure what would happen to her. Was she about to be arrested? Although the men she had consorted with had told her there was nothing to worry about, perhaps what she had been doing was, after all, against the law.

'Well?' said Hardcastle.

'I spent it with a friend.'

'I asked you *where* you had spent the weekend, not *who* you spent it with.' Hardcastle was already losing patience

with the spoilt brat seated in front of him. Marriott, who was
sitting behind the girl, hoped that the DDI would not lose his
temper. He had seen it happen before and knew it was usually
counterproductive.

'In London.' And then, sensing that this was not enough
to satisfy the coarse policeman opposite her, she continued,
'At Albany in Piccadilly. My friend's father has a lease on
an apartment there.'

'What's his name?'

'I didn't say it was a man.' Lily Musgrave still managed to
display a little arrogance, but when the DDI's fingers began
to play a slow tattoo on the edge of his desk, she promptly
clarified the statement. 'Captain Oscar Lucas. His father is
Lord Slade.'

'Is that the only time you've spent a weekend with Lucas?'

'Yes.'

'What did you think of Lord Slade's stables at Epsom?'
asked Hardcastle mildly, as if he was taking but a casual
interest in the girl's activities.

'Wonderful, and I loved the horses.' Lily paused. 'Oh dear!'
she said, and blushed to the roots of her hair.

Satisfied that he had confirmation the girl had spent the
weekend at Epsom, Hardcastle now changed tack.

'Where did Max Quilter take you after you had dinner with
him at Bellini's on Saturday the twenty-second of February?'

The suddenness of the question and its complete change
from the matter in which Hardcastle had been interested
previously, came as a shock.

'I, er, I don't know what you mean.' Lily's reply was halting
and nervous.

'And then there are . . .' Hardcastle paused to flick his
fingers. 'What was them names, Marriott?'

'Colonel Rendell, Major Toland, Mr Kelsey and a Lieutenant
Frampton of the RNVR, sir.'

At this revelation, Lily Musgrave burst into tears, and
whatever black stuff she had put on her eyes started to run
down her cheeks.

'Now, Miss Musgrave,' said Hardcastle, using the girl's
name for the first time, 'I think it's time we had the truth.

For a start, how old are you?' He knew the answer but wanted to see what the girl had to say.

'Twenty.' Despite her tears, there was a note of defiance in Lily's answer.

'I think you're seventeen. The reason I have had you brought here, Miss Musgrave, is that I am investigating these men because I believe they may have taken you away for the purpose of knowing you carnally.'

'What on earth does that mean?' demanded Lily, slowly recovering from the realization that this brutal detective seemed to know the answers to all the questions he was asking her.

'It means for the purpose of having sexual intercourse with you.'

The bluntness of the statement shocked the young girl. Despite her unconventional attitude, she was nowhere as sophisticated as she thought she was and was not yet old enough to realize that mature adults could see through her charade.

'So what?'

'Keep a civil tongue in your head, Musgrave,' snapped Mrs Cartwright.

'I take it you have had sexual relations with these men, Miss Musgrave?'

'What if I have?'

'Willingly?'

'What the inspector means, girl,' said Bertha Cartwright, before Lily had a chance to reply, 'is whether you knew that was the intention of these men when you went out with them.'

'Of course I knew. It's part of having a good time.'

Hardcastle emitted a sigh. 'You can go but I'll probably send for you again,' he said. 'One of my officers will take you home.' He glanced at Marriott. 'Arrange for Catto to take her back to Vincent Square.' After a pause, he added, 'And make sure Keeler goes too.'

When the door had closed behind Lily Musgrave, Hardcastle turned to the matron. 'Well, Mrs Cartwright, what did you think of her?'

'A right brazen little hussy, sir, who could do with being put over someone's knee and given a good spanking. I really don't know what the world's coming to.'

'I'm still not satisfied she's telling the truth, though,' commented Hardcastle, half to himself. 'I still think I'll speak to these beaux she's been giving her favours to.'

NINE

D etective Superintendent Frederick Wensley was standing at the window of his office, staring at the half-built County Hall on the other side of the river Thames. Construction of the building had begun in 1909 but ceased in 1916 because of a shortage of materials and manpower, both of which had been caused by the war.

Wensley turned as Hardcastle knocked and entered. 'I see they've started work on the new County Hall again, Ernie.'

'I wonder what that'll cost the taxpayer, sir.'

Wensley laughed; Hardcastle's reputation for parsimony was well known among officers of the Criminal Investigation Department. 'I'm sure you haven't come over to discuss the cost of building the County Hall, Ernie. What's on your mind?'

Hardcastle told Wensley about his interviews with Quilter, Lucas and Lily Musgrave, and the information he had obtained from Pickard, the maître d'hôtel at Bellini's. And he explained where he thought Sarah Gillard fitted into the Musgrave ménage, not that that was particularly relevant. 'So it looks like the end of the matter, sir, unless the girl runs off again, I suppose. Nevertheless, I will have a word with the men who've befriended her, just in case there's evidence of a breach of the Offences Against the Person Act. However, Lily denied that she had been taken anywhere by force and admitted knowing she'd have to pay for her dinner by going to bed with her benefactors, which she did willingly. Given those facts, I think we'd have a job convincing a jury.'

'I agree, Ernie. I'll let the Commissioner know the outcome and we'll write it off. Incidentally, Sir Nevil was grateful for the information about Austen Musgrave. He hadn't any idea

about the man's dubious background and apparently had met
him at his club.' Wensley sighed. 'The trouble is that Sir Nevil
is an officer and a gentleman, Ernie, and takes people on
trust, unlike the sort of nasty cynical coppers you and I are.'

'I'll let you have a written report, sir,' said Hardcastle,
standing up. 'And I'll inform you of anything of interest that
comes up as a result of my interviews with the girl's men
friends.'

'Have you got much on at the moment?' asked Wensley.
He was not checking up on Hardcastle; he knew he was a
dedicated policeman but was always interested in the workload
of his detectives.

'Not on the crime front, sir, but my youngest daughter's
wedding is looming.'

'Expensive business,' said Wensley, but added nothing
further. His only daughter had married recently, lifting the
spirits of a family that was still grieving the loss of two sons
killed in the war.

Having decided to interview Captain Oscar Lucas once more,
Hardcastle and Marriott took a cab to the In and Out Club
in Piccadilly.

The green-liveried club servant regarded the two detectives
critically. 'How may I be of assistance, Inspector?'

'I need to see Captain Lucas again,' said Hardcastle.

'I'll see if he is in the club,' said the servant.

'His car's there,' said Hardcastle, waving his umbrella at
the maroon Lagonda coupé parked in the courtyard.

'That's as maybe, but members sometimes leave their
cars here and take a cab to go out for lunch. However, if
you wait in the reception room, I'll see if the captain's
prepared to see you.'

'Pompous arse,' muttered Hardcastle and, followed by
Marriott, plonked himself down on one of the uncomfortable
sofas with which the reception room was furnished.

'I didn't expect to see you again, Inspector.' Oscar Lucas
appeared almost immediately. So quickly, in fact, that he
must have seen the two detectives being shown into the
reception room.

'I don't suppose you did,' said Hardcastle without bothering to stand up. 'Take a seat and explain why you've been lying to me.'

'I don't understand.'

Hardcastle sighed. 'Captain Lucas, I didn't come up the Clyde on a bicycle.'

'I beg your pardon?' Lucas shook his head in bewilderment.

'What my inspector means, Captain Lucas, is that when we spoke to you the day before yesterday,' said Marriott, glancing down at his pocketbook, 'you stated that you and Miss Lily Musgrave spent the previous weekend at your father's apartment at Albany in Piccadilly and dined in various London restaurants.'

'Well?'

'We interviewed Miss Musgrave yesterday and she told us that she had spent the weekend with you at your father's stables at Epsom.' Marriott's statement was not entirely accurate, but Lily had been caught out when she admitted only ever spending one weekend with Lucas. It followed, therefore, that it must have been at the Epsom stables of Lord Slade.

'And you believe her?' Lucas was not giving in easily.

'Yes, we do,' said Hardcastle. 'Apart from that, it seemed to be common knowledge around Epsom, particularly in the Spread Eagle pub.'

'I see. Well, it's not a crime, is it?'

'To quote the Offences Against the Person Act, Captain Lucas,' said Marriott, picking up the interview again, 'if you abducted Miss Musgrave with the intent of carnally knowing her, then yes, it is a crime that carries a penalty of five years' imprisonment. And she has admitted having sexual intercourse with you.'

'For God's sake, Sergeant, she was a willing partner.' Lucas's face began working and he started to shake. It was not clear whether it was the thoroughness of the police investigation into the matter and the threat of imprisonment or a renewal of the shell shock from which he was said to suffer. 'It was an innocent couple of days. She knew why she was coming down to Epsom.' A sudden thought occurred to the young ex-officer. 'I say, my father doesn't have to know about this, does he? He'd play merry hell if he found out.'

'We won't tell him,' said Hardcastle, 'but it might be a good idea to bribe the head stable lad to keep his trap shut.'

'So it was him who told you, was it?'

'No,' said Hardcastle, never willing to divulge the name of an informant, 'but I presume there *is* a head stable lad and they always seem to know everything. However, on another matter,' he continued, satisfied that Lucas had not committed any offence, 'perhaps you can tell me where I can find Colonel Rendell and Major Toland.' The question was posed in an offhand manner, giving the impression there was no doubt that the two men named by Pickard at Bellini's as dinner companions of Lily were friends of Lucas.

'I, er, well, Tom Rendell is a member here but I haven't seen him today.'

'Where does he live?' demanded Hardcastle, pressing home the advantage gained by his guesswork.

'Somewhere in Old Queen Street, I think, but I'm not too sure,' said Lucas. 'It's just off Birdcage Walk.'

'I know where it is,' snapped Hardcastle. 'Old Queen Street is on my division.'

'I don't know anyone by the name of Major Toland, though.' But Lucas looked away from the DDI when he said it. 'As a matter of interest, why d'you want to talk to Tom Rendell?'

'A cigarette case of his has come into the possession of police and I have to return it to him,' said Hardcastle.

'I could do that for you,' said Lucas. It could have been a helpful offer on his part or a device to stop the police from speaking to Rendell. If it was the latter, it was to no avail.

'If you have written authority to receive any goods on behalf of Colonel Rendell, Captain Lucas,' said Hardcastle, 'I'll be happy to hand it over. To do otherwise would be contrary to police regulations. I'm sure you came across similar rules in the army,' he added smoothly.

'Oh, I see. Yes, of course.'

'Come, Marriott, we've wasted enough time.'

Ignoring the doorkeeper, who had the courtesy to open the

door for them, Hardcastle, with Marriott rushing behind him, strode out to Piccadilly, where he hailed a cab.

'Are we going straight to Old Queen Street, sir?' asked a breathless Marriott. It was an unwise question.

Hardcastle paused, his foot on the step of the cab. 'What, and go without our usual lunchtime pint? Are you feeling all right, Marriott?'

The cab deposited the two detectives in Parliament Street and they descended to the downstairs bar of the Red Lion in Derby Gate.

Marriott had sent DC Keeler to examine the electoral roll at the public library in Great Smith Street. It was the quickest way of discovering where in Old Queen Street Colonel Thomas Rendell resided. This proposal was, of course, based on the assumption that Colonel Rendell was registered to vote, although he may have been renting the apartment and was registered elsewhere, or even not registered at all. However, on this occasion, the detectives were in luck.

Consequently, it was nigh-on three o'clock when Hardcastle and Marriott knocked on the door of Rendell's apartment.

Hardcastle had a preconceived idea of what colonels should look like, based mainly on his professional dealings with Lieutenant Colonel Ralph Frobisher, the assistant provost marshal for London District. However, the youthful man who answered the door of Rendell's apartment was probably thirty years of age at most. Tall and clean-shaven, he had the smooth appearance of a matinee idol rather than that of a soldier. Upon reflection, Hardcastle realized that he was probably one of those officers who had benefited, if that was the right word, from the death in action of his superiors. From about 1916 onwards, young men had been rapidly promoted and there were even one or two brigadier-generals who had yet to reach the age of thirty-five.

'Good afternoon.' The man cast a quizzical gaze over the two detectives, wondering who they were and why they were there. He did not have long to wait.

'Colonel Rendell?'

'Yes, I'm Colonel Rendell.'

'We're police officers, Colonel. I'm Divisional Detective Inspector Hardcastle of the Whitehall Division and this is Detective Sergeant Marriott.'

'Really? Well, I don't know why you should want to speak to me but you'd better come in.'

The sitting room of the apartment was impeccably clean and tidy, as befitted a soldier, and for that same reason was somewhat spartan in furnishing. There were a number of leather armchairs, a low table upon which were copies of *Illustrated London News* and *The Field* neatly arranged. The walls had numerous pictures, including some paintings, most of which depicted horses in hunting scenes.

'Are you a hunting man, Inspector?' enquired Rendell, having noticed the DDI's interest in the pictures.

'Alas, Colonel, I don't have the time,' said Hardcastle, as though it was a matter for regret.

It was a comment that caused Marriott to turn away and grit his teeth for fear of bursting out laughing. The thought of a red-coated Hardcastle riding to hounds was too much to contemplate.

'You'd better take a pew and tell me what this is all about.' Rendell settled himself in one of the armchairs, crossed his legs and appeared perfectly relaxed.

By way of a reply, Hardcastle took out the cigarette case that had been handed to him by the maître d'hôtel at Bellini's and placed it on the table.

'Good heavens!' exclaimed Rendell. 'I never thought I'd see that again. It was with me all through the war, only for me to lose it a couple of weeks ago. Where did you find it?'

'I didn't,' said Hardcastle. 'It was the maître d'hôtel at Bellini's who found it. You left it on the table after you'd had dinner there.'

'Oh, how super. I shall reward him next time I'm there,' said Rendell, leaning forward and picking up the case. 'It was a gift from my late father.' He glanced at Hardcastle. 'He was in the regiment, too,' he added.

'Are you still in the army, Colonel?'

'No, I've finished with all that, thank God.'

'I understand you dined with Miss Lily Musgrave on that occasion, Colonel. It was the fifteenth of February last.'

Rendell suddenly tensed. 'What exactly is this all about, Inspector? I'm sure a divisional detective inspector doesn't usually go about restoring lost property.'

'How old d'you think Miss Musgrave is, Colonel?'

Rendell glanced at Marriott and then back again to Hardcastle. 'Has this got to the point when I should have my solicitor present?' he asked.

'Have you committed a crime, then?' enquired Hardcastle blandly.

'I'm beginning to wonder.'

'I'll ask you again, Colonel. How old d'you think Miss Musgrave is?'

'She told me that she was twenty-one on her last birthday.'

'Would it surprise you to know that she is seventeen, Colonel?' asked Marriott.

'Ye Gods!' exclaimed Rendell. 'I don't believe it.'

'I can assure you she is,' Marriott continued. 'We have that assurance from Mr Austen Musgrave who, as you probably know, is a member of parliament.'

'He's even being tipped for a Cabinet post,' said Hardcastle.

'Ye Gods!' said Rendell again, and pushed a hand through his hair. 'I didn't even know her surname was Musgrave, otherwise it would have rung a bell immediately. If I remember correctly, Musgrave was responsible for the manufacture of somewhat inferior quality uniforms.'

'Yes, I believe he was a manufacturer of army clothing,' said Hardcastle, unwilling to be committed on the matter of the quality of his merchandise. 'How did you meet Miss Musgrave, Colonel?'

'At the VanDoo Club,' said Rendell promptly. 'It's in Rupert Street.'

'Yes, I know where it is. Presumably you were introduced to this young lady by Max Quilter?'

'Yes.'

'Have you ever spent a weekend away with this young woman?'

'No,' said Rendell, but it was unconvincing. 'Even supposing I had, there's nothing wrong in that, surely?'

'It depends how willing she was,' said Marriott. 'You see, Colonel, my inspector is pursuing the possibility that this young woman was deluded into spending weekends with men much older than herself, unaware that their intention was to have sexual intercourse with her. Or as the statute puts it: to carnally know her.'

Rendell remained silent for a few moments, his chin touching his chest as he gave the matter considerable thought and wondered whether he really *should* contact his solicitor. But eventually, he made a decision.

'I'd better tell you all about it, I suppose.'

'That would be a start,' said Hardcastle.

'Aren't you supposed to tell me that I don't have to say anything if I don't want to, Inspector? I'm sure I read an article in *The Times* about some new rule that's been introduced.'

'There's no need to worry about that, Colonel.' Hardcastle did not understand the so-called 'Judges' Rules' that had recently been introduced or the need for them, and therefore, typically, ignored them.

Rendell sighed. 'We have these parties every once in a while, usually on a Saturday, Inspector. We take it in turns to escort Lily to a slap-up dinner somewhere up West, and then she, er, entertains us.'

'What form does this entertainment take, Colonel?'

'I'd rather not say.'

'Who else is at these parties, as you call them?'

'I'm sorry, but I can't tell you.'

'Why? Are you all in disguise?' asked Hardcastle sarcastically.

'I'm not revealing the identity of the other guests. I'm sorry, but that's that.'

'Let me hazard a guess, Colonel,' said Marriott, fearing that the DDI was about to lose his temper. 'A Mr Kelsey, Major Toland and Carl Frampton. Frampton is, or was, in the navy.'

'I'm not saying anything.' But Rendell's expression told Marriott that he had confirmed the identity of at least some of the 'guests' at these mysterious parties.

'Very well, Colonel.' Hardcastle stood up, aware that he was unlikely to get anything else out of the ex-officer. 'We'll meet again, I think.'

'We'll walk back to the nick, Marriott,' said Hardcastle once he and Marriott were once more in the street. 'I need to clear my head.'

Hardcastle was piqued, to say the least, by Colonel Rendell's refusal to divulge the names of the others who enjoyed Lily Musgrave's entertainment, whatever form that took. Marriott took a more reasonable view, in that Rendell was quite within his rights to refuse to identify his fellow guests. It could hardly be construed as obstructing police. At least, not yet.

But Hardcastle, on occasions such as this, tended to behave like a dog with a bone, and would continue to worry it even though it was clear that there was no meat left on it. He did not intend to give up.

'I think we'll get a search warrant for the VanDoo Club, Marriott. Draw up an information and I'll swear it tomorrow morning at Bow Street.'

'Is that wise, sir?'

'Rendell refused to give any more information and that leads me to think they're up to no good. Wherever these parties take place, it could be termed a brothel, a house of ill repute. I'll not leave it, Marriott. I'm not having these toffee-nosed ex-officers running rings round me. However, I'll review the situation tomorrow. Go home, Marriott, and my regards to Mrs Marriott.'

'Thank you, sir,' said a relieved Marriott. 'And mine to Mrs H.'

'And now I have a real problem on my hands,' muttered Hardcastle, half to himself.

'A problem, sir?' queried Marriott.

'I've got to organize Maud's wedding. She's getting spliced on the twenty-second of this month and that's only a fortnight on Saturday.'

'I suppose everything's all done and dusted, sir.'

'You suppose wrong, Marriott. I haven't done a thing about it yet.'

'If there's anything I can do, sir, just say the word.'

For a long moment, Hardcastle stared at his sergeant. 'I might just take you up on that, Marriott,' he said.

TEN

Hardcastle could always find something to do in his office, and it was at least an hour after he had sent Marriott home that he left the police station. He then spent a frustrating twenty minutes standing on Victoria Embankment before the tram for Kennington arrived.

Consequently, it was just after eight o'clock that he put his key in the door of his house.

'Is that you, Ernie?'

'Yes, love. Where are you?' Hardcastle posed the usual question and received the usual answer.

'In the kitchen,' said Alice Hardcastle.

Hardcastle hung up his bowler hat and Chesterfield overcoat and placed his umbrella in the stand. Pausing briefly, he checked the hall clock against his half-hunter and, satisfied that it was keeping time, put his head round the kitchen door. He knew better than to venture further when his wife was preparing the evening meal, and no longer had an excuse for doing so. The *Daily Mail* map of the Western Front into which Hardcastle would stick little flags indicating the movement of the opposing armies had been removed from its place near the cooker on Armistice Day.

'Glass of sherry, love?' Without waiting for a reply, Hardcastle walked through to the sitting room and poured a glass of Amontillado for his wife and a whisky for himself.

'You're early tonight, Ernie.' Alice came into the room, gave her husband a kiss on the cheek and settled into her favourite armchair. 'Put a bit more coal on, there's a love,' she said.

Using the tongs, Hardcastle, aware of the soaring cost of fuel, selected a few knobs of coal and placed them carefully

on the fire. He stood up, picked up his glass and was about
to take a sip when Alice spoke again.

'I hope you haven't forgotten that your daughter Maud is
getting married a fortnight on Saturday, Ernest.'

'I'm hardly likely to.' The use of Hardcastle's full name
warned him that a rebuke was in the offing.

'Have you spoken to the vicar again? Just to make sure
that he knows what he's doing.'

'Not yet, dear, but the banns have been read.'

'Well, Ernest, I suggest you walk down to Saint Anselm's
before you've got the smell of whisky on your breath and
make sure that everything is in hand for the service. We don't
want any slip-ups, not with all Charles's brother officers there.
I've seen how it should be done in India,' continued Alice, who
was never backward in reminding Hardcastle that she had
been born in Peshawar, the daughter of a sergeant in the Royal
Garrison Artillery. 'Her young man is an officer and is used
to having things all shipshape and Bristol fashion.'

'He's in the army, not the navy,' responded Hardcastle
churlishly. 'I have been very busy, Alice, running around on
the Commissioner's orders.'

'Perhaps now he knows you exist, Ernie, he'll promote
you,' replied Alice.

Not prepared to enter into a discussion about the vagaries
of the promotion system in the Metropolitan Police, Hardcastle
opted to walk down Kennington Road to see the vicar of
St Anselm's Church. Reluctantly, he placed his glass of whisky
on the mantelshelf and returned to the hall. Donning his
overcoat and bowler hat, he seized his umbrella and departed,
somewhat irritably slamming the front door.

The Reverend Percy Lovejoy, vicar of St Anselm's Church at
Kennington Cross, was a ruddy-faced, jolly man of about thirty.
His girth indicated that he had never gone short of food; in fact,
his cassock appeared to be straining at the buttons. Shortly after
taking holy orders in 1914, he had entered the Army Chaplains'
Department on the fourth of August where his ministrations as
a padre had taken him right into the front-line trenches, and he
had been highly respected by colonels and corporals alike.

On his release from the army at the end of the war, Lovejoy had been offered a choice of the livings of St Anselm's in Kennington, and another in a fashionable part of Cheltenham. It was characteristic of the man that he had unhesitatingly chosen Kennington where he had established a reputation as a caring clergyman. His concern for his parishioners went far beyond that normally expected of an incumbent, and he was not afraid, literally, to get his hands dirty. Now that he was a civilian clergyman, he never mentioned his military service, and if anyone asked him what he had done in the war, he would wave a hand in the air and mutter something about his having got in everyone's way.

'My dear Mr Hardcastle.' Lovejoy opened the door of the vicarage. 'Do come in, my dear fellow.' He conducted Hardcastle into the living room where a log fire was crackling in the hearth. 'Let me take your hat and coat, and I'm sure you'd not be averse to a glass of whisky, eh?'

'Very kind, Vicar,' murmured Hardcastle.

'A bottle of The Glenlivet recently came my way,' said Lovejoy, adopting an innocent expression but with an impish twinkle in his eye. Having poured substantial measures of malt whisky, Lovejoy took out his pipe. He reached across to a side table and picked up a brass box bearing a likeness of Princess Mary. Thousands of such boxes had been sent to sailors and soldiers at Christmas 1914, but Lovejoy now kept tobacco in his. 'Have a fill, my dear fellow,' he said, handing the box to Hardcastle. 'I know you're a pipe-smoker.'

Once the two men were settled by the fire with their pipes well alight and they had talked about the topics of the moment, such as the conference at Versailles, rising prices and how little was being done for wounded ex-servicemen, Lovejoy poured more whisky.

'I'm sure your good lady wanted you to make sure everything was in hand for a fortnight on Saturday, eh, Mr Hardcastle?' Lovejoy guessed that Alice Hardcastle had sent her husband to see him with that specific instruction, despite having discussed it with Hardcastle at some length seven or eight weeks ago.

'She was born in India of a military family, you see, Vicar.

And now that young Maud is to marry an army officer, Alice is concerned that everything goes according to plan.'

'Well, my dear fellow, you can put her mind at rest. I've been in touch with the bridegroom, Captain Spencer, and we talked about his brother officers wanting all that military ceremonial stuff. Well, why not? There's not a great deal of happiness in the world right now, so why not allow them to let their hair down, eh what?'

'I'm very pleased to hear you say that, Vicar. You know what women are like over weddings.'

'Yes, I do.' Lovejoy shook his head solemnly. 'Unfortunately there aren't too many weddings these days, and all too many funerals with all this wretched Spanish influenza. And there are an awful lot of war widows, Mr Hardcastle, and I can't see them getting married again. The sad fact is that there aren't enough men of marriageable age left. It's very depressing. The powers that be came out with all this talk about a war to end all wars, and some rubbish about a land fit for heroes, but I haven't seen any evidence of it yet. Lord Derby made all manner of promises to the chaps who were conscripted under his scheme in 1916, but he seems to have been talked out of it, presumably by Lloyd George. But then, I think it was Field Marshal Haig who said that Derby was like a feather pillow in that he bore the mark of the last person who sat on him.'

'I couldn't agree more, Vicar,' said Hardcastle warmly. It was not often that he found someone who shared his views of what he perceived to be a rapidly deteriorating world. 'Thank you for the whisky and your reassurance about the arrangements. I knew it would be all right, but Mrs Hardcastle tends to fuss over things like that.'

'Indeed, women do, you know, but I have to say that I was agreeably impressed by your daughter and her fiancé. They seem to have their feet firmly on the ground. I understand that Miss Hardcastle nursed during the war.'

'Yes, at Dorchester House, Vicar. That's where she met her future husband and nursed him back to health.'

'Excellent,' said Lovejoy. 'Sounds like a firm foundation for a successful marriage.' He shook hands. 'I'll see you on the day, Mr Hardcastle.'

'Yes,' said Hardcastle. And with a wry smile, added, 'I can't see any way of avoiding it.'

Lovejoy threw back his head, laughing loudly. 'I fear not,' he said.

'But seriously, Vicar, perhaps you would join us at the reception after the service. I've arranged for a bottle or two of whisky to be tucked away.'

'I look forward to it,' said Lovejoy.

On Friday morning, by way of a change, Hardcastle entered the police station by the front door rather than through the station yard, much to the surprise of the station officer.

'All correct, sir,' said the station sergeant, scrambling quickly to his feet.

'Anything happened overnight, Higgins?'

'A couple of drunks off Trafalgar Square, sir, and one female for soliciting prostitution in Whitehall.'

Hardcastle stopped. 'In *Whitehall*?' he exclaimed. 'What happened – did she get lost? She should have asked a copper the way to Shepherd Market.'

'She was trying it on with the foot-duty sentry in Horse Guards Arch, sir.'

'They should have deemed her under the Lunacy Act,' said Hardcastle. 'What happened?'

'The corporal of the guard called the PC on the beat and he nicked her.'

'Well, I hope the station officer knew the wording of the charge.' Hardcastle was still chuckling when he went upstairs to his office. It was almost unheard of to find prostitutes in Whitehall, especially at night when there were few people about. On the other hand, Shepherd Market on the St James's Division was a well-known haunt of ladies of the night, as they were euphemistically known.

Passing the detectives' office, Hardcastle shouted for Marriott.

'Good morning, sir.' Marriott appeared in the DDI's doorway.

'We're going back to the VanDoo Club, Marriott. It's time we put the wind up the galloping major. But we'll go via Bow Street and get a search warrant, just in case Quilter wants to stand on ceremony.'

'On what grounds can we apply for a search warrant, sir?' Marriott was concerned that, one day, Hardcastle would over-step the mark and get them both into serious trouble.

'Based on information received, I have reason to believe that Quilter is running a bawdy house, contrary to the Licensing Act 1910. There, that good enough for you, Marriott?'

'Information received, sir?' Marriott was certain that Hardcastle was off on one of his flights of fancy again.

'You heard what Colonel Rendell said, Marriott, or more to the point what he didn't say. When I asked him what happened at these parties, he clammed up. No, Marriott, there's something fishy going on at the VanDoo Club and I intend to find out what it is.'

'But shouldn't we leave that to Mr Sullivan of C Division, sir?'

'I don't think so, Marriott,' said Hardcastle, just managing to restrain himself from criticizing a senior officer to a junior one. 'Fetch Wood in here.'

'Sir?' Detective Sergeant Herbert Wood had been a police-man very nearly as long as Hardcastle. He was a year away from his pension, had neither hope nor desire for further promotion and the DDI did not frighten him.

'Round up a couple of DCs, Wood, and station yourselves within shouting distance of the VanDoo Club in Rupert Street by half past ten, but discreetly, mind. I might be executing a search warrant on the premises if the owner don't play ball. You can hang about in Rupert Street until Sergeant Marriott calls you. I might not need you, but at least it'll put the wind up the local villains.'

It was close to eleven o'clock by the time that Hardcastle, armed with a search warrant, and Marriott arrived at the VanDoo Club. This time the front door was locked. Hardcastle hammered on it repeatedly with the crook of his umbrella.

A surly individual, at least sixty years of age with wispy grey hair barely covering his head and wearing a waistcoat and a green baize apron, eventually opened the door.

'We ain't open,' he said and attempted to slam the door.

'Police,' said Hardcastle, 'and you're open to me.' With

that he shoved open the door, striking the retainer and almost knocking him to the floor. 'Where's Quilter?' he demanded once the retainer had recovered.

'In his office,' said the man churlishly, and disappeared.

'I don't think he likes the police, Marriott. Something tells me he's got a bit of form.'

The two detectives mounted the flight of stairs and pushed open the door of the owner's office. Quilter had his back to the door and was holding a young woman in a tight embrace. She looked no older than twenty, but Hardcastle would readily admit that it was difficult to guess a woman's age now that they had developed the habit of plastering their face with the new cosmetics.

The woman tensed at the arrival of the two men and Quilter swung round, an angry expression on his face at the intrusion.

'I thought I told you—' And then, recognizing Hardcastle, said, 'Oh, it's you, Inspector. I didn't know you were coming this morning.'

'That's because I didn't tell Station Sergeant Goddard so that he could forewarn you, Major.' Hardcastle had already formed the opinion that Goddard was not to be trusted, and was certain that he was accepting bribes.

'I'll telephone you later, Diane,' said Quilter, turning back to the woman. 'Now run along, there's a good girl.'

Once Diane had departed, Quilter faced the detectives. 'This is rather inconvenient, Inspector,' he began.

'Yes,' said Hardcastle, 'I can see that.'

'It would have been better if you'd telephoned to make an appointment.'

'I've no doubt,' said Hardcastle, sitting down uninvited in one of Quilter's chairs, 'but it's not my practice to give advance notice to people whose premises I'm about to search on a warrant.'

'What?' Quilter was genuinely shocked. 'A warrant? Why on earth would you want to search my club?'

'On suspicion of running a bawdy house, Major, or in plain language, a brothel.'

'But that's ridiculous. What possible evidence do you have?'

'That's what I'm here for, Major. To find some evidence.

On the other hand,' Hardcastle continued, taking out his pipe and slowly filling it, 'you could make it easy on yourself by telling me everything I want to know.'

'I think I need a drink,' said Quilter, crossing to a cabinet and pouring himself a stiff whisky. He held up the bottle. 'Can I interest you gentlemen?'

'No, thank you.' Hardcastle had a strict rule: he would take a whisky from anyone except a suspect and, right now, Quilter fell into that category.

'Well, what it is you want to know, Inspector?' asked Quilter, lighting a cigarette.

'It has come to my notice,' Hardcastle began pompously, 'that Lily Musgrave has been providing some form of entertainment to a group of men, including you,' he added, taking a guess, 'all of whom are members of this establishment. My informant refused to say what form this entertainment took, so I can only conclude that something immoral is going on. And that makes it an offence.'

'What are you driving at?' asked Quilter nervously. It was obvious from his demeanour that he had something to hide.

'If I find that's the case, you'll be prosecuted and this tawdry establishment will be shut down.'

Quilter emitted a sigh and poured himself another whisky. 'I can assure you that everyone, including the girl, was a willing participant.'

'Are you going to tell me what's going on, Quilter, or do I have to call up the three police officers I've got nearby so they can take this place apart? You could start by telling me where I can find these men.' Hardcastle turned. 'Read out them names, Marriott.' He had already briefed his sergeant to include the name of Colonel Rendell, not wishing to indicate that he had already interviewed him, for fear that Quilter would recognize him as the informant.

'Colonel Rendell, Roland Kelsey, Major Toland, Captain Lucas and Carl Frampton.' Marriott closed his pocketbook and looked up.

'Good God! How on earth did you find that out, Inspector?'

'Because I'm a detective, Quilter.' Hardcastle glanced at his sergeant. 'I think you'd better get the other officers in,

Marriott. It looks as though we're going to have to do a proper search.' Turning back to Quilter, he said, 'I don't think we'll be finished in time for you to open up tonight, Major.'

'All right. All right.' Quilter held up a placating hand. 'Each week we take it in turns for one of our group to give Lily dinner at one of the best West End restaurants. Then we all gather at one of our group's houses and Lily does an act for us.'

'What sort of an act?' asked Marriott.

There was a pause before Quilter answered. 'She stands on a table and slowly undresses,' he said diffidently.

'I presume she finishes up naked?' said Hardcastle.

'Of course.' Quilter gave a rueful grin.

'And where does this sordid business take place?' asked Hardcastle, making no secret of his distaste at what he considered to be the excesses of the upper classes.

There was a pause, and then, 'At Tom Rendell's place.'

'And where is that?' asked Hardcastle, feigning innocence.

'Old Queen Street.'

'And the other names? They are all involved, are they?'

'Yes, they are, Inspector. But the girl's quite willing so it's not an offence, is it?'

Hardcastle could not immediately think of any crime that had been committed. In law, the girl was old enough not to come within the compass of legislation affecting children and young persons. It was not a public performance, and it would be difficult to prove that Lily Musgrave was being paid for her performance, even though there was little doubt that her reward was a slap-up dinner at the best the West End had to offer in the way of fine dining. But he was not prepared to give up yet.

'We'll have to see what the Director of Public Prosecutions has to say about it, Major. However, I'm duty bound to inform Lily's father. You may recall that he's an MP.' Having delivered that barbed reminder, Hardcastle stood up. 'We'll return to the station, Marriott, and start writing reports.' He paused for a moment. 'After we've interviewed these other men. And you can start by giving my sergeant their addresses, Quilter.'

Max Quilter crossed to a safe, unlocked it and took out a

sheet of paper. Slowly he dictated the addresses that Hardcastle had asked for.

ELEVEN

'**D**id you dismiss Wood and his men from Rupert Street, Marriott?' asked Hardcastle once the two of them were back at Cannon Row.

'Yes, sir.' *Perhaps one day, he'll stop telling me how to do my job,* Marriott thought.

Hardcastle took out his half-hunter and glared at it as though it were guilty of some heinous crime. 'Now's as good a time as any, Marriott. We've seen Lucas, and we've seen Colonel Rendell, but who's the nearest after him?'

Marriott glanced at his pocketbook. 'Major Nigel Toland, sir, at Wellington Barracks. I imagine that Toland is a serving officer in the Grenadier Guards which is the regiment currently deployed to public duties from there.'

'Oh dear!' exclaimed Hardcastle. 'Well, that's walking distance. It's at the bottom end of Birdcage Walk.'

'I'll get my coat and hat, sir.' Marriott forbore from answering the DDI's observation about the location of the barracks for fear he may make an impertinent remark.

'There's no need to rush, Marriott. We'll have a pie and a pint in the Red Lion before we go anywhere.'

After more than four years wearing khaki, the Brigade of Guards was once again resplendent in its pre-war red tunics.

'Gentlemen?' The sergeant surveyed the two arrivals in the guardroom. He knew instinctively that they were not officers; in fact, it was clear that they were not in the army at all.

'I'm Divisional Detective Inspector Hardcastle of the Whitehall Division, Sergeant. My sergeant and me would like a word with—' He paused and flicked his fingers. 'What's his name, Marriott?' He knew perfectly well who he was looking for but it was a foible of his that he liked to appear absent-minded. On the other hand, though, it had deluded more than one criminal into making a confession because he thought the DDI had forgotten what he had said previously.

'Major Nigel Toland, sir.'

'Ah, yes, that's the chap.' Hardcastle returned his gaze to the guard commander. 'That's who we want to see, Sergeant.'

'He should be in his office, Inspector. I'll get a runner to take you over there.' Turning his head, he shouted for someone called Harris.

'Sarn't?' A young guardsman came rushing out from the rear of the guardroom, skidded to a halt and snapped to attention.

'All right, lad, all right,' said the sergeant, holding up a hand. 'Take it easy. The bloody guardroom ain't on fire. Take these two police officers to Major Toland's office. D'you think you can manage that without getting lost?'

'Where's his office, Sarn't?'

'God give me strength! He's the second in command of the bloody battalion, you pitiful blockhead. Which fool accepted you for the finest regiment in the British Army, answer me that, eh? And put your bloody titfer on. Can't go walking about naked.' The sergeant shook his head. 'I don't know where we get 'em from, Inspector. Right, Harris,' he continued as the soldier reappeared now with his cap on. 'Are you quite ready, lad? I don't want to put you to any trouble or upset any arrangements you might have. Right, double away!'

Harris set off at a fast pace across the barrack square towards the office block but slowed down when he realized that Hardcastle and Marriott were not keeping up with him. Finally, the trio reached Toland's office.

Harris knocked, strained his ears for a reply and, having received a summons to enter, threw open the door and crashed to attention on the bare boards immediately inside the major's office.

'Sir, your leave to speak, if you please, sir,' he cried as he saluted.

'Yes, what is it?'

'Sir, there are two police officers here to see you, please, sir. Your leave to show them in, sir?'

Without waiting to hear a reply, and already tiring of this
military ritual, Hardcastle pushed past Harris and introduced
himself and Marriott.

Toland stood up behind his desk and waved a hand of
dismissal at Harris. 'Please take a seat, gentlemen,' he said
smoothly, affording the detectives a welcoming smile, 'and
tell me how I may help you. One of our chaps got himself
into trouble, eh?' Hardcastle guessed that the Guards major
was in his mid-thirties. Immaculate in blue frock coat with a
red sash around his waist, he was a full six foot tall with an
aquiline nose and pomaded hair. During the interview, he
frequently brushed his guardee moustache with the back of
his hand.

'No, Major Toland,' Hardcastle began, 'it's about a young
lady by the name of Lily. I'm given to understand that you
have taken her out to dinner on several occasions.'

Suddenly the false bonhomie vanished. 'Yes, dammit, I have,
but I'm not married and I don't see that my social arrangements are any concern of the damn police.'

'In addition to that,' Hardcastle continued, quite undeterred
by the major's brusqueness, 'you often attend a party at a
private house where the young lady in question disrobes fully
for the entertainment of you and your friends.'

'Where on earth did you get that slanderous cock-and-bull
story from, Inspector?' Toland brushed at his moustache. 'Just
give me the name of the scoundrel who told you and I'll see
the damned fellow in court. Or was it the wretched woman?
Trying a bit of blackmail, is she, eh what?'

'Are you denying it?' asked Hardcastle mildly.

'Certainly I'm denying it.'

'Read out them names, Marriott.' Hardcastle ignored the
major's protestations.

'Captain Oscar Lucas, Major Max Quilter, Roland Kelsey,
Colonel Tom Rendell and Lieutenant Carl Frampton of the
Royal Naval Volunteer Reserve.' Marriott read the names out
slowly, carefully enunciating each one.

'Do those names mean anything to you, Major Toland?'
asked Hardcastle.

'Now look here, Inspector—'

'Before you say something you later regret, Major,' said Hardcastle, rather formally, 'you might like to know that the young lady in question is only seventeen years of age.'

'She told me she was twenty-four. What is she? A professional tart?' Toland sneered.

'No,' said Hardcastle. 'As a matter of fact, she is the daughter of Mr Austen Musgrave.'

'He's a member of parliament who is tipped to become Secretary of State for War,' put in Marriott. Apart from the vague suggestion made by Inspector Crozier of the Palace of Westminster police that Musgrave was in line for a Cabinet appointment, there was no suggestion as to which particular post. But as the Secretary of State for War was the political head of the army, Marriott thought that mentioning it would be a good way of bringing the pompous major down a peg or two.

Up to that point, Major Toland had remained standing, presumably to give him a psychological ascendancy over these two policemen. But now, he sat down suddenly, the arrogance vanishing, and his face a picture of contrition.

'Oh my God!' he exclaimed, tugging fiercely at his moustache. 'I'd no idea. Is there any way in which this can be kept quiet, Inspector?'

'All I can tell you, Major, is that I'm preparing a report for the Director of Public Prosecutions about the entire matter,' said Hardcastle, with a degree of satisfaction. 'It will be for him to decide,' he added. But he knew the likelihood of a prosecution was remote. 'Good day to you, Major Toland.'

'Where to now, Marriott?' asked Hardcastle, once they were back in Birdcage Walk.

'Is there any point in interviewing any more of these men, sir? I mean, are we likely to learn any more than we already know?'

'Shan't know until we ask, Marriott.'

'Roland Kelsey lives in Wilton Street, sir,' said Marriott, suppressing a sigh.

'Wilton Street,' said Hardcastle. 'Henry Gray used to live there, at number eight.'

'Who was he, sir?' Marriott feared he was about to get another short history lesson.

'He wrote *Gray's Anatomy*,' Hardcastle replied airily. Seeing Marriott's puzzled expression, he added: 'It's a medical textbook. However, what does this Kelsey do for a living? Any idea?'

'No, sir, and Quilter didn't know.'

'In that case, we're about to find out.'

Roland Kelsey's house was a four-storey property in a Georgian terrace.

Hardcastle and Marriott alighted from their cab and, for a few moments, the DDI stood looking up at the house and nodding slowly.

'Well, Marriott, we'll see what Mr Kelsey has to say.' It took only two paces to cross the narrow pavement and Hardcastle rapped loudly on the knocker.

'Good afternoon, gentlemen.' Attired in morning dress, the butler had the bearing of one who had been in service all his life.

'We're police officers,' announced Hardcastle, 'and we want to speak to Mr Roland Kelsey.'

'I'm Roland Kelsey,' said the butler. 'What's this about?'

'It might be better if we spoke inside.' Although somewhat taken aback by this revelation, Hardcastle showed no signs of his surprise.

'Perhaps so,' said Kelsey, and led the two officers into the entrance hall before turning sharply to the right, opening a door and descending a flight of stairs to the basement.

Once in the servants' quarters, Kelsey took the two detectives into his pantry.

'Please take a seat, gentlemen. Has a member of the household staff got into trouble with the police?'

'I'm Divisional Detective Inspector Hardcastle of the Whitehall Division, and information has come my way that you have been entertaining a young woman by the name of Lily to dinner at West End restaurants. Usually on a Saturday evening. It is understood that you first met this young woman at the VanDoo Club in Rupert Street.'

'Me, sir?' Kelsey burst out laughing. 'Good God, Inspector, where d'you imagine I'd get the money to dine young women in expensive restaurants? Apart from anything else, I'm married. To the cook here.'

'Read them names to Mr Kelsey, Marriott.'

Marriott took out his pocketbook and read out the names, although he was now so familiar with them that he could have recited them from memory.

Kelsey looked at the two detectives with a bemused expression on his face. 'I've never heard of any of these gentlemen, Inspector. Anyway, butlers don't mix with colonels and majors socially or any other way for that matter, and I've certainly never been to anywhere called the VanDoo Club.'

'Was your master a soldier by any chance, Mr Kelsey?' asked Marriott.

'Only very briefly, sir. He volunteered at the very start as a medical officer but received a chest wound at the retreat from Mons and was invalided out. They said they couldn't risk him facing a gas attack so he went back to being a doctor. He has what you might call a society practice in Harley Street.'

'What's his name?' asked Hardcastle.

'Doctor Jack Rylance.'

'Does he ever go out by himself on a Saturday evening, Mr Kelsey?' Marriott asked.

'Quite often, sir. You see, the doctor's not married. He's only a young man comparatively speaking – twenty-seven, he is – and between you, me and the gatepost, I think he likes to play the field. Still, I daresay he'll settle down one day.'

'Is he here now?' Hardcastle enquired.

'No, sir. As a matter of fact, you just missed him. Well, by an hour or so. He's gone off for a weekend in the country. He has a cottage in Lancing in West Sussex. He owns a market garden there and he goes down from time to time to keep an eye on things. He's just bought a Rolls-Royce – a beautiful car, it is – but he hasn't taken on a chauffeur as yet. Mind you, I think he quite likes driving the thing himself.'

'Thank you, Mr Kelsey,' said Hardcastle, as he stood up. 'There's obviously been a misunderstanding. I'm sorry to have troubled you.'

'Not at all, sir. I'll show you out.'

Hardcastle was silent all the way back to the police station, his head bowed in thought. It wasn't until he reached his office that he expressed a view about the abortive visit he and Marriott had made to Wilton Street.

'I think that young Doctor Rylance has been using his butler's name in case his own gets into the newspapers.'

'Indeed, sir, I think you're right,' said Marriott, who had come to that conclusion almost as soon as he and the DDI had started talking to Kelsey.

'A smart practice in Harley Street by day and watching a young girl take off her clothes by night. Rylance is a bit of a Jekyll and Hyde if you ask me, Marriott.'

'What do we do now, sir?'

'This is all getting interesting. I think we'll go looking for Lieutenant Carl Frampton of the RNVR.'

'Very good, sir.' But there was no enthusiasm in Marriott's voice. He thought that Hardcastle was wasting his time.

'I wonder if he's a member of the In and Out Club.'

'Is there a reason why he should be, sir?'

'Of course, Marriott. Its proper name is the Naval and Military Club.'

'There's also The Rag, sir.'

'The *what*?'

'The Army and Navy Club in St James's, sir, but it's known informally as The Rag.'

'Oh, yes, of course, that one. I'd quite forgotten it's called The Rag. Yes, you could be right, Marriott. We'll give that a try.'

'But I've also heard that some RNVR officers have started their own club. It's called the RNVR Auxiliary Patrol Club.'

'Remind me where that is.'

'At the moment in Pall Mall, sir. Apparently they've leased rooms at the Marlborough Club until they can get premises of their own.'

Hardcastle said nothing immediately. He was always irritated when Marriott produced detailed information of that sort, but would at once be irritated if he had *not* found it out. As Hardcastle would frequently remind him, that was what a first-class sergeant was supposed to do.

'Is Frampton a member of any of these clubs, then, Marriott? Have you found that out yet?'

'Not yet, sir.'

'Well, you'd better do so. I don't want to waste my time traipsing round the clubs of Pall Mall making enquiries like a door-to-door salesman.'

Ten minutes later, Marriott tapped on the DDI's office door. 'Frampton is a resident member of The Rag, sir.'

'How did you find that out so quickly, Marriott?'

'I telephoned the secretary, sir.'

'Really?' said Hardcastle. 'Not very efficient, I'd have thought. How did you know you were actually talking to the secretary if you didn't see him, eh? It could have been the hall porter for all you know.'

'He assured me he was the secretary, sir.'

Hardcastle chose not to prolong that discussion. 'We'll interview Frampton,' he said. 'Tomorrow.'

Lieutenant Carl Frampton was about twenty-five years old and, he told the detectives, a single man. The war got in the way of any lasting relationships, he said, apparently with some regret. As Marriott had predicted, but had not dared put into words, the interview with the former naval officer revealed nothing fresh about the parties at which Lily Musgrave 'entertained' the guests by taking her clothes off in exchange for a dinner bought for her by one of them.

Just before the two detectives left the Army and Navy Club, Marriott posed a question.

'Lieutenant Frampton, you obviously know Mr Roland Kelsey.'

'Yes, of course, but you knew that already.'

'Would you be so good as to describe him for my inspector.'

Frampton placed the tips of his fingers together and leaned back in his chair, a pensive expression on his face.

'Somewhere in his mid-twenties, I should think. Probably about five foot eight or nine, with gingery hair. I suppose you'd call it auburn.'

'Was he clean-shaven?'

'No,' said Frampton as he stroked his beard. 'He had
a well-trimmed moustache. He stooped a bit when he was
walking, too.'

The two detectives left the club and eventually turned
into Whitehall. 'That was obviously Doctor Rylance that
Frampton was describing,' said Hardcastle without compli-
menting Marriott for having thought of a question that
had not occurred to him. 'I think we'll have a word with
Rylance next week.'

'Yes, sir.' Marriott wished he had not asked Frampton.

On Monday morning, Hardcastle and Marriott caught up with
Dr Rylance just as he was about to leave Wilton Street for
Harley Street. He explained that his panel of patients did not
appreciate early morning appointments. In fact, he said,
most of them preferred the afternoon or even the early evening
to consult him. As Frampton had suggested, he was about
five-foot-eight-inches tall and by the look of him in fairly
good shape. Apart from a longish scar on his jawline and a
lack of lobes on his ears, there was nothing else particularly
outstanding about him.

He invited them into his first-floor drawing room before
cheerfully admitting that he used his butler's name when he
attended Lily Musgrave's little soirées, as he described them,
but was sorry if he had caused Kelsey any embarrassment.
He would apologize to him and in future use an entirely
fictitious name. His clientele, he said, would be unlikely to
consult a doctor who indulged in what they would doubtless
see as debauchery of the worst possible kind, hence the
duplicity.

At two o'clock that afternoon, Hardcastle crossed to Detective
Superintendent Frederick Wensley's office at New Scotland
Yard.

'I thought I'd tell you what's happened so far before I begin
to prepare my written report, sir.' He told Wensley about the
parties and what went on there, and handed him a list of
the names of the participants. 'Much as I hate to say this, sir,

I cannot see that any offence has been committed, either by Miss Musgrave or by the men who wined and dined her in exchange for her giving a performance for them.'

'Nor can I, Ernie,' said Wensley, 'but I'll forward your report to the Assistant Commissioner L Department. He might want to send it to Wontner's, our legal advisers, but I doubt that anything will come of it.'

'D'you think I should inform Mr Austen Musgrave of my findings, sir?'

'No,' said Wensley sharply. 'We're not allowed to tell him anything because Lily Musgrave, although she's not yet reached her majority, is not a child or a young person. I'll inform the Commissioner, and if he wants to tell Mr Musgrave then that's a different matter. But in view of what you told me about Musgrave's dubious business dealings, I doubt if Sir Nevil will want to talk to him again.'

When Hardcastle returned to Cannon Row, he sent for Marriott and told him the outcome of his interview with Mr Wensley.

'That looks like it, then, sir.'

'Yes, it does.' But Hardcastle was disappointed that no one would be prosecuted for what, at best, he saw as disreputable behaviour.

Although not in quite the same category, Marriott recalled the Force instruction that forbade police from interfering with 'the innocent amusements of the working classes'. Of course, the group of officers and ex-officers they had been dealing with could hardly be categorized as working class.

'By the way, sir,' said Marriott, 'there was a piece in *The Times* this morning that might be of interest to you.'

'About Musgrave?'

'No, sir. It announced that ex-Detective Superintendent Patrick Quinn, late of Special Branch, has received a knighthood.' Marriott closed the door before the outburst he knew this piece of information would cause the DDI.

TWELVE

During the days following the closure of the Lily Musgrave affair, concerning which the Force's legal advisers had recommended no action be taken, nothing of great importance happened to occupy the professional mind of Divisional Detective Inspector Ernest Hardcastle. There had been a break-in at the premises of a jeweller's establishment in Artillery Row where known thieves had obligingly left their fingerprints, but apart from a few cases of pickpocketing – known to the police as larceny person – little had occurred to whet the DDI's appetite. Consequently, Hardcastle had reached that point where he was becoming bored. Events at home, however, were far from tranquil. And on Tuesday the eighteenth of March, Hardcastle finally yielded.

'I'm still struggling to find a suitable place for my daughter's wedding reception, Marriott,' Hardcastle admitted in a rare acknowledgement of his own fallibility. 'Mrs Hardcastle is getting a bit impatient.'

That was putting it mildly. In fact, Alice Hardcastle had become quietly very annoyed, her voice dropping to the measured low tone that Hardcastle recognized only too well as a warning of criticisms yet to come. She had crushingly observed that at work, Hardcastle had only to flick his fingers to get things done, but on those occasions when he had to do it himself, they somehow didn't seem to get done. It's a simple enough matter, she had added. And in case you had forgotten, she continued, it's your daughter's wedding we're talking about, *to an army officer*, and it's on Saturday, not next year.

'Would you like me to make a few enquiries, sir?' Marriott was loath to become involved in the domestic matters of the Hardcastle family but he knew instinctively that if the DDI was in a bad mood about Maud Hardcastle's wedding, he was likely to be in a bad mood with the detectives at Cannon Row police station, if not all of A Division.

'You could do, Marriott, but I doubt you'll have much more luck than me,' said Hardcastle.

Marriott smiled. 'I'll see what I can do, sir. Where is the service to be held?'

'Saint Anselm's at Kennington Cross.'

'You'll want the reception to take place as near to there as possible, then, sir, and it'll need to be somewhere that provides good service.'

'Exactly, Marriott.'

'How many guests are you inviting, sir?'

Hardcastle had to give that question some thought; in fact, he had not even considered it. 'About twenty, I suppose,' he said after a minute or so.

'I'll make some enquiries, sir.'

'Good of you, Marriott,' said Hardcastle grudgingly, 'but not in duty time.'

'Of course not, sir,' responded Marriott, deciding immediately that he would ignore that admonition. After all, if the DDI wanted him to find a suitable venue for Maud's wedding reception at such short notice, Marriott was not going to do it in his own time.

It was, perhaps, proof of Marriott's detective ability that he had an answer for the DDI within the hour.

'I think I might have found a suitable place, sir,' said Marriott. 'I spoke to my opposite number at Kennington Road nick and he suggested the Royal Oak which is about a hundred yards down Kennington Road. It's just past your house, as a matter of fact. They have a private room on the first floor that will accommodate as many as thirty or forty guests and they do silver service. It's highly recommended.'

'I'm obliged, Marriott.' Hardcastle did not know what was meant by 'silver service', and did not intend to enquire, certainly not of a sergeant. But Alice would know.

'Well, Ernest?' Alice Hardcastle was seated in an armchair in the sitting room, putting the finishing touches to the hem of Maud's wedding dress.

'All arranged, love.'

'How did you manage that so quickly? And while you're thinking up an answer, you can pour me a glass of sherry.'

Hardcastle poured the drinks and sat down opposite his wife. He then told her about the Royal Oak, its private room and the fact that it provided silver service.

'I should hope so,' said Alice. 'Nothing less will do. Have you inspected the place yet?'

'No. As a matter of fact it was Marriott who made all the enquiries for me.'

Alice Hardcastle placed her glass of sherry carefully and deliberately on a side table and stared at her husband. 'Did I hear that correctly, Ernest? You sent your *sergeant* to make the arrangements?'

'I was very busy, Alice, love,' said Hardcastle, hoping to deflect the criticism that was implied by the tone of censure in Alice's voice.

Suddenly, Alice threw back her head and laughed. 'Well, if Sergeant Marriott picked the place it'll be all right. Frankly, Ernie, I think you'd be lost without him.' She paused. 'You have invited him to the wedding, I hope?'

'Well, er, no,' said Hardcastle hesitantly. 'He is only a sergeant.'

'So were you once,' Alice reminded her husband pointedly. 'Of course you must invite him. And his wife. What's her name, by the way?'

'I've no idea.'

'You've no idea?' Alice sounded scandalized. 'He's your right-hand man and you don't even know his wife's name? I've really no idea how you get your men to work for you. You won't find it that easy once you get women police officers in the Force. They won't be pushed around.'

'Women police officers!' scoffed Hardcastle and laughed. 'That'll be the day.'

'Come along, Ernie,' said Alice, draining her glass and standing up. 'We'll walk down to the Royal Oak and interview the cook.'

'But I haven't started my whisky yet,' complained Hardcastle.

'That's all right,' replied Alice, 'you can buy one when we get there. That'll be something, won't it? Ernie Hardcastle buying a drink.'

Although it was a Tuesday, the Royal Oak was surprisingly full. Nevertheless, the moment Hardcastle and Alice entered the private bar they were spotted by the landlord.

'I don't often see you in here, Mr Hardcastle, and with your good lady, too, I see. Allow me to buy you both a drink.'

'Very kind, I'm sure,' murmured Alice and asked for a sherry. Hardcastle opted for a whisky.

'It's always a pleasure to see local residents patronizing the old Royal Oak,' said the landlord.

Particularly if they happen to be a senior detective who might do you a bit of good, thought Hardcastle. 'We'd like to talk to you about our daughter's wedding,' he began.

'Ah, yes,' said the landlord, whose name, he reminded Hardcastle, was Henry Wade, 'on Saturday, I believe.'

'How did you know that?' asked Hardcastle suspiciously.

'I had a telephone call from your Mr Marriott, asking a few questions which, I'm pleased to say, I was able to answer to his satisfaction, I trust.'

'As it stands at present, we shall be looking at twenty-two covers, Mr Wade.' Alice Hardcastle, tiring of the niceties that were being exchanged between her husband and Wade, decided to intervene.

The use of the technical term 'covers' immediately warned the landlord that Mrs Hardcastle was not a woman to be trifled with.

'Of course, madam.'

'And I shall not be looking to pay more than five shillings per head, either.'

'Oh, I'm quite sure the Royal Oak can accommodate you handsomely at that price, madam. Perhaps if I were to introduce you to my cook, you could discuss the finer points of the menu with him, so to speak. If you care to follow me, I'll show you the way.' As Wade moved towards the door, he issued an order to the barman: 'Have another whisky and another sherry brought up for sir and madam. On my account.'

The trio mounted the stairs to the first floor and Wade opened a door that led straight into what he described as the banqueting suite.

'As you can see, this room will easily accommodate the numbers you quoted, madam.' Wade obviously saw little point in including Hardcastle in this conversation. Mrs Hardcastle knew exactly what she wanted. 'If you wait for one moment, I'll fetch the cook.'

'This seems quite suitable, Ernie,' said Alice, looking around with a critical eye. 'With linen napery it should impress Charles's parents and his friends.'

'This is Maurice Shooter, the cook, madam.' Wade returned with a small man who, although possessed of an English name, had a thin moustache that gave him the appearance of being Italian and who was clutching a foolscap-sized book. 'Perhaps you'd care to listen to his suggestions.'

'I'm not interested in his suggestions, Mr Wade. I'll tell Mr Shooter what is required. All I need from you is an assurance that this room will be spotlessly clean on Saturday and that the linen napery is freshly laundered. There will be linen napery, won't there, Mr Wade?'

Wade recognized that not as a question but as an order. 'Of course, madam.'

'A chair, please,' commanded Alice, looking around.

'Oh, I do apologize, madam.' Wade scuttled across the room and fetched two chairs.

Alice produced a sheet of paper from her handbag. 'This is what I require, Mr Shooter. Oh, thank you,' she said as a waiter appeared with the Hardcastles' drinks on a tray. 'Now, where was I?' she continued, examining her list again. 'To start, I would want scallop Saint Jacques or smoked salmon with dill, pickled cucumber and crème fraiche.' She waited until Shooter had finished writing and then cast a querying glance at him.

'Yes, madam. Easily arranged,' said Shooter nervously. 'What about the main courses?'

'I thought lobster tail poached in a suitable dressing.'

Shooter nodded. 'I would suggest a purée of seafood lobster emulsion, madam.'

'I'll leave that to you, then, Mr Shooter.' Alice made it sound like a magnanimous gesture on her part. 'Now for the meat course.' She consulted her notes again. 'Roast baby Welsh lamb with crispy rosemary oats, baby potatoes roasted in duck fat and creamed spinach. Can you manage that or is it a little too ambitious?'

'I most certainly can,' confirmed Shooter, scribbling furiously and looking slightly affronted that Mrs Hardcastle thought that such a main course was beyond his capabilities. 'And to follow, madam?'

'Ices or sorbets I think would be just right. And cheese, of course.'

'Of course, madam. And tea or coffee as required?' Shooter raised an eyebrow.

'Thank you.'

'Now, what about wines, Mr Hardcastle?' asked Henry Wade hopefully.

'We'd better have a selection,' said Alice, deciding that arrangements of this nature were beyond her husband. 'But I daresay some of the men would prefer beer. Perhaps you'd arrange to have that available.'

'Most certainly,' said the unctuous Wade, his hands slowly revolving around each other. 'And may I suggest champagne? We are fortunate to have obtained a couple of cases of Moët. It's been very difficult to get hold of because of the war.'

'The champagne has been taken care of, Mr Wade,' said Alice, causing Hardcastle to raise his eyebrows. It was the first he had heard of any champagne. 'And there will be a croquembouche provided. Perhaps the necessary dishes and cutlery will be available.' She lapsed into thought for a second or two. 'You do know what a croquembouche is, I suppose?'

'Of course, madam.'

'And I trust there'll be no question of corkage for the champagne. There will be a number of army officers here, you see. In fact, our Maud is marrying one and I think they deserve a little leniency after all they've been through, don't you?' Alice smiled disarmingly.

'I wouldn't dream of it, madam.' Wade knew that the bride's family would be footing the bill, not the army officers in question, but decided it would be impolitic to argue with a woman as formidable as Mrs Hardcastle.

'Most satisfactory,' proclaimed Alice Hardcastle, rising to her feet.

'Er, the time on Saturday, madam?'

'We'll be sitting down at a quarter past two, Mr Wade.' It was a statement that brooked no argument.

'What's all this about champagne, Alice, love?' asked Hardcastle once they were back home.

'Charles's fellow officers managed to bring some home from France at the end of the war and they put it by for the wedding, as a present to the bride and groom, and apparently one of their clever army cooks has produced the croquembouche.'

Hardcastle had not the faintest idea what a croquembouche was but decided not to display his ignorance. 'How d'you know all this, Alice?'

'Strangely enough, Ernie, Charles talks to Maud, and Maud talks to me because you're never here. And even when you are here, you never listen.' That rebuke delivered, Alice went on. 'Now, you have arranged the cars, I hope?'

Hardcastle looked triumphant. 'I've arranged for a Rolls-Royce to take Maud to the church, and it will take the couple from the church to the reception.'

Alice frowned. 'And just how did you manage to get hold of a Rolls-Royce, Ernest Hardcastle?'

'It's a 1912 Silver Ghost shooting brake,' said Hardcastle, avoiding the question of how he had managed to hire such a car for the day. 'And you needn't worry about the cars for the groom and the other guests. It's all taken care of.'

'I sincerely hope so, Ernest.' Alice had been married to Hardcastle for quite long enough to be able to gauge his efficiency, or lack of it. She also knew that his bluff confidence often turned out to be a pious hope rather than an endorsement of the true situation. But it was too late now.

The day of the wedding dawned gloomily. The temperature struggled to reach a few degrees above freezing point and there were spasmodic falls of wet snow. However, bad weather was not going to dampen the spirits of the young couple.

Hardcastle was sitting in an armchair when Maud came downstairs. He was not a man easily taken aback, but the sight of his twenty-year-old daughter in her bridal gown left him speechless.

Maud's ankle-length white satin dress was topped by a tunic with tasselled points to her waist. The veil was held by an orange blossom wreath, and white stockings and shoes completed the picture of a fashionable young bride.

'You look beautiful, lass. You really do us proud.'

'You can thank Mother, Pa,' said Maud. 'She made the whole outfit.'

Hardcastle turned to his wife. 'Well done, Alice, love. I do believe our little girl's grown up.'

'I'll get my hat,' said Alice, turning away quickly. 'Are you girls ready to go?' she asked sharply as Kitty Hardcastle came down the stairs with Charles Spencer's sister, Lavinia, the other bridesmaid.

Kitty handed Maud her bouquet. 'Good luck, sis,' she said and gave her a kiss on the cheek. 'Off you go.'

The passenger door of the Rolls-Royce was held open by a liveried chauffeur. Waiting in Kennington Road were most of the Hardcastles' immediate neighbours, delighted to have a diversion from their drab lives after four weary and worrying years of war.

A sad reminder of that war was the ruined house opposite. Just over eighteen months previously it had fallen victim to a German bomb that had killed Arthur Hogg and the family's two children, and left the widowed Bertha bereft of her reason and confined to a lunatic asylum.

The onlookers cheered and waved, shouting, 'Good luck, Maud!' as the youngest Hardcastle daughter stepped into the car, accompanied by her proud father. A policeman from Kennington Road police station had magically appeared in the busy road and stopped the traffic to allow the smooth departure of the bridal limousine.

* * *

At the door to St Anselm's Church, Walter Hardcastle stood with his fellow usher, Private Cyril Townsend of the Loyal Regiment, who on every other day of the year was the groom's army batman.

Captain Charles Spencer, in khaki service dress and sword, waited nervously at the altar, constantly fingering the cross-strap of his Sam Browne. Next to him was Geoffrey Wainwright, his best man.

The organist began Richard Wagner's *The Bridal Chorus,* and there was a shuffling of feet as the congregation stood for the arrival of the bride.

The Reverend Percy Lovejoy, looking as though he was thoroughly enjoying himself, began the service. The bride and groom made their responses in a firm voice that implied they really meant what they were saying. The parties retired to the vestry and signed the certificate and the register, and suddenly it was all over.

The bride and groom emerged from the church into a brief shaft of March sunlight that had managed to penetrate the clouds. A number of Charles Spencer's fellow officers lined both sides of the pathway and formed an arch with their drawn swords. Confetti was thrown, photographs were taken, and with much laughter the entire group made its way to the Royal Oak for the reception.

Mindful of Alice's advice that he should keep his speech short, and to remember that he was not about to give evidence at the Old Bailey, Hardcastle stood up to welcome the guests. He said a few complimentary words about Maud and made the usual trite comments about gaining a son rather than losing a daughter before proposing the toast to the bride and groom.

As the wedding breakfast was served, Henry Wade, the landlord, hovered close by, conscious that Alice Hardcastle was casting a critical eye over every dish. But even she could find no fault.

Charles Spencer was every bit the suave army officer when it came to delivering his speech. He thanked Ernest and Alice Hardcastle for arranging the reception and making all the other arrangements, but in saying how appreciative Maud and he were of everything they had done to make this day such a success, he acknowledged how much his new father-in-law had contributed. Alice Hardcastle coughed discreetly. Laughing, Charles quickly added that he was about to learn that the real strength of any family rested with the lady of the house, and he knew that today's major contribution had come from his new mother-in-law.

As was customary on these occasions, the best man, Captain Geoffrey Wainwright, spoke in less-than-glowing terms about his brother officer, saying that he didn't deserve such a talented, beautiful girl as the new Mrs Spencer, and that he regretted that he hadn't been wounded himself, otherwise he and Charles might today have been occupying opposite places.

But then he caused a brief stir. Reading the cards and telegrams of congratulation, he picked up a blank piece of paper, frowned and pretended that it too was a telegram. 'This is addressed to Captain Charles Spencer, MC, The Loyal North Lancashire Regiment. You are to report forthwith to the regimental depot at Fulwood Barracks, Preston, for immediate embarkation.'

There was a hubbub of conversation. The shocked look on Charles Spencer's face was matched by Maud's crestfallen expression.

But then, smiling, the best man relented. 'The telegram goes on to say that Captain Spencer is to leave his new and attractive wife in the sole care of Captain Geoffrey Wainwright for the seven years Spencer will be in India.'

In the laughter that followed, Charles Spencer was heard to make dire threats to the detriment of Wainwright's well-being.

After the formalities were over, Hardcastle shared more than one large whisky with the vicar and moved on.

Sighting Marriott and his wife, he crossed the room and slapped Marriott on the back. 'Glad to see you here, Charlie, old man,' he said cheerfully. 'And this must be Linda.' He beamed at Marriott's wife and shook hands with her. 'It's nice to meet you at last, Mrs Marriott.'

'Her name's Lorna, sir,' corrected Marriott.

'So it is, m'boy, so it is.' Hardcastle laughed and moved on.

'I thought you said he was a miserable old devil to work for, Charlie,' said Lorna.

'And he usually is, love, but I've never seen him drunk before.' Marriott shook his head, unable to believe what he had just witnessed. 'D'you know, that's the first time he's ever used my Christian name. In fact, I didn't know he even knew it.'

As the reception drew to a close and talk was of the departure of the bride and groom for their honeymoon, Charles Spencer approached Maud's parents and thanked them once again for making the day such a great success.

But then he surprised his father-in-law. 'I'm pleased that you arranged for Percy Lovejoy to conduct the service, sir,' he said. 'That was very thoughtful.'

'It was pure coincidence, Charles,' said Hardcastle. 'It just so happens that he's the vicar of Saint Anselm's.'

'And a very happy coincidence it is, too, sir, in the circumstances. He won the Military Cross for venturing out into no-man's-land under enemy fire and bringing a wounded officer back to his own lines.'

'I didn't know that, Charles,' said Hardcastle. 'He never mentioned it.'

'No, he's not the type to,' said Spencer, 'but the wounded officer in question was me. And as you know, Maud took over and nursed me back to health.'

THIRTEEN

It was some three weeks after the wedding, by which time the newly-weds had returned from their honeymoon in Cornwall and settled into a house in the officers' married quarters area of Aldershot, that Charles Spencer was notified of an opportunity in Germany.

'I've been offered a job that's come up on the staff in Cologne with brevet promotion to major,' Spencer explained to his in-laws during a brief visit he and Maud paid to

Kennington. 'As it's a step up, albeit without the pay for the rank, I'd be a fool to refuse, and there is excellent accommodation there. I'm sure that Maud will love it.' He glanced at his wife as if seeking reassurance. 'It's a beautiful city.'

Alice Hardcastle was not so sure, but now that Maud was a married woman, she would have to make up her own mind. Alice knew from her father's frequent moves in India that army wives were treated in much the same way as camp followers had been a century earlier. But she also realized that Maud, being an officer's wife, would enjoy conditions far superior to those which Alice's mother had endured at the hands of the British Army in India. That was forty years ago; things might be different now. And occupied Germany was not India.

However, the domestic upheaval of Charles and Maud was not to worry Ernest Hardcastle, for on Tuesday the fifteenth of April, he was summoned to New Scotland Yard to see Detective Superintendent Frederick Wensley.

'She's gone again, Ernie.'

'Who's gone again, sir?'

'Lily Musgrave.'

'She seems to be making a habit of it, sir, but surely this time we can hand it over to the Uniform Branch to deal with, can't we?'

'It could be a little more serious this time, Ernie,' said Wensley, waving Hardcastle to a chair. 'It seems she told her father she was going to spend the weekend with Captain Oscar Lucas at Epsom. When Musgrave contacted Lucas, Lucas confirmed that she had been there that weekend but had left on the Sunday evening. That in itself strikes me as a bit odd. Are we to believe that she returned to London alone? And if so, how? There are times when the younger generation baffles me, Ernie. If you or I had left a girl to make her own way home, that would have been the end of that romance.'

'What was the date of the weekend she went to Epsom, sir?'

Wensley glanced down at a notepad. 'She arrived there on Friday the fourth of April and left on Sunday the sixth, but it was some days later before Musgrave got in touch with Lucas. You know this Captain Lucas, of course.'

'Yes, sir, I know Lucas and I wasn't very taken with him.

He's said to be suffering from shell shock but I've got my doubts about that.' However, Hardcastle knew nothing of the condition that had affected so many soldiers and was only now being taken seriously, albeit reluctantly, by the army's high command. 'In view of what I discovered about those parties she'd been to, sir, I suppose it's possible she's turned professional and joined her mother on the stage at the Brighton Hippodrome. To be perfectly honest, I think Marie Faye's way of life would appeal to Lily. When I went to see Miss Faye last month, she was entertaining an ageing stage-door johnnie in her dressing room, and I think I interrupted a bit more than just a chinwag.'

'I wondered if that's where she might've gone, Ernie,' said Wensley, 'so I spoke to the Chief Constable of Brighton and asked him to make urgent enquiries. He called back within the hour to say that one of his officers had interviewed Marie Faye and she claimed not to have seen her daughter in months.'

'Does the Commissioner know about this latest turn of events, sir?'

'I mentioned it to him but he's no longer interested. I think the information you obtained about Musgrave, coupled with what he's now heard from other sources, made him decide not to have anything further to do with the man. He said we were to deal with this latest Musgrave affair in the same way as we would deal with any other enquiry.'

'That's something, I suppose, not to have the Commissioner on our backs.'

'But even so, I'm giving it to you, Ernie, because at least you know something of the background to the case.'

'When were we told that she was missing, sir?' Hardcastle was not at all pleased to be saddled once again with finding the missing Lily Musgrave but it would have been unwise to protest, particularly to Wensley.

'Yesterday morning.'

'So Musgrave waited about a week before making up his mind there was something to worry about.'

'I think it shows what sort of parent he is,' commented Wensley.

'I'd better go and see him, then, sir.'

'Keep me informed, Ernie.'

'Of course, sir.' Irate at having been given what he believed to be a footling enquiry, Hardcastle stormed down the corridor and across the courtyard to his police station. As he passed the door to the detectives' office, he shouted for Marriott.

'That bloody Musgrave girl's gone missing again, Marriott.' Hardcastle repeated what he had been told by Wensley. 'Why the hell her damned father can't use a bit of discipline to keep the silly little bitch under control, I don't know. But now we've got to start looking for the wretched girl simply because her father can't be bothered. For a start, Marriott, we'll go and interview Musgrave, and then I'll work out where we go from there.'

'I'll get my hat and coat, sir.' Marriott decided that it would be unwise to fuel the flames of Hardcastle's anger any further. When the DDI was in a bad mood, it boded ill for anyone who got in his way, and that included the detectives under his command.

'Good morning, Inspector. I thought we might be seeing you again, sir. I take it you wish to see the master. Step inside, sir, and I'll enquire if he's at home.'

'Don't bugger me about with all that "I'll enquire if he's at home" claptrap, Crabb,' said Hardcastle. 'I'm not in the mood for it. Find him now, and I don't care if you have to drag him out of bed, no matter who he's sharing it with.'

'Yes, sir, of course, sir,' said Crabb nervously, and ushered the detectives into the morning room before dashing off in search of his master.

It was only a matter of minutes before Austen Musgrave appeared wearing a gold silk dressing robe with black lapels and maroon slippers with turned-up, pointed toes that lent them a vaguely oriental appearance.

'Inspector Hardcastle, how good of you to come so promptly.'

'A bit quicker than the ten days it took you to inform the police that Lily was missing, Mr Musgrave,' said Hardcastle bluntly.

'Yes, well, the fact is that this time Lily told me where she was going. I think that after her last little escapade which finished up involving the police, she realized that she should keep me informed of where she would be. And she told me she was spending the weekend with Captain Oscar Lucas and his family at Epsom. As Lucas is the son and heir of Lord Slade, I naturally thought it would be perfectly all right. I mean, what with him being a peer of the realm and all that.' Musgrave emitted a nervous little laugh.

'Ye Gods!' exclaimed Hardcastle, staggered at the man's naiveté.

'I telephoned Lord Slade's residence last Friday and spoke to Captain Lucas. He said that he hadn't seen Lily since Sunday the sixth of April when she left Epsom.'

'I suppose the Commissioner didn't tell you what Lily had been up to when she was with Lucas and his ex-officer friends,' said Hardcastle, deciding it was time to tell Musgrave about his daughter's reckless behaviour, no matter what the Elephant thought.

'No, I haven't spoken to Nevil since my conversation with him the first time Lily went missing, Inspector. I tried calling him two or three times but I was told that he was unavailable. Anyway,' continued Musgrave airily, 'I suppose Lily was just out enjoying herself like all young women these days.'

'She was acquainted with a group of men she met at the VanDoo Club, a Soho dive. These men would take it in turns to escort her to dinner at a West End restaurant, usually on a Saturday,' said Hardcastle, relishing the moment, 'and by way of payment, she would then entertain them at one of the men's houses by standing on a table and taking all her clothes off in what has been described as a seductive manner.'

If Hardcastle had imagined that Lily's father would be outraged by this revelation, he was disappointed.

Musgrave threw back his head and laughed. 'I can see she's following in her mother's footsteps,' he said. 'That sort of entertainment is very popular in the United States, you know, Inspector. Over there, they call the girls burlesque strippers.'

'In short, then, Mr Musgrave,' said Marriott, contributing to the interview for the first time since he and Hardcastle had arrived, 'you have no idea where your daughter might be.'

'No, I'm afraid not, Sergeant,' said Musgrave cheerfully. It appeared that he was not in the least bit worried by his wayward daughter's activities or her disappearance, but nevertheless expected the police to find her.

'We'll do what we can to trace her, Mr Musgrave,' said Hardcastle, 'but I can't make any promises. In law, she is of an age when she can please herself what she does or where she goes. If, for some reason, she doesn't want to be found, then she won't be. And even if we do find her, we're not allowed to tell you where she is if she doesn't want us to.'

'I'm sure the Commissioner would want you to make an exception in this case, Inspector,' said Musgrave smoothly.

'One of the rules that govern the police force in this country, Mr Musgrave,' said Hardcastle, 'is that the Commissioner can't tell me how to investigate a crime. I'm only answerable to the law. But as a member of parliament, you'd know that. Good day to you.' And with that, Hardcastle left Musgrave wondering why his daughter's disappearance had been described by the DDI as a crime.

Once the two detectives were outside and Hardcastle was peering, in vain, for a cab, Marriott asked, 'What's next, sir? Do we go to the In and Out Club and see Lucas again? If he's there, of course.'

'No, we don't, Marriott. We'll start our enquiries where they ought to be started. At Epsom. And we'll start this afternoon.'

With no regard whatever to the amount of money that it was costing the Receiver to the Metropolitan Police, Hardcastle and Marriott took a cab first to Brixton police station, the headquarters of W Division, with the intention of going on to Epsom afterwards. It was a matter of courtesy that Hardcastle should inform DDI Fowler that he was making enquiries on his bailiwick.

'So, that's the situation, Connie,' said Hardcastle once he had explained the latest twist in the Lily Musgrave affair.

'Sounds like a right lash-up to me, Ernie,' said Fowler, pouring more whisky for A Division's DDI and his sergeant, 'and I'm not sorry you've copped it. I must remember to buy the Elephant a drink next time I see him.' It was a standing joke among senior CID officers that Wensley only occasionally took a drop of alcohol and that it would cost little to buy him a drink. 'Out of the goodness of my heart, though, I'm willing to lend you Gandy, as he's familiar with that neck of the woods.'

It was Detective Sergeant Harold Gandy who had prepared the report for Hardcastle when Lily Musgrave first went missing.

'Thanks all the same, Connie,' said Hardcastle, 'but I've given up pussy-footing about. If Lucas doesn't come up to snuff I'll probably nick 'im for obstruction.'

Fowler laughed. 'That's more like the Ernie Hardcastle I knew. I thought for a minute you'd gone soft up there on your poncey A Division.'

Slade House lay about halfway between Epsom High Street and the famous racecourse that was home to the Derby. A long drive led up to the house itself, and the extensive stables were some way behind it, together with an exercise paddock.

The butler who opened the door was wearing morning dress so old that it had faded to grey in places. He must have been well past sixty years of age, was stooped and gave the appearance of someone who should have retired from service years ago.

'Good afternoon, sir.'

'We're police officers,' announced Hardcastle, 'and we're here to see Captain Lucas.' He did not for one moment expect to find Lucas there on a Tuesday and his visit was primarily to speak to Padraig O'Reilly, the head stable lad. But he was to be surprised.

Staggering a little and holding on to the door for support, the butler stepped back a few paces. 'Do come in, sir. I'm sure the captain's about somewhere.' His croaky voice seemed to match his decrepit physique. 'I thought for a moment you might be wanting to see His Lordship but he's in Ireland. He spends most of his time there, you see, on account of the horses. He's very keen on the horses, is His Lordship, sir. Oh, yes, very keen. He even had a horse running in the Derby afore the war.' He paused to give the matter some consideration. 'Yes, 1913, that was. Same race as that one when that young lass threw herself in front of the King's horse, that were, sir. Killed herself, she did.' The butler nodded knowingly.

'Yes, I'm sure that's all very interesting,' said Hardcastle, fearing the butler was embarking on a discourse about racing that could go on for a while, 'but we are a little short of time.'

'Ah, yes, you would be, sir,' said the butler. 'It's amazing how the time flies, particularly when you're getting older. *Tempus fugit*, as they say.' All the while he was speaking, he was shuffling towards the inner part of the house. Eventually he opened a door. 'This is the morning room, sir. If you'll wait in here, I'll see if the captain's about.' He paused. 'Of course,' he added thoughtfully, 'he might be in London. Soon find out, though.'

Hardcastle paused on the threshold. 'Was there a young lady staying here the weekend before last?'

The butler continued to walk away as he answered the DDI's question. 'Like as not, sir. There seems to be young lasses here most weekends, and young gentlemen, too. When His Lordship's not here, of course.' And with that unsatisfactory reply, he disappeared through a door on the far side of the large hall.

Some ten minutes passed before the door to the morning room opened again.

'I thought I might be getting a visit from you, Inspector,' said Lucas. 'Do sit down, please.'

'I spoke to Austen Musgrave this morning about the disappearance of his daughter, Captain Lucas.' Hardcastle was determined to take advantage of this unexpected meeting with Lucas.

'Yes, I had a telephone call from him last week. He was querying whether his daughter had spent the weekend here.'

'And did she?' As was his practice, Hardcastle was checking everything he had been told so far, including the information he had received from Detective Superintendent Wensley.

'Yes, she was here. And that's what I told Mr Musgrave.'

'Your butler suggested that there were young women and young gentlemen here most weekends.'

Lucas laughed. 'Anything Sidebottom says has to be taken with a pinch of salt, Inspector. I'm afraid his mind's going and the guv'nor only keeps him on out of charity. He was a very good trainer years ago.'

'Why should I believe anything you tell me, Captain

Lucas?' Hardcastle fixed Lucas with a penetrating stare. 'After all, you've lied to me before.'

'I think I've always been quite straight with you, Inspector,' protested Lucas, but he sounded far from convincing.

'The last time I interviewed you, I asked you where Colonel Rendell lived.' Hardcastle glanced at his sergeant. 'Just read the note you made at the time, Marriott.'

'You said you *thought* Rendell lived in Old Queen Street, Captain Lucas, but claimed not to be sure,' said Marriott.

'Did I say that?' asked Lucas innocently.

Hardcastle did not bother to respond to that question. Instead, he countered it with a statement. 'You knew perfectly well where Colonel Rendell lived because you'd been to parties there – parties also attended by Lily Musgrave when she entertained you by taking off all her clothes.'

'That's not true.' Lucas attempted to convey outrage at the suggestion but it lacked conviction.

'I can produce half-a-dozen witnesses who are willing to testify that you were. But,' continued Hardcastle, 'I'm not here to talk about that. I'm here to talk about Miss Musgrave's disappearance and where she is now.'

'I have no idea,' said Lucas, but he was now giving signs of being rattled by the DDI's probing.

'Musgrave was under the impression that she was here as your guest the weekend before last?'

'She was here, Inspector, but as a guest at the party that was held here.' At last, Lucas had decided to tell the truth. 'Not as my personal guest.'

'And did you tell Austen Musgrave that? He believed that she *was* here as your personal guest.'

'I don't know what gave him that idea, because when I invited Lily, I told her that she would know most of the people here.'

'The last time we spoke to you, Captain Lucas, you admitted having sexual intercourse with this seventeen-year-old girl,' said Marriott. 'Where did this take place?'

The sudden change of direction, and Marriott's soft-voiced delivery, further unnerved Lucas. 'The first time it was in my bedroom on the first floor,' he replied nervously.

'So sexual intercourse occurred more than once, did it?' asked Marriott.

'Yes. Several times, in fact. There were a few times in the hayloft at the back of the stables.'

'Good God!' exclaimed Hardcastle.

'And on each of these occasions, your father was in Ireland, was he?' continued Marriott.

'Yes. As I said before, he'd play merry hell if he found out.'

'That's a pity,' commented Hardcastle drily. 'We may have to talk to him at some stage.' But it was an empty threat designed to discomfit Lucas even further.

'Oh my God!' exclaimed Lucas, clearly concerned at the prospect. 'Do you have to?'

'How many times has Miss Musgrave been down here altogether, Captain Lucas?' asked Marriott.

'Three in all,' said Lucas unhesitatingly.

'So this story you told us originally about using your father's flat in Albany to bed this young woman was untrue, was it?'

'Yes.' Lucas had the good grace to look shamefaced about the admission. 'To be perfectly honest, I wouldn't dare, Sergeant. If the guv'nor found out I'd been using his flat to bed some girl he'd blow his top.'

'I imagine so.' Marriott glanced across at Hardcastle.

'I don't think we need to bother you any further, Captain Lucas,' said the DDI as he and Marriott stood up.

Lucas stood up, too, and shook hands. 'Goodbye, Inspector.' He sounded relieved.

Hardcastle paused as if a sudden thought had occurred to him. 'Would you mind if I had a look around your stables, Captain Lucas? I'm rather taken with racehorses. Lovely creatures.'

'By all means, Inspector. You'll find the head stable lad there somewhere. He knows more about the animals than I do. Padraig O'Reilly is his name. He might even give you a tip for next week's Brighton meeting. Allow me to show you out by the back door. That's the quickest way to the stables.'

'How long have you had an interest in racehorses, sir?' asked Marriott once Lucas had closed the door on him and Hardcastle.

'Ever since I decided that the head stable lad might be a useful source of information, Marriott. I don't think Lucas is being open with us at all. He pretends to be innocent and naïve but I think he's far sharper than he lets on. After all, you don't go through the war without developing a bit of cunning.'

'Can I help you, sir?' The man who approached the detectives pulled briefly at the peak of his cloth cap. He was short and bow-legged, and wore a tweed hacking jacket, breeches and riding boots. He had the rugged appearance of a man between forty and fifty but was probably no older than thirty.

'I'm Divisional Detective Inspector Hardcastle and this is Detective Sergeant Marriott.'

'You'll be from Epsom, I'm thinking. Padraig O'Reilly at your service, gentlemen. A look at the horses, is it?'

'I'm investigating a serious matter, Mr O'Reilly,' said Hardcastle, not bothering to correct O'Reilly's inaccurate assumption, 'and our conversation must remain confidential. Not even Lord Slade or the captain must know of it, otherwise the question of criminal conspiracy might have to be considered. Do you understand?'

'Oh, indeed I do, sir.' O'Reilly appeared to be suitably impressed, even slightly worried.

Marriott was uncertain what the DDI was driving at when he talked of criminal conspiracy but decided that it was a device to scare the head stable lad into keeping quiet.

'You remember Miss Musgrave coming down here, Mr O'Reilly, don't you?'

'Indeed I do, sir. As beautiful a young filly as ever I did see. I think the captain's a lucky fellow to have a peach of a girl like that on his arm. Fair smitten, he is.'

'Yes, he was just saying the same thing,' said Hardcastle affably, as though he had only come here to discuss the girl's attributes.

'Has she been here often, Mr O'Reilly?' asked Marriott.

'Oh, at least a half-dozen times, sir.'

'And was she here the weekend before last?'

'The weekend before last? Now, let me see. That'd be the fifth of April, the Saturday, I'm thinking. That was the weekend of the Kempton Park meeting. We never had anything running in that. Yes, I do believe she was here. In fact, I know she was here.'

'And when did she leave, Mr O'Reilly?'

'Sure, it must've been the Monday morning. Mind you, sir, I never saw her going but I remember cook telling me – when I went in for me meal – that the young lady hadn't been down for breakfast. Is that a help with this – what was it you called it, sir? Criminal conspiracy?'

'Very much so, Mr O'Reilly,' said Hardcastle warmly. 'And as I said, this must remain confidential between us.'

'I'm glad to have been of help to you, sir.'

The two detectives walked back to their waiting cab.

'Are you going to confront Captain Lucas with that, sir?' asked Marriott.

'No, Marriott, I'll keep that up my sleeve for the time being. Apart from anything else, Lucas would know who'd told us and I want to keep O'Reilly as a useful informant. I think there's more to this business than meets the eye.'

FOURTEEN

On the following morning, Hardcastle sent for Marriott. 'I want two reliable officers that I can send down to Epsom, Marriott.'

'To Slade House, sir?'

'No, to the racecourse and to Epsom town itself. What was the name of that pub that's popular with the racing folk? Gandy mentioned it in his report.'

'The Spread Eagle, sir. Might I suggest Catto and Keeler, sir? They were the two that I sent to bring the Musgrave girl back here last month.'

'Not Catto. I want someone trustworthy.'

Marriott knew it was no good arguing. 'What are these officers to do in Epsom, sir?'

'Keep their eyes and ears open,' said Hardcastle. 'If the

tittle-tattle is as good as Gandy says it is our men might just pick up something about the goings-on at Slade House. I'm bloody certain that Lucas wasn't telling the truth when he said that Lily wasn't his personal guest at the weekend in question. And then we have Padraig O'Reilly, who I think could be a useful source of information. Finally, there's Sidebottom, the butler, who said there are men and women there almost *every* weekend. Mind you, Marriott, I don't think he knows A from a bull's foot. But someone might know something.'

'Who d'you suggest we send, then, sir?'

'Wood's a mature man,' said Hardcastle after a moment or two. 'What about Wilmot?'

'Up at the Bailey this week with a robbery, sir.'

'So he is, so he is. What's the name of that Irish fellow at Rochester Row? A chap in his forties.'

'I think you mean Liam Bodkin, sir, a DC.'

'That's the fellow,' said Hardcastle, rubbing his hands together. 'Just the man to get alongside Padraig O'Reilly. Provided the head stable lad gets in the pubs around Epsom, but I've yet to meet an Irishman who doesn't enjoy the occasional wet. Get in touch with Mr Neville, the DI at Rochester Row, tell him I want to borrow Bodkin for a few days and to send him over *tout de suite.*'

'But Bodkin might be on another job, sir.' It was Marriott's job to point out administrative problems of that sort, as he had just mentioned Wilmot's case at the Central Criminal Court.

'Then tell Mr Neville to take him off it, whatever it is, Marriott.' Hardcastle was beginning to display a measure of exasperation. 'Those two are smart enough detectives to find out if something odd's going on. And I'm sure there is. Fetch 'em in when Bodkin gets here.'

It was half an hour later when Detective Sergeant Wood was followed into the DDI's office by Detective Constable Liam Bodkin, another long-serving CID officer who, like Wood, was not far off retirement. Consequently, neither of them was the slightest bit intimidated by Hardcastle, who they regarded as something of a dinosaur, even though the three of them were of comparable age.

Hardcastle outlined what he required of the two detectives.

'How long d'you want us to stay down there, sir?' asked DS Wood.

'As long as it takes,' said Hardcastle, a comment that would have beset Catto with a nervous paroxysm. But not Wood.

'That's not very helpful, sir,' said Wood. 'It might take a day or it might take a week. And what about expenses?'

'You can go down to Epsom by train, Wood, and you can charge the difference between that fare and the fare you normally charge to go from here to your home address.' Hardcastle knew the regulations regarding claims for expenses almost word perfect. But so did Wood.

'I live in Victoria, sir. I travel to and from work by bicycle. So I presume I can charge the whole fare between London and Epsom.'

'I'm in the same boat, sir,' put in Bodkin. 'I live in the section house over the nick in Rochester Row. All I have to do is walk downstairs to get to work.'

'Oh, very well, then,' said Hardcastle tetchily, convinced that these two officers were being deliberately obstructive, 'but make sure the Metropolitan Police gets value for its money.'

'When d'you want us to start, sir?' asked Wood, ignoring the DDI's last petty comment.

Hardcastle took out his half-hunter, gave it a brief wind and dropped it back into his waistcoat pocket. 'It's a quarter to ten now. You should be able to get down there by midday.'

'I never thought the guv'nor would give us a job like this, Bert,' said Bodkin as he pushed open the door of the Spread Eagle Hotel in Epsom High Street. 'But I thought you might've tried to get our drinks included in expenses as well.'

'I'm sure we'll be able to slip them in somehow, so that the guv'nor doesn't notice.'

Both officers had changed into clothing better suited to a country district like Epsom, but it was more for comfort than a concern about being recognized as policemen.

'What'll it be, gents?' asked the barman in the saloon bar.

'A couple of pints of your best,' said Wood.

'Coming up, sir.' The barman pulled two pints of the best bitter and placed them in front of the two detectives. 'Down for the racing, are you, gents?'

'The racing?' queried Bodkin, his face a picture of innocence. 'Of course I'm interested in the racing,' he added, adopting his native Galway accent. 'Where is it, then?'

'Up at Tattenham Corner.' The barman seemed to have difficulty appreciating that this man, and an Irishman at that, did not realize that they were in the very town where the world-famous Derby was held.

'Unfortunately, we've got other fish to fry today,' said Bodkin. 'We're in the mole-catching business, you see. Got a job down at the Woodcote Park golf course but we thought we'd stop off here for a pint and a bite to eat. If you hear of anyone wanting a mole-catcher, tip me the wink and there'll be a drink in it for you.'

'Are you sure about that job at Woodcote Park?' asked the barman. 'It's occupied by the Canadian Army and the last I heard they had their tents all over the golf course.'

'Bloody hell!' exclaimed Bodkin. 'Did you hear that, Bert?' He shook his head. 'I reckon we've been taken for a ride. Who was it who said this job was going? Anyway,' he continued, trying to avoid any further questions, 'what've you got to eat in this wonderful establishment?'

'We do some very good sandwiches,' said the barman. 'Ham, chicken, cheese, turkey. I'll get you the menu.'

'Don't you do any fourpenny cannons?' asked Wood.

The barman looked bewildered. 'What on earth's a fourpenny cannon?'

Wood laughed. 'We should've remembered we're in the country now, Liam.' He turned back to the barman. 'That's what we call a steak-and-kidney pie up the Smoke. But you country folk wouldn't know that.'

The barman laughed. 'Well, you should've said so. Of course we've got 'em, and Cornish pasties, too. A couple of your fourpenny cannons, then, gents? Nice and hot.'

After the steak-and-kidney pies were served, Wood bought more beer for himself and Bodkin. He also bought a drink for the barman on the grounds that barmen are good listeners, and with the right sort of cultivation can also be useful informants.

'I've heard that there's a big house near here owned by a lord, so they tell me. I was wondering if he'd have any work for us. In the mole-catching business, like.'

'You're likely talking about Slade House,' said the barman. 'There are racing stables there, too, and they're owned by Lord Slade. But I don't know if he has trouble with moles. Well, talk of the devil, here's His Lordship's head stable lad just walked in. Padraig O'Reilly's his name. Excuse me, gents. I'll see what he wants.'

'I'll pay for it,' volunteered Bodkin. 'Tell him it's from one Irishman to another.'

Once he had been served with a pint of Guinness and the barman had pointed out Wood and Bodkin, O'Reilly moved along the bar to join them.

'The barman tells me I have you to thank for the drink, friend, and he tells me you're from dear old Ireland.'

'That I am. Liam Bodkin's the name.' He held out a hand.

'Padraig O'Reilly.' The head stable lad shook hands.

'And this is my mate, Bert Wood,' said Bodkin. In a stage whisper, he added: 'But he's a Londoner.'

'Top o' the morning to you,' said O'Reilly, shaking hands. 'Jim the barman said you're in the mole-catching business.'

'That we are,' said Bodkin, 'but there's not a lot of work about these days. We thought we'd been lucky enough to get a job down at Woodcote Park this afternoon but the barman's just told us there's Canadian troops camped all over it.'

'Where are you from?' asked O'Reilly, signalling for another round of drinks.

'Galway,' said Bodkin. 'And yourself?'

'Waterford. Other side of Ireland.'

'The barman was saying you're from the big house.' Bodkin decided to push O'Reilly in the hope of getting some useful information. The last thing that Wood and Bodkin wanted was work as mole-catchers. Neither of them knew anything about the trade.

'I'm head stable lad at Slade House,' said O'Reilly proudly.

'I caught the eye of His Lordship just after the war, me being in the North Irish Horse and looking for work.'

Bodkin laughed. 'And you from the South, boyo. What were you doing in the North Irish Horse?'

'I like horses,' said O'Reilly, not wishing to get into a fight with a fellow Irishman about having fought for the English.

'Well, I'll not hold it against you. Now, will you have a short to go with the black stuff?'

'I'll take a Bushmills, God bless you. There are so many Irishmen about the place, what with trainers and jockeys and stable lads, that the landlord makes sure there's always a case or two in the stockroom, especially now that the racing is coming back to England after the war.'

Bodkin signalled to the barman to pour a large Irish whiskey for O'Reilly but wisely did not order any more beer for himself and Wood.

'And is it a good billet you've got with His Lordship?' asked Bert Wood.

'Well, yes and no,' said O'Reilly, adopting a confidential tone. 'Lord Slade's more often across the water than in England but his son is always about the place when he's not up in London town doubtless bedding some filly. That's Captain Oscar Lucas. Now there's the broth of a boy. He has the run of the place while His Lordship's away and you'd be surprised at the parties he has there.'

'Really? What sort of parties are they? I suppose they come down for the horse riding.'

'Riding? Bless you no, Liam,' said O'Reilly, laughing. 'The captain fills the house with young fellows, all ex-officers from the war, and the prettiest colleens you ever did set eyes on. Oh, it's a riotous time they'll be having with young girls running about the house half-naked, laughing and screaming while the young blades chase 'em from room to room. Every weekend, so it is. And the drink flows like water.'

'It sounds like great fun,' said Wood. 'Does the captain let you join in?'

'That'll be the day. Mind you, I've even come across them in the hayloft. I had to have a word with the captain about that on account of them frightening the horses.'

Bodkin nearly burst out laughing at O'Reilly's naïve comment. 'Does His Lordship ever join in, Padraig?' he asked and, noticing that O'Reilly's speech was slightly slurred now, ordered another Bushmills for him.

O'Reilly laughed. 'If His Lordship was to see the goings-on he'd have fifty fits, so he would. No, when he's in residence the house is as quiet as a grave.'

'And is he there now? I'm not being nosey but I've never heard tell the like of this before,' said Bodkin. 'I never believed that things like this could go on in respectable houses.'

'Well, the weekend before last,' continued O'Reilly, warming to his subject now that he had a captive audience, 'there was the usual party up at the house, all young fellows and girls as usual. I don't know what was different about it but a week or so later we had the police down asking all sorts of questions about what went on. They spent about two hours with the captain,' he said, exaggerating wildly, 'and then they came down to the stables asking me all sorts of questions. I knew it was something serious because this inspector was talking about a criminal conspiracy, so he was. Whatever that is, but I didn't believe a word of it otherwise I wouldn't be telling you gentlemen all about it.'

'I don't see what's wrong with a few youngsters enjoying themselves,' suggested Wood, who only just stopped himself from defining a criminal conspiracy for O'Reilly's benefit.

'Nor I,' said O'Reilly. 'Not that I told the police anything, on account of me not liking them all that much.' After a pause, he added, 'And the same goes for the RIC back home. But he was a fierce-looking fellow, this policeman who came to the house. Said his name was Harlow or Harding, something like that. No, I tell a lie. It was Hardcastle. A terrible man, so he was.'

'What did he want to know, then?' Bodkin asked.

'I don't rightly remember now but he seemed to be interested in one particular lass, not that he told me her name, and I never knew any of their names anyway. But he particularly wanted to know if she'd been there. I told him there was a girl and that she must've gone home because I never

saw her after Sunday afternoon when I saw her crying her
eyes out in the garden of the big house.'

'What was wrong with her, then?' asked Wood.

'I don't know. I asked her if she was all right and she said
she was, then she ran indoors but I never saw her again. Cook
told me that she hadn't been down for breakfast and, as I
said, I never saw her again.' O'Reilly took a turnip watch
from his waistcoat pocket. 'Glory be, will you look at the
time. Thank you for the drinks, my friends, and I hope you
find some mole-catching to do. God bless you, but I must be
off.'

'That was all very interesting, Liam,' said Wood once
O'Reilly had departed. 'I'll bet the guv'nor didn't know
anything about these parties and, what was it our new-found
friend said, "girls running about the house half-naked"? I
think I was born too soon.'

'Me too,' agreed Bodkin, his Irish accent once again hardly
noticeable. 'So what do we do now, Bert?'

'There are at least four other pubs nearby but I'm not sure
we'd learn any more by visiting them, especially as we've
had the tale from the horse's mouth, in a manner of speaking.
I think it's best if I find the local nick and telephone DS
Marriott. See what the guv'nor wants us to do next.'

'Why not telephone Mr Hardcastle direct, then?' asked
Bodkin.

'Because he hates the bloody telephone, Liam, and is likely
to lose his temper with anyone who tries to talk to him on
it. It's much safer to speak to Charlie Marriott, then he can
have a word with the guv'nor.'

'I've just spoken to DS Wood, sir,' said Marriott.

'Is he back, then?'

'No, sir, I spoke to him on the telephone.'

'Oh, have we still got those things?'

Marriott decided that there would be no profit in pointing
out that Hardcastle had one on his desk. It had been placed
there on the orders of higher authority but Hardcastle had no
intention of using it.

'They had a few drinks with Padraig O'Reilly in the Spread

Eagle at Epsom, sir,' said Marriott, and summarized what DS Wood had learned.

Hardcastle nodded. 'I think we're getting somewhere, Marriott. Where are Wood and Bodkin now?'

'Standing by at Epsom nick, sir, waiting for further instructions.'

'I don't think they can learn any more by wasting their time down there. Tell them to come back and report to me.'

'Did O'Reilly tell you how many people were at this party the weekend before last, Wood?' asked Hardcastle when Wood and Bodkin were once again in his office.

'No, sir, but I got the impression from what O'Reilly was saying that there were quite a few. I'd take a guess at probably eight or ten.'

'Did he say whether Lily Musgrave was one of them?' Hardcastle had been told by Lucas that Lily was there but as usual was comparing one story with another.

'He'd no idea, sir,' said Bodkin. 'He didn't know the names of any of the guests, except, of course, for Captain Lucas.'

'Tell me again what O'Reilly said about this one girl he found crying in the garden.'

'He said that there was one girl he remembered because he saw her on the Sunday afternoon crying her eyes out in the garden. He then said that she must've gone home because he never saw her after that. But he also said that he told you all that, sir.'

'He told me about the girl not appearing for breakfast but he didn't say if it was Lily who was crying in the garden. Either there's a bloody conspiracy going on or half the people at Slade House are doolally tap.' Hardcastle stared at Wood. 'Did you get a description of this girl?'

Wood stared back and remained silent for a moment or two. 'O'Reilly thought that Bodkin and I were mole-catchers, sir, not police officers. To have asked him for a description might have made even O'Reilly suspicious.'

'What are you proposing to do next, sir?' asked Marriott hurriedly. He realized that Hardcastle had posed a stupid question but hated being seen to have done so. In circumstances like that the DDI's reaction was always unpredictable.

'What I'm going to do next, Marriott, is go home and think about it. I'll see you here at half past eight tomorrow morning.'

'What about us, sir?' asked Wood.

'You can go about your normal duties, Wood.'

'See me in my office before you go, Sergeant Wood,' said Marriott.

When Wood and Bodkin joined Marriott in the detectives' office, Marriott closed the door.

'The DDI was very pleased with what you and Bodkin found out, Bert.' Marriott was always conscious of the fact that Hardcastle never offered a word of praise when one of his officers did a good job, and tried to make up for it by pretending the DDI had mentioned it in their absence.

'I've been too long in the Job to fall for that, Skip,' said Wood. 'Between you and me, the DDI isn't bothered how hard we sweat our guts out so long as he gets what he wants.'

Marriott grinned but made no comment about Wood's truism. 'Leave the door open on your way out, Bert.'

FIFTEEN

Hardcastle arrived home at just after eight o'clock. As usual, he checked the hall clock against his half-hunter and then pushed open the door of the sitting room. Alice was seated in her own particular armchair near the fire, knitting a scarf, but to Hardcastle's surprise, Walter was also at home. Normally, the family's only son, who worked as a postman out of Lambeth Road letter office, would be on the last post walk, as postmen called their final round of the day. If, on the other hand, he was on the early turn, he'd be at a local pub with some of his workmates at this time of the day.

'I'm surprised to see you at home, Wally,' said Hardcastle as he poured sherry for his wife and a whisky for himself. 'D'you want a Scotch or a beer?'

'I'll have a Scotch, please, Pa.'

Alice waited until Hardcastle had settled in his chair and taken a sip of his whisky before making her announcement. 'Wally's got something to tell you, Ernie.'

'He's got a tongue in his head, hasn't he? He doesn't need an introduction like a singer of comic songs at the Alhambra.'

'Oh, for pity's sake, Ernest, just listen for once,' said Alice sharply. 'You're not at work now.'

'Don't tell me you've suddenly got engaged, Wally.' Hardcastle ignored his wife's jibe. 'This marriage thing seems to be catching on. Still, at least we won't have to pay for the wedding this time.'

'No, I'm not engaged, Pa.'

Hardcastle leaned forward in his chair, a stern expression on his face. 'You haven't got a girl into trouble, have you?'

'Oh, for heaven's sake, Ernest, d'you always have to see the worst in people?' Alice was becoming increasingly impatient with her cantankerous husband.

'No, Pa, nothing like that.' Walter was finding that imparting his news was a struggle.

'Well, what is this important information you wish to tell me about?'

'I've joined the Metropolitan Police, Pa.'

Hardcastle put his whisky glass on a side table, almost spilling it as he did so. 'You've done *what*?' he exclaimed.

'Don't tell me you're going deaf, Ernie,' commented Alice drily.

'But why didn't you tell me?' spluttered Hardcastle.

'I just did.' Wally paused, and then grinned at his father. 'Sir!'

'You can hardly blame the boy for wanting to follow in your footsteps, Ernie,' said Alice, who sensed a row brewing. 'But he knows how opposed to the idea you've always been and he didn't know what your reaction was likely to be. Although, he could probably have guessed,' she added as an afterthought.

'But how come they accepted you, Wally? You're supposed to be twenty to apply and you've only just turned nineteen.'

'I don't know, Pa. Perhaps they took one look at my name and decided that another Hardcastle in the Force would definitely be an asset.'

Alice burst out laughing. 'There, Ernie, you've got no answer for that, have you?'

Then, to the surprise of both Alice and Walter, Hardcastle levered himself out of his chair and shook hands with his son.

'Congratulations, Wally. It's a hard life but a rewarding one. Have another Scotch.'

'Good grief!' exclaimed Alice. It was not often that she saw her husband accepting a controversial situation so phlegmatically.

'Thanks, Pa.' Walter was also surprised that his momentous announcement had been accepted so placidly by a parent known for his shortness of temper.

'When d'you start training?' Hardcastle settled back in his chair. 'Have we got Peel House back from the Dominion Forces yet?'

'Yes, but it's being used to train women police patrols now.' To stem the predictable outburst that the family knew would follow any mention of women in the police, no matter in what role, Walter said, 'The men are being trained at Eagle Hut in the Aldwych. And I start on Monday.'

'Dinner's ready,' said Alice.

After dinner, Walter announced that he was going down to the pub for a drink with his mates.

'I thought you were going to bite Wally's head off, Ernie,' said Alice. 'He was very nervous about telling you.'

'I'm very proud of him, Alice,' said Hardcastle, much to the surprise of his wife. 'Despite knowing that I didn't much care for the idea, he had the guts to go ahead and do what he wanted to do. He'll make a good copper.'

'It's his future wife I feel sorry for,' said Alice, and picked up her knitting again.

Hardcastle was in his office by eight o'clock the following morning. Marriott joined him at exactly eight thirty.

'Good morning, sir.'

'My Walter's bloody well joined the Force, Marriott. What d'you think of that?'

'He'll do well, sir.' Risking a reproof, Marriott grinned, and added, 'If he's anything like his father.'

Hardcastle looked up suddenly and stared at Marriott but made no comment about his sergeant's unashamed flattery, although he was secretly pleased at the compliment.

'What are we going to do about Lily Musgrave, sir?'

'I intend to interview Captain Lucas one more time. And this time I'm going to get the truth out of him. If he buggers me about, Marriott, I'll nick him for obstructing the police. For a start, you can get on that telephone thing you're so fond of and find out if he's at the In and Out Club or if he's still at Slade House. A bit *tout de suite.*'

Marriott was back twenty minutes later. 'Lucas is at the In and Out, sir. He returned to London from Epsom yesterday apparently.'

'Good.' Hardcastle stood up and put on his coat and hat, then seized his umbrella. 'Now's as good a time as any, and we'll go and interfere with his leisurely breakfast. No doubt, being one of the gentry, he breakfasts later than us mere mortals.'

'I'll go down and find a cab, sir.' Marriott was disturbed by Hardcastle's mood of hostility towards Captain Oscar Lucas, particularly as it existed before the DDI had even started to question him. In Marriott's experience, hectoring a witness usually produced the answers the witness thought his interrogator wanted to hear rather than the truth.

It was half past nine when Hardcastle and Marriott arrived at the Naval and Military Club in Piccadilly.

'I believe he's having breakfast, Inspector,' said the club servant who opened the door.

'What did I tell you, Marriott?' said Hardcastle, and turned back to the servant. 'Perhaps you'd fetch him out, then. I want to talk to him.'

'But he may not have finished his breakfast yet, Inspector. The members don't like being interrupted at meal times.'

'I don't give a damn,' said Hardcastle. 'Just fetch him. We'll be in the reception room.' Without waiting for a comment, Hardcastle pushed past the doorkeeper and sat down on one of the uncomfortable settees with which the room was furnished.

Five minutes later, Lucas appeared, clutching a copy of *The Times* and clearly in a mood to match Hardcastle's ill temper. 'I take grave objection to this high-handed attitude, Inspector, and frankly, I'm getting a little tired of your harassment. What is it you want this time?'

'Sit down, Captain Lucas,' said Hardcastle, in such a manner that brooked neither refusal nor further argument. 'I want the truth from you about what's been going on at Slade House, and I want it now, otherwise I shall arrest you and charge you with obstructing the police in the execution of their duty.'

'I don't know what you mean.' A tic in Lucas's left eyelid began and he pressed a finger against it.

'Well, let me put it to you straight,' said Hardcastle. 'I have learned that the weekend Lily Musgrave was at your house in Epsom, there were several men and women there, and that a riotous party was held where half-naked girls were being chased through the house. And I'd remind you she's not been seen since.' He said nothing further, but waited to see what Lucas would say.

'That's true. There was a party and it did get a bit out of hand.' Lucas decided that Hardcastle knew too much about that particular weekend.

'You seemed rather vague about Lily's departure when I spoke to you at Slade House. When did she leave?' Rather than upbraid Lucas for his previous mendacity, Hardcastle pushed home his advantage.

'I don't know exactly. I know she was there on the Sunday evening but I didn't see her again after that.' Lucas took out a cigarette case and lit a cigarette. He did not offer the case to Hardcastle or Marriott. 'It tends to be like that. People come and go, more or less as they please.'

'Why was Lily crying her eyes out in the garden on the Sunday evening of that weekend?' asked Hardcastle, although he was only guessing it was Lily.

'I didn't know anything about that.' The question had come as a surprise to Lucas and it was confirmed by his shocked reaction.

'I want the names of all those attending this party of yours, Captain Lucas. And I do mean everyone.'

'And if I'm not prepared to tell you?' Lucas raised his head slightly and peered down his nose at the DDI.

'In that case you leave me no alternative but to arrest you.' Hardcastle paused. 'On the other hand, I could ask Lord Slade what he knows about this whole affair.'

The threat of speaking to his father was obviously far more worrying to Lucas than the prospect of being arrested. Hardcastle imagined that, with his money, Lucas would probably be able to field an army of smart lawyers who would argue that he was not guilty of obstruction at all. But smart lawyers would not help him if Lord Slade took a sudden decision to disinherit his son of the considerable Slade estate.

'All right. They were—'

As Lucas began to recite the names, Hardcastle held up his hand. 'Write them down for me in Sergeant Marriott's pocketbook, Captain Lucas, and don't forget to add details of where I can reach them.'

Lucas was able to write the names and addresses of the guests without any hesitation; they were obviously all well known to him.

Hardcastle cast a cursory glance over the names and handed the book back to Lucas. 'Sign it,' he said. 'Very well, Captain Lucas, I'll let you get on with your breakfast.'

'I've had that list typed out, sir,' said Marriott, and handed it to the DDI. 'Isn't there a possibility that Lucas will contact these people and that they'll manufacture some excuses and alibis, sir?'

'I'm sure they will, Marriott. I'm sure they will. Then we'll at least have a conspiracy to charge them with in the absence of something more serious, and concocted alibis are easier to disprove.' Hardcastle, hands in his pockets and puffing furiously at his pipe, was standing at his office window glaring down at a train passing through Westminster Underground station below. 'I'm going to prepare an information for the Bow Street magistrate,' he said, turning suddenly. 'I intend to search Slade House, its grounds and stables tomorrow, Friday. And if the search lasts all weekend,

I don't care what social arrangements of Lucas's little gang
it buggers up.'

'But what d'you hope to find, sir?'

'Lily Musgrave's body, Marriott.'

On the Friday morning, confident that his search warrant
would be granted, Hardcastle sent for Marriott.

'We'll need four officers to assist us in the search, Marriott.
We'll take Wood, Bodkin and Lipton. I suppose Wilmot's still
up at the Bailey?'

'Not today, sir, but the case is still running.'

'In that case, I suppose it'd better be Catto, but keep an
eye on him.'

'Yes, sir,' said Marriott wearily. 'Is it wise to take Wood
and Bodkin, sir? O'Reilly thinks they're mole-catchers.'

Hardcastle laughed. 'If we're lucky, they'll turn out to be
rat-catchers now. Anyway, it doesn't matter any longer what
O'Reilly thinks. It's a rum set-up down there, and for all I
know O'Reilly might be mixed up in this business. Once
you've detailed the officers I mentioned, tell Wood to
assemble them in the road outside the entrance to Slade
House but to keep them out of sight. I'll give you a time
later on.' He pulled out his watch. 'Time we were off to Bow
Street, Marriott.'

'The court's not sitting today, sir.'

'Not sitting? Why not?'

'Today is Good Friday, sir. No courts are sitting, which
is why Wilmot's not at the Bailey. I thought you'd realized
that, sir.'

'Of course I did, damn it!' exclaimed Hardcastle. 'It'd
temporarily slipped me mind. But it's essential that we search
Slade House without delay. Well, don't keep me in suspense,
Marriott. What arrangements have you made to get me a
warrant?'

'The nearest stipendiary available this morning is Mr
Archibald Prevett who normally sits at Rochester Row police
court. I think you know him, sir.'

'Of course I know him. Taken two or three jobs in front
of him. Where's he live?'

'In Chadwick Street, sir.'

'See if you can find a cab. I suppose the cab drivers' religious principles don't prevent them from working on a Good Friday,' said the DDI sarcastically.

Hardcastle knocked on Archibald Prevett's door at a couple of minutes after ten o'clock.

'Good morning, Mr Hardcastle.' Prevett himself opened the door. 'Step inside.' The magistrate showed the DDI and Marriott into his morning room. 'What can I do for you this morning?'

'I apologize for disturbing you on a bank holiday, sir, but I'd be obliged for a search warrant.' Hardcastle handed over his 'information'.

Prevett read quickly through the document. 'Lord Slade's place, eh?' he said, but made no further comment. He handed Hardcastle a copy of the New Testament. 'You don't need the card with the words on it, do you, Mr Hardcastle?' he asked with a chuckle.

'No, sir.' Hardcastle held the book in his right hand. 'I swear by Almighty God that this information is true to the best of my knowledge, and I will true answer make to any such questions as the court shall demand of me.'

But the magistrate had no questions. He signed the warrant and handed it to the DDI. 'I hope you find what you're looking for, Mr Hardcastle.'

'I have every confidence, sir,' said Hardcastle. It was not a confidence shared by Marriott.

'Are you after my job, Ernie?' asked Fowler when Hardcastle appeared, yet again, in the W Division DDI's office at Brixton police station. 'You're up and down to my bailiwick like a fiddler's elbow. And on a Good Friday, too.'

'I'm not ready to be put out to grass yet, Connie.' Having indulged in the usual badinage that was the precursor to any conversation between policemen, Hardcastle got down to business. 'As a courtesy, I thought I'd let you know that I've got a warrant to search Lord Slade's place down at Epsom.'

'That should put His Lordship in a wax, Ernie. I hope he ain't religious. What are you looking for anyway – evidence of racehorse nobbling?'

'No, a dead body. If I do, Connie, it'll be your job as it's on your manor, unless you want me to take it over.'

'Is this all connected with your Lily Musgrave job?' asked Fowler.

'Yes, it is.' Hardcastle went on to explain briefly what Wood and Bodkin had learned from Slade's head stable lad and the outcome of his interview with Captain Oscar Lucas. 'And if I'm right, it'll be her body I find.'

'I'm only a simple policeman, Ernie, and this all sounds much too complicated for me,' said Fowler with a laugh. 'As far as I'm concerned, you can have it. Anyway, I'm sure Mr Wensley wouldn't want this job split between two DDIs. But it might be as well to square it with him before you go to court. If you get to court,' he added, knowing how often policemen were disappointed in their quest for evidence.

'I was wondering if you could spare me a couple of your detectives to lend a hand, Connie. I've got four of my lads on their way to Epsom now but some help would be appreciated.'

'I'll tell you what I'll do, Ernie,' said Fowler, 'I'll let you have Gandy, and as he's the first-class sergeant at Epsom he knows the ground like the back of his hand and he can pick another DC from his lot down there. By the time you get to Slade House he'll he waiting for you nearby.'

'I'm much obliged, Connie, and I'll let you know how we get on.'

'Gandy can do that, Ernie.' Fowler glanced at Marriott. 'On your way out, Skipper, ask my clerk to come in and I'll get Gandy up on his pins. That'll ruin his Good Friday for him.'

'What does Mr Fowler want a clerk for, Marriott?' muttered Hardcastle, but then he stopped, realizing that he was obliquely criticizing a senior officer to a junior one.

It was almost two o'clock that afternoon by the time Hardcastle was able finally to address his team in the road near the entrance to Slade House.

'How well d'you know the stable area, Gandy?'

'Been there a few times, sir,' said Detective Sergeant Gandy.

'You start searching the stable area, then. Take your own man with you, and you can have DS Wood and Bodkin. That'll give O'Reilly a surprise. The rest of you come with me, and when we've finished searching the house we'll start on the grounds and what's not been covered in the stables. But wait until I've served the warrant.'

Hardcastle, accompanied by Marriott and Catto, walked up the drive and knocked loudly on the front door. When Sidebottom opened it, he peered closely at the DDI.

'I've seen you somewhere before, sir.'

'Yes, you have. It was last Tuesday when I came down to see Captain Lucas.'

'D'you want to see him again, then?' asked Sidebottom.

'If he's here.' Hardcastle was surprised that Lucas was back at Slade House but perhaps he was anticipating the return of A Division's senior detective.

'Come in, sir, and I'll see if I can find him. Oh, there's three of you,' Sidebottom exclaimed as Hardcastle was followed by Marriott and Catto.

It was not long before Lucas appeared in the drawing room. 'What on earth d'you want now, Inspector? Am I to be hounded constantly by you until you find this wretched Musgrave girl?'

'That's it in a nutshell, Captain Lucas. And it would help me, and might even help you, if you were to tell me what you know about her disappearance from this house the weekend before last.'

'I've told you all I know,' said Lucas in a tired voice, 'and I really think it's time I consulted a solicitor about this badgering of yours. You have absolutely nothing to indicate that I know anything about this girl.'

'If I were you, Captain Lucas, I'd wait until we've finished before you speak to your solicitor. You might have something really important to discuss with him then.'

'Such as?'

'This for a start.' Hardcastle took out the search warrant and held it up. 'This is a warrant signed by a stipendiary magistrate empowering me and my officers to search this house, its grounds and stables.' As Lucas went to take the warrant, Hardcastle drew it back out of his reach. 'You may read it but not take it.' The DDI had known of careless detectives who had handed over a warrant only to see it cast into the fire.

'A search warrant,' exclaimed Lucas. 'But what on earth do you hope to find?'

'Evidence that will indicate where Miss Lily Musgrave has gone,' said Hardcastle. 'Or that suggests she didn't go anywhere. In which case, I hope to find her dead body.'

Lucas slumped into an armchair, his face ashen, and the tic in his left eyelid began again. 'You're not seriously suggesting that she's been murdered here in this house, are you?'

'That's exactly what I'm suggesting, Captain Lucas. Catto, go down to the road and tell DS Gandy and the rest of them to start.'

SIXTEEN

'Right, Bert,' said DS Gandy as he and DS Wood and the other two arrived at the stables, 'we'll make a start.'

Padraig O'Reilly emerged from one of the stalls and immediately recognized DS Wood and DC Bodkin. 'Don't tell me you and Liam have been given the job of catching moles on the estate, Bert. Does His Lordship think I don't know how to put paid to the little beggars?'

'Sorry to disappoint you, Padraig,' said Wood, 'but we're not mole-catchers, we're police officers, as are these gentlemen,' he added, indicating the other two detectives. 'And I think you know Sergeant Gandy, anyway.'

O'Reilly's chin dropped. 'Holy Mary, mother of God!' he exclaimed, taking off his cap and scratching his head. 'And why in the name of old Ireland were you spinning me that yarn about the mole-catching when I was in the Spread Eagle the day before yesterday?'

Confronted by four policemen, two of whom he thought were mole-catchers, he was clearly having difficulty grasping what was going on.

'It was so we could get you to tell us all about the goings-on up at the big house the weekend before last, Padraig. And like the good fellow you are, you did just that.' Wood saw no reason to keep the truth from O'Reilly any longer because he would have found out sooner or later. And right now it might be of some advantage to question the head stable lad while he was still coming to terms with the deception perpetrated on him by the police.

'How well d'you know these stables and grounds, Paddy?' asked Gandy.

'Like the back of my hand,' said O'Reilly, 'despite only having been here since last November. Why d'you ask? And, by the way, the name's Padraig, not Paddy.'

'Oh, I *am* sorry,' said Gandy with mock sincerity. 'Well, *Padraig*, have you noticed any disturbance in the earth anywhere around the stables or in the grounds?'

But O'Reilly was prevented from giving an answer by the clatter of a horse's hooves on the cobblestones behind the assembled group. As a stanhope drew to a halt, a man alighted. He was of middling height, but lean and probably somewhere between sixty and seventy years of age; it was difficult to estimate with any degree of accuracy. His tweed hacking jacket, riding breeches and highly polished boots were of good quality and his bristly moustache and heavy, unkempt eyebrows lent him a fierce expression that was matched by his character the moment he opened his mouth.

'Good day to you, My Lord,' said O'Reilly, whipping off his cap and half-bowing.

'What the devil's going on here, O'Reilly?' Lord Slade pointed his riding crop first at the luckless head stable lad, and then waved it in a circular movement as if encompassing the entire estate. 'Unharness the damned horse, will you, and feed the brute. And the carriage needs a damned good cleaning, too. A bit of elbow grease, that's what it needs. Who does it?'

'It's Makin, My Lord, the new stable lad.'

'Well, put your boot up his arse and tell him to get the job done properly, otherwise you can kick the bugger out without any pay.' Slade turned his attention to the four detectives. 'Who are you, and what the hell are you doing snooping around my stables, eh? If I thought for a minute you were tampering with their feed, I'd have the police on you in a second.'

'We *are* the police, Lord Slade,' said Gandy.

'The police?' Slade's monocle dropped from his eye. 'What the devil are you doing here on Good Friday, then? And what was this about a disturbance in the grounds you were talking to O'Reilly about, eh?'

'I think it might be for the best if you spoke to our inspector, Lord Slade,' said Wood. 'He's searching the house at the moment.'

'Searching *my* bloody house?' spluttered Slade, his red face becoming even redder as, in a rage, he danced about waving his riding crop. 'Who is this damned man who has the audacity to come down here and search me damned house, eh? Answer me that.' He could hardly get the words out, such was his loss of self-control.

'It's Divisional Detective Inspector Hardcastle of the Whitehall Division, Lord Slade.'

'Whitehall? What the hell's a Whitehall man doing down here at Epsom poking about in me damned property, eh? Answer me that.' But without waiting for an answer, Slade strode off towards the house, thrashing his right boot with his riding crop and muttering 'Whitehall!' over and over again.

'I think you've upset His Lordship,' said O'Reilly. It was a masterful understatement of the effect the arrival of the police had had on Slade, particularly when he had learned that his house was being searched.

Hardcastle was still talking to Captain Oscar Lucas when the door to the drawing room flew open, crashing back on to an ornamental table.

'What the hell's going on here, Oscar, eh? Answer me that, boy.'

'I presume you're Lord Slade,' said Hardcastle before Lucas had a chance to reply.

'I wasn't talking to you, whoever you are.'

'Well, I'm talking to you,' snapped Hardcastle. 'I'm a police officer and I'm about to search this house, the stables and the grounds. Anyone, and I mean *anyone*, who gets in my way will be arrested for obstructing me in the execution of a justice's search warrant granted by the Chief Metropolitan Magistrate at Bow Street police court this morning.' The DDI thought that naming the chief magistrate was more impressive than talking of a stipendiary who had been disturbed at his home.

'Good God!' exclaimed Lord Slade, recognizing in Hardcastle a man who refused to be bullied by his blustering. He sank on to a leather Chesterfield, one of three with which the room was furnished. 'Well, who are you? Some damned fellow down at the stables said you were from Whitehall.'

'That's correct. I'm Divisional Detective Inspector Hardcastle of the A or Whitehall Division.'

'Well, that don't explain what you're doing here.'

Hardcastle sat down on the settee facing the one occupied by Lord Slade. His son Oscar, looking increasingly anguished, occupied the third settee. 'I'm looking for the body of a young woman.'

'A body? A young woman? What on earth are you talking about, Inspector? Perhaps you'd better explain what the hell this business is all about.'

Beginning with Austen Musgrave's original complaint to the Commissioner that his daughter Lily had gone missing, Hardcastle launched into a full account of what he had learned so far. 'In view of the fact that this young woman was not seen after the evening of Sunday the sixth of April, and that none of the people I've interviewed admit to seeing her leave these premises, I can only conclude that she's dead and her body is secreted somewhere on your estate.'

Lord Slade leaned back against the cushions of his settee, apparently deep in contemplation. But he did not remain tranquil for long.

'What the hell have you been playing at while I've been

across the water, boy?' Slade shouted at his alarmed son. 'You can answer that later this evening, assuming this officer has not clapped you in irons. In the meantime, ring the bloody bell and tell that excuse for a butler to get some whiskey up here. I take it you're not averse to a few fingers of Jameson, Inspector?'

'Not for me, thank you, Lord Slade. I have work to do.' Hardcastle was not against drinking, even Irish whiskey, but he always refused to take a drink from someone who might turn out to be culpable in the crime he was investigating. And he had no reason, at the moment, to rule Lord Slade out of what was fast becoming an extremely complex enquiry.

Once Sidebottom had managed to find a bottle of whiskey and some glasses, and Lord Slade had a substantial measure in his own glass, he appeared calmer.

'Get rid of Sidebottom, boy,' Slade said to his son. 'The man's a bloody liability.' That domestic problem resolved, he turned to Hardcastle. 'When I was down at the stables, Inspector, I heard one of your men asking O'Reilly if he knew of any part of the stable or grounds that had been disturbed. What was that about, eh?'

'If ground has been disturbed recently, it's possible that we might find Lily Musgrave's body there,' said Hardcastle bluntly.

Oscar Lucas paled at this prospect, despite having been through the war and doubtless witnessed violent death many times. But when the victim was someone with whom he had admitted having sexual intercourse, it presumably made a difference. On the other hand, Hardcastle, who had not missed Lucas's reaction, thought it might betray guilty knowledge.

Lord Slade, however, was unaffected by the statement and appeared to take a more technical view of the problem facing Hardcastle.

'I was born here, Inspector, and I know every square inch of this estate. Supposing you and I take a stroll around the grounds and I'll tell you if anyone's been messing about with the earth. How would that suit you?'

'That would save me a lot of time, and if we're lucky, it

would prevent any further disruption to you and your family by a search of the house.'

'Bugger the family,' said Slade. 'It's time it was disrupted. Anyway, they're all in Ireland apart from the boy here. Her Ladyship won't come near this place, nor will my two girls. Probably just as well if people go about murdering people, eh?'

'We don't know that for sure, Lord Slade, but a search might resolve the question one way or another.'

'Or it might not resolve it at all, eh?' said Slade, demonstrating that he had a keen brain, despite all the bluster and the exaggerated gesticulating. Once the peer had finished his whiskey, he struggled out of his settee with much squeaking of the leather.

'Let's see if we can find you a dead body, Inspector.'

'You come with me, Marriott,' ordered Hardcastle. 'Catto and Lipton, you stay here and keep an eye on Captain Lucas.'

'Am I under arrest, then?' asked Lucas, plaintively.

'Not yet, boy,' muttered Slade and, turning to Hardcastle, said, 'Quickest way to get to where we're going, Inspector, is out of the back door.' He strode through to the hall and, pausing only to select a walking stick from the six or seven in the stand, led the way to the rear of the building.

It soon became apparent that Lord Slade knew his own land intimately. He also knew the less open areas and started there, seemingly enjoying himself in seeking the whereabouts of a dead body.

'If anyone's looking for somewhere to bury something, Inspector, this is the sort of place I'd choose.' He led the way between a group of oak trees to an enclosed area surrounded by dense gorse. 'I thought this might be a good place,' he said, 'but it's obvious nothing's been disturbed. Never mind. Follow me.'

And so the quest continued. Moving from one sheltered part of the extensive estate to another, Slade spent most of his time staring at the ground. But it was all in vain until he decided to return to the house by way of a slightly different route that took them through the kitchen garden.

Slade stopped, quite suddenly, and pointed with his walking

stick. 'If that ain't disturbed earth,' he said, indicating an area in the centre of the garden close to a row of young runner bean plants on cane poles, 'then I'm the Flying Dutchman. Just look at that, Inspector. You can see someone's been at it.'

'It certainly looks fresh, Lord Slade,' agreed Hardcastle, but wondered why a disturbed patch in the middle of a kitchen garden should have particularly attracted the peer's interest. It seemed a fairly logical place for anyone to dig. But perhaps that would make it less suspicious.

Slade turned and shouted for someone called Winters.

Moments later, a man of about sixty emerged from the door to the kitchen. Attired in an old smock and corduroy trousers with straps around the knees, he was wearing what appeared to be army-issue boots.

'You wanted me?' asked the man, casually touching his shapeless felt hat with the forefinger of his right hand.

'Of course I wanted you,' said Slade. 'That's why I called your name. This is Winters, my head gardener, Inspector. He's a surly bugger but what he doesn't know about the grounds isn't worth knowing and he could teach Capability Brown a thing or two about gardens.' He turned back to his gardener. 'Winters, this is Inspector Hardcastle.'

'Oh, ah!' Winters took an old clay pipe out of his pocket and started to fill it.

'Have a look at that patch of earth, Winters,' Slade said, pointing with his walking stick, 'and tell me about it.'

'Someone's been at it,' said Winters without moving an inch. 'And afore you say owt else, it weren't me.'

'But you're the only one who has anything to do with the kitchen garden, Winters.' Slade was beginning to sound a little frustrated but his obvious tetchiness had no effect on the head gardener.

'That's right. And as it weren't me, it must've been someone else. Is that all, then?'

'Get a shovel and dig it up. The inspector here wants to know what's down there.'

'That won't be necessary, Lord Slade,' said Hardcastle. 'If what I think is down there, it needs to be a police officer who

uncovers it. It's essential for continuity of evidence. All I
need from Winters is a couple of shovels. And if he's got a
riddle, that might be useful. Oh, and a trowel.'

'Well, you heard the inspector, Winters. Get to it.'

Muttering inaudibly, Winters ambled towards a shed in the
corner of the kitchen garden and took out the items that
Hardcastle had requested.

'Marriott,' said Hardcastle, 'fetch Wood and Bodkin up
here from the stables. They can start turning this soil over.'

It took about half an hour of careful digging, the two officers
taking it in turns while Hardcastle and Marriott stood watching.

'I think we've found it, sir,' said Wood, standing up and
taking the opportunity of a brief respite to ease his aching
back by leaning on his shovel.

Hardcastle stepped closer to the excavation and leaned
down so that he could see more closely. Wood had uncovered
a hand.

The DDI stood up again. 'Use the trowel from now on,
Wood, so's you don't cause any post-mortem injuries that
might confuse the pathologist.'

'Of course, sir.' Wood, like Marriott, was an experienced
detective with many years' service and always tried to hide
his resentment at being told how to do his job. But occasionally it did boil over.

'Marriott, get hold of Doctor Spilsbury and ask him if he
can spare the time to come down here.'

'Yes, sir.' Marriott turned to Slade. 'Are you connected to
the telephone, Lord Slade?'

'Well, of course I am,' said Slade. 'Isn't everyone? It's up
at the house. Be quicker if you went through the kitchen,
Sergeant Marriott. Cook will show you the way.'

It took a further twenty-five minutes of painstaking
removal of the soil before the entire body of a woman was
revealed.

'That's Lily Musgrave, without a doubt,' said Hardcastle,
staring down at the girl's face. He stepped back and put his
hands in his pockets. 'All I've got to do now is find out which
of the young gentlemen who was here the weekend before
last was responsible for her death.'

'Or which of the young women, sir,' said Wood.

'Oh, so you think it's a woman who was responsible, do you, Wood?' Hardcastle abhorred a junior rank offering an opinion and he did not bother to hide the tinge of sarcasm in his voice.

'I don't know that it's *not*, sir. Yet. Any more than I know it's murder. Yet.'

Hardcastle glowered at Wood, but Wood was retiring from the Force in six months' time and what Hardcastle thought of him was of no consequence.

'D'you want the body removed, sir?' asked Wood.

'No, I think we'll wait for Doctor Spilsbury to arrive. I once dealt with a case of arsenic poisoning where there wasn't enough left in the body for conclusive proof of murder but there was in the ground surrounding it. That's why we'll leave it where it is and the good doctor can decide what he wants done next.' Hardcastle glanced at Slade. 'I really need something to cover the body with, Lord Slade, just in case it rains before the pathologist gets here.'

'Winters!' roared Slade.

Once again, Winters emerged from the kitchen door. 'What now?'

'Find a clean tarpaulin for the inspector, large enough to cover the diggings.'

'I might get my tea in peace in a minute,' muttered Winters.

'I swear to God, I'll sack that man for his impertinence one day,' said Slade.

It was close to seven o'clock by the time that Dr Bernard Spilsbury arrived at Slade House and it was already dark. Winters was despatched to obtain a lantern.

Spilsbury spent some time on his hands and knees examining the body as closely as was possible in the light of a hurricane lamp.

'There's nothing further I can do here, Hardcastle. You can safely remove the cadaver.'

'Where would you like it put, sir? I daresay Lord Slade has somewhere convenient.'

'Not at all satisfactory. I couldn't conduct a post-mortem

examination in a greenhouse,' said Spilsbury jocularly. 'How far is the nearest hospital, Lord Slade?'

'About two miles, Doctor. It's in the Dorking Road.'

'Excellent. All we need now is a means of transport to get it there.'

The grumbling Winters was summoned once more and told to find someone called Scudder.

'And tell him to bring the brake as near as he can to the kitchen garden,' said Slade.

Five minutes later, a light brown Rolls-Royce shooting brake drew to a halt at the entrance to the kitchen garden. There was a look of envy on Marriott's face as he studied the classical lines of the vehicle, its gleaming acetylene lamps and its beautifully crafted wooden bodywork.

'You wanted the brake, milord?' The chauffeur, attired in a grey livery consisting of a tunic, breeches, leather gaiters and a peaked cap with a cockade, strode up to Slade and saluted

'Will this do, Doctor?' asked Slade, indicating the shooting brake.

'Handsomely, Lord Slade. A fine motor car, if I may say so.'

'Had it from new since 1910. It was 1910, wasn't it, Scudder?'

'Yes, milord.'

'Good. This is Doctor Spilsbury. He has a body for you to take to Epsom hospital in the Dorking Road.'

'Very good, milord.' Scudder replied without emotion or question, as though transporting dead bodies at nigh-on eight o'clock at night on Good Friday was an everyday occurrence.

'I take it you'll want to go with the body, Doctor?' asked Slade.

'Yes, and so will Mr Hardcastle and his sergeant.'

'Marriott,' said Hardcastle, 'get hold of Gandy and tell him to telephone Epsom hospital and advise them that Doctor Spilsbury will be arriving shortly with a body and will need facilities for conducting a post-mortem.'

To Hardcastle's astonishment, Scudder went to the back of the shooting brake and withdrew a stretcher. 'D'you always carry a stretcher in your shooting brake, Lord Slade?' he asked.

'Only since last year, Inspector,' said Slade. 'One of me

guests managed to shoot a beater up the arse with both barrels. Damned careless, but he was never a very good shot. I put the word around and I doubt he'll be asked to any more shoots. I mean to say, it's all right to shoot a fellow guest up the arse, but it's not the done thing to go about shooting your beaters. Or anyone else's, for that matter. Damned bad form.'

SEVENTEEN

I t had taken some time for Detective Sergeant Gandy to convince the staff at Epsom hospital that the famous Dr Spilsbury was actually on his way with a body. Especially as it was eight o'clock on a Good Friday evening.

Bernard Spilsbury had first come to the notice of the general public four years previously when his evidence in what became known as the Brides-in-the-Bath case resulted in the conviction for murder of George Joseph Smith. Smith's counsel, the equally famous Sir Edward Marshall Hall, had argued eloquently that the deaths were accidental drownings, but Spilsbury proved conclusively that they were not. Since then, every case in which he had been involved attracted the attention of the newspapers and the public, many of whom thronged the public gallery of any court in which he was to give evidence.

Lord Slade's Rolls-Royce shooting brake stopped at the main entrance to the hospital. Spilsbury alighted first, followed by Hardcastle and Marriott.

The man standing on the steps was of medium height and perhaps a little overweight. He had not taken a great deal of trouble with his appearance, apart from his carefully arranged 'fold-over' hair. The crumpled suit he was wearing had seen better days, and a watch chain drooped between the lower pockets of his waistcoat. His shoes had not been polished for some time, and although his bow tie was of a sober pattern, the soft collar of his scrupulously clean white shirt was showing signs of fraying. Part of a stethoscope hung untidily from one of the side pockets of his jacket.

He stepped forward, his hand outstretched. 'I'm Arnold Hughes, Doctor Spilsbury, chief of medicine. Welcome to my hospital. Although we're a charitable foundation, I'm pleased to say that we boast many facilities that are the envy of other similar establishments.' Using both hands, he tightened his bow tie, a habit that he was to repeat from time to time. 'Just tell me what you require and I'll do my best to provide it.'

'Thank you, Doctor. I'm sorry to impose on you at this late hour, but in criminal cases there is always some urgency, as I'm sure you understand, which is why Divisional Detective Inspector Hardcastle and Detective Sergeant Marriott of the Metropolitan Police are with me. Incidentally, the Home Office will pay for any of the facilities I make use of, and as you're a charity, I daresay I can persuade them to make a donation in addition. Although,' Spilsbury added with a smile, 'getting money out of the Home Office is like getting blood out of a stone.'

'That's extremely kind of you, Doctor Spilsbury.'

'Now then, what arrangements do you have for conducting an autopsy, Doctor?' Spilsbury rubbed his hands together.

'There is an examination room adjacent to the mortuary,' said Hughes. 'I'll show you the way.'

'Thank you. And do you have a couple of porters available who can bring my cadaver into the examination room?'

'Of course.' Hughes issued instructions to a uniformed attendant standing nearby. 'I wonder if I might ask a great favour of you, Doctor Spilsbury?'

'By all means.'

'Would you allow me to observe your post-mortem examination?'

'Most certainly, Doctor. In fact, I always welcome a second pair of eyes. They sometimes see something I've missed.'

'Thank you.' Hughes doubted that Spilsbury ever missed anything during the course of an autopsy.

The facilities were quite adequate for Spilsbury's purpose. The mortuary attendant was ready with a rubber apron and rubber gloves, and said that if there was anything else Dr Spilsbury needed, he should just ask.

After forty minutes, during which time Hardcastle was obliged to abstain from smoking his pipe, there was a grunt of triumph from Spilsbury.

'This looks like the little devil, Hardcastle.' Using a pair of forceps, Spilsbury carefully removed a round of ammunition from the girl's cadaver and placed it in a kidney-shaped enamel bowl. 'I'm as certain as can be that the round penetrated the aorta. Death would have been instantaneous, and from the angle of penetration, it is possible that the assailant was slightly taller than his victim, assuming that both were standing and facing each other. To go further would be unwarranted conjecture.'

'And the time of death, Doctor?' Hardcastle asked, not that there was much doubt in his mind.

'Judging by what you've told me so far,' continued Spilsbury, 'it is compatible with the condition of the cadaver, and the circumstances under which it was secreted, that death could have occurred during the weekend of the fifth to sixth of April. I hope that helps, my dear Hardcastle.'

'Indeed it does, sir.' Although, in Hardcastle's view, it did not help a great deal, but he forbore from saying so. All the men he had interviewed so far were taller than Lily Musgrave. He peered closely at the bullet. 'I'd say that was a four-point-five, Doctor.'

'I agree, Hardcastle. No doubt about it in my book, but I suppose your ballistics fellow might disagree; it's in their nature to disagree, you know. Still, that's not my job. However, I'll make sure that there are no more of those things in the poor young lass's body. And then I'll see if there's anything else that may assist you. Why arc you looking so gloomy?'

'Most of my suspects are former officers in the army or the navy, Doctor, and the Webley forty-five was a standard issue weapon, certainly for army officers. I'm not sure about the navy.'

'The Royal Navy issues them, too, sir,' said Marriott helpfully. 'It's going to make it difficult to trace.'

'Means you're going to be busy, then, Marriott,' snapped Hardcastle, irritated at being corrected by his sergeant, especially in the presence of so distinguished a pathologist as Spilsbury.

'I suppose she wasn't pregnant, was she, Doctor?'

'No, she wasn't.' Spilsbury glanced at Hardcastle, knowing that the DDI always had a reason for posing a question. 'Why d'you ask?'

'She was described by one of her male admirers as a young woman of "easy virtue", and another of those admirers claimed to have had sexual intercourse with her three times, but in my view, probably more often. From what I've learned about this little club, I imagine he wasn't the only one she obliged.'

'She certainly wasn't a virgin, but perhaps she was just lucky not to finish up pregnant,' said Spilsbury as he sewed up the girl's body. 'It might be a good idea to have the cadaver removed to my hospital at Paddington tomorrow morning, Hardcastle, just in case there are any more questions you or the coroner need answering. And it might be as well if I were to have another look at it in the morning, but that said, I think it's fairly safe to say that death was due to a gunshot wound. In the meantime,' he said, turning to Hughes, 'might the police impose on your goodwill by keeping the cadaver in your mortuary overnight, Doctor Hughes?'

'Most certainly, Doctor Spilsbury. I'll arrange it immediately.'

'There will have to be a police guard on it until it's removed to Paddington tomorrow, Doctor Hughes,' said Hardcastle. 'It's a question of continuity of evidence.'

'I'll get hold of Sergeant Gandy and arrange a guard and transport, sir,' said Marriott. 'Doctor Hughes, might I use a telephone?'

'Of course. The attendant here will show you where it is.'

Spilsbury took out a letter containing a bill from his tailor and made a few notes on the back of the envelope about the examination he had just conducted.

Hardcastle was in his office, as usual, by eight o'clock on the Saturday morning. After lighting his pipe, he shouted for Marriott.

Catto appeared in the doorway. 'Er, Sergeant Marriott's not in the office, sir.'

'Well, where is he? Has he arrived yet? What's going on, Catto?' Hardcastle made it sound as though the unavailability of Marriott was entirely Catto's fault. At least, that was how Catto saw it.

'Oh, yes, sir, he's here, sir, but he's not here,' stuttered Catto, 'if you know what I mean.' Seeing the DDI's deepening frown, he added, 'But he went straight across to Mr Franklin's office.'

Detective Inspector Percy Franklin was the Metropolitan Police's ballistics expert. Closeted in a small room near the top of Scotland Yard, his evidence was vital in any murder case that involved firearms.

'Tell Sergeant Marriott to see me the moment he gets back, Catto. Now get about your duties.'

'Yes, sir.'

Less than five minutes later, Marriott knocked on Hardcastle's open door.

'Ah, Marriott. What did Mr Franklin have to say about our bullet?'

'He confirmed that it was a military issue round, four-point-five calibre, sir. Once we have the weapon, he said he'll be able to compare the striations on the round to the rifling in the barrel of the revolver.'

'He always says that,' muttered Hardcastle gloomily, 'but no more than I expected him to say. Now, Marriott, we have the unpleasant task of telling Mr Austen Musgrave that we've found his daughter.'

It was nine o'clock when Hardcastle and Marriott alighted from their cab outside Musgrave's house in Vincent Square.

'Good morning, sir,' said Crabb as he opened the door. 'I'm afraid the master hasn't risen yet.'

Hardcastle stepped past the butler. 'Get him now, Crabb. This is a matter of some importance.'

'Well, sir, I'm not sure that I ought to—'

'Don't argue with me, Crabb, just do it,' said Hardcastle wearily. 'Sergeant Marriott and I will be in the morning room.'

Crabb hastened away, muttering to himself. He did not like the inspector and was sure that the inspector did not like him. He was also concerned that the inspector might discover that he was falsifying the wine account. He also suspected Mrs Briggs, the cook, was not being altogether honest when it came to rendering the monthly household accounts to the master. Not that they needed to have worried; Musgrave only cast a cursory glance over any of the household accounts. What both he and Mrs Briggs most feared, albeit separately, was that one day Sarah Gillard might become mistress of the house.

It was at least twenty minutes before Austen Musgrave appeared in the morning room. On this occasion, he was wearing a dressing gown of bright red silk that was only long enough to cover his knees. And, unlike the last time he had received Hardcastle, he was barefooted and tousle haired.

'This is an unearthly hour on a Saturday to call on me, Inspector,' snapped Musgrave. 'For God's sake, man, you could have come later, surely?' He had a frown on his face, as though he expected underlings like mere policemen to be aware of the customs of the leisured classes. The real reason, which Hardcastle had guessed anyway, was that Musgrave had been forced to leave a bed in which the amorous Sarah Gillard was impatiently awaiting his return. Not only to his displeasure but to her displeasure also.

'I'd advise you to sit down, Mr Musgrave, before I go on.' Hardcastle ignored the reproof.

'You make it sound as though this is something serious, Inspector.' Nevertheless, Musgrave sat down on one of the settees, his face expressing the sudden realization that Hardcastle may have grave news.

'I'm afraid your daughter Lily is dead, Mr Musgrave,' said Hardcastle bluntly. He had long ago decided that there was no easy way to inform people of the violent death of a close relative. It was perhaps a legacy of the Great War that sudden death had become all too commonplace during the four years and three months of its duration. And regrettably was continuing with the advent of the Spanish influenza pandemic.

Musgrave did not immediately react to the news, other than

to sit quite still, a stunned expression on his face. He remained like that for two or three minutes, during which time Hardcastle and Marriott relaxed in armchairs. None of them spoke.

'What happened, Inspector?' Musgrave asked eventually.

'She was murdered, sir. Shot. Her body was found in a shallow grave at Slade House where she'd gone with Captain Oscar Lucas the weekend before last.'

'Have you arrested Lucas yet?'

'No, Mr Musgrave, I haven't.'

'Why not?' Musgrave demanded, the frown returning.

'Because there is no evidence at this stage to prove that he was responsible for your daughter's death.' Hardcastle went on to explain about the party that had been held at Slade House and that there had been a number of guests, any one of whom could have been responsible.

'Would it help if I spoke to Sir Nevil Macready, Inspector?'

'Certainly not. I think I explained the other day that the Commissioner is not empowered to tell me how I should investigate a case of murder or who I should arrest.' Hardcastle did not mention that the Commissioner was unlikely to see Musgrave again and would most certainly not return any future telephone calls from him.

'I need to arrange the funeral,' said Musgrave absently.

'I'm afraid you'll have to wait for the coroner to release your daughter's body, sir.'

'Yes, I suppose so.'

The door to the morning room opened. Sarah Gillard stepped inside and paused, a hand still on the handle. It was, without doubt, a rehearsed theatrical entrance, but she had been told by Crabb who was in the morning room with Musgrave. Her long, black satin robe was neither peignoir nor housecoat; it was more like an evening gown, the like of which Hardcastle had never before seen. Her long hair was loose around her shoulders, but in such a way that she had obviously taken some trouble in carefully disarranging it before coming downstairs, and her face had been treated to some of Mr Max Factor's products. Satin slippers completed the carefully devised ensemble. Hardcastle had the impression that Sarah Gillard never did anything without careful forethought.

'Austen, darling, what is it? You look awful.'

'Lily's dead, murdered,' said Musgrave flatly.

'Oh, you poor dear darling, how dreadful.' Sarah Gillard leaned down to put an arm around Musgrave's shoulders and shot an accusing glance at Hardcastle. 'Why was this allowed to happen? I would have thought that you could have prevented it, especially as you knew the poor, innocent girl was missing. Austen told me that your Commissioner was taking an interest in your investigations.'

'I'll let you know when Lily's body is released, Mr Musgrave.' Hardcastle completely ignored Sarah Gillard's rantings and stood up.

But Sarah was unwilling to leave the matter alone. 'Have you arrested someone for this crime?' she demanded haughtily, thrashing around for someone to blame.

'No, madam,' snapped Hardcastle. 'Nor do I expect to do so in the near future.'

'Well, what on earth are you doing about it? Shouldn't you be out looking for this killer?'

'I'll have him dancing on the hangman's trap before very long, but these things take time, Miss Gillard. It's not a theatrical mystery that can be solved in three acts with two intervals. We'll let ourselves out, Mr Musgrave. Come, Marriott.'

As Hardcastle and Marriott walked out of the room and into the hall, Sarah Gillard could be heard complaining bitterly to Musgrave about 'that man Hardcastle's disgraceful insolence'.

'That woman's got her foot in the door, Marriott, and she ain't going to let go,' said Hardcastle, as they walked around Vincent Square in search of a cab.

'Bring me that list, Marriott. The names of the men who attended the parties where the naked Lily Musgrave did her song and dance act.'

'One moment, sir. It's on my desk.' Marriott crossed to the detectives' room, picked up the list and returned to the DDI's office. 'There you are, sir.'

'As well as Lucas, there were Colonel Rendell, Major Toland, Lieutenant Frampton and Doctor Rylance using his butler's name.' Hardcastle read the names aloud. 'And, of course, Major Quilter. He's too good to be true.'

'Have you discounted Rylance's butler Kelsey altogether, sir?'

'Just a cat's paw, Marriott. Just a cat's paw. He was not very happy when he found out that the doctor was using his name and he'd be even less happy if he knew *why* he was using it. No, we can forget him. Now, they were all at Slade House for the weekend that Lily was murdered. Who were the others?'

'According to Lucas, sir, there was only one other and his name was Harvey, sir – Randolph Harvey.'

'Is he an ex-officer as well?'

'Lucas didn't know, sir. Or at least he said he didn't know. And then, of course, there were the six young women including Lily Musgrave.'

'One for each man,' said Hardcastle.

'Not exactly, sir. There were seven men but only six women.'

'You're right, Marriott,' said Hardcastle in a rare admission of his sergeant's mathematical superiority. 'Have we got the women's names?'

'Yes, sir, but d'you think that one of them was a murderess?'

'Who's to tell? It's a funny world we're living in now, Marriott,' said Hardcastle phlegmatically. 'This bloody war's changed everything. But we'll leave them for the time being, although they'll have to be seen in case one of them saw or heard anything.'

'When do we start to interview the men, sir?'

Hardcastle pulled out his half-hunter. 'I'll decide that after we've had our lunch, Marriott. After all, there's no hurry. The poor lass is dead.'

'Hello, Inspector.'

Hardcastle put down his pint of bitter and turned. 'What are you after, Simpson?'

Charlie Simpson, a reporter on the *London Daily Chronicle*, spent much of his time in the Red Lion, the public house adjacent to New Scotland Yard, in the hope of picking up a snippet. Fortunately for Simpson, there were detectives who would tell him anything he wanted to know for the price of a large whisky, but to his regret, Hardcastle was not one of them.

'I've heard whispers about a topping down Epsom way, Mr Hardcastle. I was wondering if you knew anything about it?'

'Why should I know anything about what goes on in Epsom, Simpson? Apart from the Derby. I'm in the Whitehall Division. Mr Fowler's the CID officer responsible for that area, as you undoubtedly know.'

'Yes, but I heard your name mentioned, Mr Hardcastle.'

'That don't surprise me, Simpson. I'm a very popular man. Just ask my sergeant here. Ain't that true, Marriott?' Hardcastle enquired jocularly.

'Very true, sir. Highly popular,' said Marriott drily.

'Now, if you'll excuse me, Simpson,' said Hardcastle, 'I'm having my lunchtime pint and I get very tetchy if people go about interrupting it.'

'I heard that an MP's daughter was the one that got murdered. Any truth in that?' persisted Simpson.

Hardcastle turned his back on the reporter.

'What we'll do, Marriott,' said Hardcastle when they were back in the DDI's office, 'is send for each of these men, and we'll start with Lucas.'

'He's probably still down at Epsom, sir, it being Saturday.'

'He's got a Lagonda, Marriott. It won't take him long to get here. Telephone him. Or telephone Lord Slade if he's there and ask him to send his boy up here.'

'And if he refuses, sir?'

'Then I'll ask Mr Fowler to send his newest detective constable round to Slade House to nick him.'

In the event, Captain Oscar Lucas did not argue. An hour after Marriott had telephoned Slade House he presented himself at Cannon Row police station.

'There's a man called Lucas at the front office counter, sir.' The constable stood in the doorway of the DDI's office.

'Yes, I thought there might be, lad,' said Hardcastle. 'Bring him up.'

Looking very nervous, Lucas appeared moments later,

still wearing the tweeds that he had been wearing the previous day.

'Was it really necessary to send for me on a Saturday afternoon, Inspector?' Lucas was incapable of making more than a half-hearted protest.

'It saved me having to go down to Epsom to arrest you, Lucas. Sit down and tell me what you know about Lily's murder.'

'I don't know anything about it, Inspector.'

Hardcastle adopted a sceptical expression. 'D'you really expect me to believe that this young woman was murdered at your home and you know nothing about it?'

'It's true, Inspector,' pleaded Lucas desperately.

'You didn't hear a revolver shot at any time over the weekend? I take it you know what that sounds like,' observed Hardcastle sarcastically.

'No, I heard nothing, and yes, I would know what it sounded like.'

'Where d'you keep your forty-five Webley revolver, Lucas?' the DDI asked suddenly.

Lucas opened his mouth in surprise. 'What makes you think I've got a revolver, Inspector?'

'I don't have time to discuss the matter, Lucas. Almost every ex-officer I've come across hung on to his issue revolver.'

'But they have to be accounted for. How am I supposed to have kept a revolver?'

'Quite simple, Captain Lucas,' said Marriott. 'I know for a fact that after every big attack the battlefield is littered with abandoned weapons. Rifles for the most part but also a sprinkling of officers' sidearms.'

'It's down at Slade House,' admitted Lucas.

Hardcastle glanced across the office at Marriott. 'Be so good as to get on the telephone instrument to Epsom nick and ask Gandy to go up to Slade House and seize Captain Lucas's revolver, and then to get someone to bring it up here, *tout de suite*.' He turned back to Lucas. 'In the meantime, Captain Lucas, you will be detained here on suspicion of murdering Lily Musgrave.' The DDI looked over his desk. 'Pick him up, Marriott,' he said, seconds after Lucas had fallen to the floor in a dead faint.

EIGHTEEN

Hardcastle glanced at his watch and decided that to send for Major Max Quilter at seven o'clock on a Saturday evening would cause the club owner a great deal of inconvenience. That pleased Hardcastle, who was becoming increasingly impatient with the attitude of the men with whom he had been dealing of late. It seemed to him that they believed themselves to be above the law, and that included Austen Musgrave, MP, the victim's father.

'Who have we got in the office, Marriott?'

'Catto and Lipton, sir,' replied Marriott promptly. It was his job to know where all the detectives were at any given time.

'They'll do. Send them round to the VanDoo Club and ask Major Quilter if he'd be so good as come to the station. Immediately. And if he refuses, they can have the pleasure of nicking him on suspicion of murdering Lily Musgrave.'

It was exactly the sort of task that Catto enjoyed. Having been given specific directions by Sergeant Marriott as to where he would find Quilter's office, Catto ignored the doorman of the VanDoo Club in Rupert Street, apart from thrusting his warrant card in the man's face, and he and Lipton moved swiftly through the club's premises. Although it was a Saturday evening, and many of the club's usual clientele were spending the weekend in the country, there was still a sizeable crowd of drinkers and dancers.

Needless to say, Catto and Lipton were not in evening dress and their purposeful stride towards Quilter's office led quite a few of the revellers to correctly suspect that they were police officers. Thinking that a raid was about to take place, some of them made swiftly for the nearest exit, just to be on the safe side. It was not that they were worried about appearing at Great Marlborough Street police court on Monday; in fact, it would be quite a hoot, but ten o'clock in the morning really was an unearthly hour at which to have to get there. Particularly as next Monday was Easter Monday.

When Catto opened the door of the club owner's office, he found that Quilter was entertaining a young woman. Draped languidly on a settee and sipping champagne, she was displaying a little more leg than was regarded as seemly. At least by those people who still clung to Victorian values in a rapidly changing post-war society where younger women were seeking emancipation and renewing their demand for the right to vote.

'Who the hell are you and what d'you want? This is a private part of the club.' Quilter rose aggressively from behind his desk. 'You're not members.'

'We're police officers, Mr Quilter.'

'It's *Major* Quilter.'

'Doesn't really make any difference, *Major*,' Catto continued, 'to the fact that you are required at Cannon Row police station right now for an interview with Divisional Detective Inspector Hardcastle.'

'Well, you can tell Hardcastle to go to hell. I've got a business to run. If he wants to see me he can call here between ten and eleven on Monday week. I shall be staying with friends until then.'

Catto was thoroughly enjoying himself. 'Did you bring the handcuffs, Gordon?' he asked, casually addressing the question to Gordon Lipton.

Lipton made a show of patting his pockets. 'No, I must've forgotten, Henry. I'm awfully sorry.'

For the first time since the arrival of the two police officers, Quilter began to look uneasy at this little charade being played out by Catto and Lipton.

'In that case, I suppose we'll have to manage without them.' Catto turned back to Quilter. 'As you decline to accompany us voluntarily, Major Quilter, I have no alternative but to arrest you on suspicion of the murder of Lily Musgrave on or about the fifth or sixth of this month.'

'What the hell are you talking about?' Quilter sank into

his chair, his face suddenly losing its colour. 'Are you telling me that Lily is dead?'

At that point, the young woman reclining on the settee decided that it would be beneficial to her well-being to leave this distasteful scene. 'I'll leave you to get on with your lovely policemen friends, Max, darling,' she said, slurring her speech and standing up somewhat unsteadily. 'I'll see you around, lover.' And with that disingenuous farewell, she left the office as quickly as the limitations of her skirt and her intake of champagne allowed.

'For God's sake, I know nothing of the murder of Lily Musgrave,' protested Quilter.

'Which is it to be, then?' asked Catto, ignoring Quilter's protestation of innocence. 'Are you coming voluntarily or do we have to arrest you and have you conveyed to Scotland Yard in a Black Annie?' The Cannon Row detectives often unnerved their suspects by ominously mentioning Scotland Yard rather than naming their police station. The fact of the matter was that suspects were never taken to the Yard. It was not a police station and had no facilities for detaining prisoners.

'Thank you for sparing the time to come in,' said Hardcastle with mock sincerity as Marriott showed Max Quilter into the DDI's office.

'After your officers threatened to arrest me, I didn't see that I had much option,' said Quilter.

'Threatened to arrest you, did they, Major Quilter? Surely not.' Hardcastle raised his eyebrows. 'Good gracious! There was no need for them to have done that. I'm sure you'd have been willing. Do have a word with them, Marriott. Can't have my men going around threatening people. Now, do sit down, Major Quilter.'

'I suppose they were also lying when they said that Lily Musgrave had been murdered.' Quilter sprawled in the chair and took out a gold cigarette case from which he extracted a Turkish cigarette.

'Alas no. She was murdered just over two weeks ago at Slade House in Epsom.'

'I really don't see how you expect me to know anything about that, Inspector. And I can only presume that's why you had me dragged down here.'

'I thought you might know something about it as you were at Slade House that weekend, along with six other men from your unsavoury little group, and six young women, including the unfortunate Lily Musgrave.'

Quilter sat forward in his chair. 'Who told you I was there?' he demanded.

'Oscar Lucas,' said Marriott, who was standing behind Quilter. 'In fact, he's told us quite a lot. Despite your denials, we now know that you had sexual intercourse with Lily more than once. We also know that you and others were present at Colonel Rendell's house in Old Queen Street on several occasions when Lily entertained you all by taking off her clothes.'

'Oscar Lucas has peached on the lot of you, Quilter,' said Hardcastle, further adding to the club owner's discomfort. 'And now you can tell me where you keep the army issue Webley revolver Lucas said you neglected to hand in when you resigned your commission.' Lucas had made no such statement, but Hardcastle always found it useful to 'gild the lily' slightly and lead his suspects into believing that their so-called friends had turned on them. He knew, better than most, that there was no honour among thieves. And even less among murderers, for that matter.

'Damn the man,' muttered Quilter. 'No more than I expected from someone in the Connaught Rangers. All right, so I hung on to my revolver for personal protection. There are some very nasty characters, mainly Maltese, running rackets in the West End, and they'll stop at nothing, and I do mean nothing. But I daresay you know all about that, Inspector.'

'You still haven't told me where it is, Quilter.'

'At the club, of course.'

'Did you take it with you when you spent the weekend at Slade House?'

'Of course not. Why would I need a gun down there?'

'Very well, Quilter. I'll send two of my officers to your club to take possession of your revolver. You can tell Sergeant Marriott here exactly where it is.'

'What right have you to take it?'

'Have you got a licence for it?'

'No.'

'Then you've answered your own question,' said Hardcastle, by no means sure that Quilter had contravened the Pistols Act, but certain that Quilter would not know either. 'Marriott, send Catto and Lipton to fetch the major's firearm, once he's told you where it is. And you'll be detained here until they get back, Quilter.'

'Are you charging me?'

'Not yct.'

'Then you can't keep me here.'

'I can easily charge you with suspicion of murder, if that's what you want,' said Hardcastle.

And so it went on. Over the next few days, Hardcastle and his detectives interviewed most of the men who had been at the now infamous Slade House party.

Each of the party-goers who had held on to his service-issue revolver surrendered it voluntarily, albeit reluctantly. Detective Inspector Percy Franklin, the ballistics expert, had compared each weapon against the round that had killed Lily Musgrave but none of them had matched. Lieutenant Carl Frampton, of the Royal Naval Volunteer Reserve, had been released from active service once hostilities had ceased and had not retained his sidearm, archly pointing out that the navy was stricter about such matters than the army.

The men who had been interviewed about revolvers were also asked what, if anything, they had seen or heard during the fateful weekend of Lily's death. None of them could assist, apart from one or two of them who told Hardcastle that they had last seen Lily after dinner on the Sunday. Each one had presumed that she had gone to bed with one of their number, but did not know who.

There were, however, two of the men who had yet to be traced. The whereabouts of the mysterious Randolph Harvey seemed to be unknown. No one admitted having invited Harvey to Slade House, and that included Oscar Lucas, although he had put the man's name on the list. He could now not recall why he had done so. Colonel Rendell said that he thought he was at one of the parties at his house at Old Queen Street when Lily performed her risqué cabaret, but was by no means certain.

Hardcastle decided to widen the enquiry by having the women interviewed. One by one, they were spoken to, but not one of them was prepared to admit having any knowledge of Lily's murder. None of them knew where she had gone after dinner on the Sunday. By dint of persistent questioning, each of the girls was persuaded to disclose with whom they had slept on that fateful night. This revealed an interesting fact: none of them had slept with Dr Jack Rylance, the Harley Street physician.

It therefore became a matter of some urgency to interview Rylance. Detective Constable Henry Catto was despatched to Wilton Street to bring the doctor to the station, either voluntarily or under arrest.

Rylance's butler, Roland Kelsey, told Catto that his master was undertaking a tour of the battlefields in France and was believed to be somewhere in the area around the river Somme. Rylance, said Kelsey, should be returning on Sunday the twenty-seventh of April. Weather in the English Channel permitting, of course.

Therefore, at ten o'clock on the morning of Monday the twenty-eighth of April 1919, Hardcastle and Marriott knocked on the door of Rylance's Wilton Street house.

'I'm afraid you've just missed him, Inspector,' said the butler.

'Where's he gone then?'

'To his Harley Street consulting rooms, Inspector. At least, that's where he said he was going.'

'Did you by any chance tell him I was looking for him, Kelsey?' asked Hardcastle.

'Yes, I did, sir. Last night when he arrived back from France. The ferry was held up and consequently the boat train was late in arriving at Victoria, at the South Eastern and Chatham terminal, that would be, sir.'

'What is the exact address in Harley Street, Kelsey?' asked

Marriott, and then wrote down the details at the butler's dictation.

'I ain't happy about Doctor Rylance, Marriott,' said Hardcastle as the two detectives walked down Wilton Street towards Grosvenor Place in search of a cab. 'And come to that, I ain't too happy about his butler, either.'

The address that Kelsey had given the detectives appeared at first sight to house several members of the medical profession. But Dr Jack Rylance's name did not appear on any of the brass plates at the entrance.

Nevertheless, Hardcastle entered the building and rang the bell of the first door on the right.

A middle-aged woman in horn-rimmed spectacles, her grey hair fashioned into coils that covered her ears, known colloquially as 'earphones', opened the door and studied the two men.

'Can I help you?' she asked.

'We're police officers, madam,' said Hardcastle, raising his hat. 'I'm looking for a Doctor Jack Rylance.'

'Well, this isn't his practice,' said the woman, in a tone that implied Hardcastle could not read.

'No, I understand that, but the address we were given for Doctor Rylance was this house.'

'I'm afraid I've never heard of him, and I've been the receptionist here for twelve years.' The woman's attitude softened slightly. 'I would ask the doctor but he has a patient with him at the moment.'

'Do you, by any chance, have a copy of the *Medical Register*?' asked Marriott.

'Of course,' said the woman in a rather superior manner. 'Would you like to examine it?'

'If we may,' said Hardcastle, taking back the initiative from his sergeant.

'Come in.' The receptionist held open the door and, once the two detectives were in the reception room, she crossed to a bookcase and took down a heavy volume.

Hardcastle skimmed quickly through the pages and then looked up. 'He ain't there, Marriott.'

'D'you know anything else about this doctor, apart from believing he practised at this address?' asked the receptionist, becoming suddenly quite helpful. 'He may only just have registered, you see, although this is the latest edition,' she added, indicating the *Medical Register.*

'As a matter of fact, I know very little about him,' admitted Hardcastle, 'but he told us he had been an army medical officer during the war.'

'In that case, you might try the Royal Army Medical College at Millbank. He may still be practising as an army doctor.'

Although Hardcastle thought that to be unlikely, he thanked the receptionist and he and Marriott left.

'I knew there was something not quite right about that fellow, Marriott,' said Hardcastle as he looked up and down the street. Seeing a cab, he waved his umbrella.

'Where to, guv'nor?' asked the driver.

'D'you know the Royal Army Medical College in Millbank?'

'Course, I do, guv'nor. Here, you ain't got that Spanish flu, have you? I wouldn't want to catch any of that.'

'The only thing you're likely to catch is a dose of the Commissioner's elbow,' snapped Hardcastle as he and Marriott got in.

As the Commissioner of Police licenced London cabs, the driver knew exactly what that pithy comment meant. He said nothing, but vented his annoyance on the taximeter by savagely yanking it down.

The librarian at the Royal Army Medical College consulted several lists and ledgers.

'The only Jack Rylance on the list, Inspector, was a Lieutenant Colonel Jack Rylance, a regular officer of the Royal Army Medical Corps, who was killed at Vlamertinge in 1917 when a shell hit a forward dressing station.'

'You're sure about that?' asked Hardcastle.

'Positive,' said the librarian. 'If I may make a suggestion, you could try the War Office. It's possible that there was a Jack Rylance associated with medical services. For example, the Army Service Corps provided ambulances and there were entire companies of them, usually commanded by a captain. I'm sorry I can't be of more help.'

'You can't help us if the fellow don't exist,' said Hardcastle, with unusual magnanimity.

'Thank you for your assistance, ma'am,' said Marriott.

'I had hoped that our frequent visits to Colonel Frobisher might've come to an end when the Armistice was signed, Marriott,' said Hardcastle as the cab deposited them at Horse Guards in Whitehall. He raised his bowler hat in acknowledgement of the mounted sentry's salute as they passed into the archway, even though he was not entitled to the compliment.

'I daresay Colonel Frobisher felt the same way, sir,' ventured Marriott, and received a sharp sideways glance.

The dismounted sentry also saluted and Hardcastle again raised his hat before pushing open the door of the office of the Assistant Provost Marshal of London District that was in the archway itself.

'Haven't seen you in a while, Inspector.' In the outer office, Sergeant Glover, the APM's chief clerk, was seated behind a desk laden with files.

'Is Colonel Frobisher in, Sergeant Glover?' asked Hardcastle.

'Colonel Frobisher's retired, Inspector. He'd actually served more than his pensionable time but like so many was kept on until the war was over. Left us last year, on December the thirty-first, to be precise.'

'Who's taken his place, then?'

'Major Sinclair, a General List officer, Inspector.'

'A major, Cyril?' queried Marriott.

'They decided we only needed a *deputy* assistant provost marshal in London District, now the fisticuffs with Fritz is over, Charlie. But knowing the army, they'll have changed their minds again in a few months' time. Anyway, Inspector, I take it you'd like a word with the major?'

'Yes. We have an interesting query for him.'

'In that case, it'll probably be me who finishes up solving it, Inspector.' Glover stood up. 'I'll show you in.'

'George Sinclair, Inspector.' The DAPM was a tall, slim man, possibly six foot two and about thirty years of age and with a moustache. He was immaculate in blue patrols, the plain form of undress uniform occasionally worn by soldiers in peacetime. 'I've heard all about you from Ralph Frobisher. He told me that you're always asking difficult questions.' Sinclair laughed, shook hands and invited the two detectives to sit down. 'What can I do to help?'

Hardcastle explained about the mystery of Jack Rylance and the result of those enquiries he had made so far.

'The only other information we had, and that was from Rylance's butler, was that he owned a Rolls-Royce. He was also said to own a cottage and a market garden in Lancing. We'll be asking the police in Sussex to make enquiries to ascertain whether that is true. I'll advise you of anything relevant we hear that might help.'

'It certainly does seem something of an enigma, Inspector,' said Sinclair thoughtfully after he had finished taking copious notes of Hardcastle's problem. 'And it's a pretty big job you're asking me to do for you. Is the man actually wanted by the police?'

'He is suspected of murdering a young woman, Major.' Hardcastle had already decided that Rylance was indeed a suspect or, at best, had a few questions to answer.

'Is he, by Jove! I don't suppose you have a description of the man, do you? That might help if more than one Jack Rylance served in the army.'

'I do, as a matter of fact, because we interviewed him once. Read the major the note you made when we saw Rylance at Wilton Street, Marriott.'

'Aged between twenty-five and thirty, he was about five-foot-eight-inches tall, with auburn hair and a trimmed moustache, Major,' Marriott began, 'and he was rather stooped when he walked, as though he'd spent all his life going through low doorways. It's possible, I suppose, that it's the result of a war wound, and as Mr Hardcastle told you, the butler said that Rylance had been wounded at the retreat from Mons and discharged from the army as unfit for further service. As far as his weight was concerned, I'd estimate that he was about ten stone and in pretty good shape. There were two particular features that I noticed: his ears don't have lobes and he has a scar running along the jawline on the left-hand side of his face. About four inches long, I'd say.'

Sinclair wrote down the details and leaned back in his chair. 'I must say that's a very detailed description, Sergeant Marriott,' he said, putting the cap on his fountain pen and dropping it casually on the desk.

'We are professionals, Major,' said Hardcastle rather pointedly.

Sinclair laughed, much to Marriott's relief, and then surprised Hardcastle. 'Would you care to join me in a drink, Inspector, and you too, Sergeant? To celebrate our future cooperation. Not that we policemen ever need an excuse for a drink, eh?'

'Very kind, Major,' murmured Hardcastle, immediately forming a favourable view of the new provost officer.

Sinclair crossed to a wall cabinet and took out a bottle of Johnny Walker Black Label and three glasses. 'I take it you don't want water?' he enquired, implying that the very idea was anathema.

For the next half an hour, Sinclair regaled the two detectives with stories about the last three months that he had spent as town major of Bonn, a small community some twenty or so miles outside Cologne.

'He seems quite a decent fellow,' said Hardcastle as he and Marriott walked back up Whitehall towards Cannon Row police station. 'In all the years we knew Colonel Frobisher, he never offered us a drink.'

NINETEEN

Following their lunch at the Red Lion, Hardcastle and Marriott returned to the police station. For some twenty minutes, the DDI sat at his desk in deep thought before standing up and crossing the corridor to the detectives' office.

'Catto!' he barked.

'Sir.' Catto leaped to his feet, knocking over his chair as he did so, and wondering, as ever, what he had done wrong.

'When you went to Wilton Street to bring Rylance back here, who answered the door?' asked Hardcastle, waving down the other occupants of the office who had stood up at the arrival of the DDI.

'The butler, sir. Man by the name of Kelsey.'

'What time of day was that?'

'Ten thirty in the morning, sir.'

'What clothes was he wearing, Catto?'

'Clothes, sir?'

'For God's sake, Catto,' snapped Hardcastle, 'it's a perfectly straightforward question. They're the things people put on before they go out. It saves them from being arrested for an outrage on public decency.'

'Ah, yes, sir. I see, sir.' Catto was immediately seized by a paroxysm of nerves, a condition always brought on by being in the DDI's presence. 'He was wearing plus-fours, a Paisley-patterned pullover and socks, sir. And a spotted tie and white shirt. He looked as though he'd been playing golf, sir.'

'Well done, Catto,' said Hardcastle. 'A good description.'

'Yes, sir. I mean, thank you, sir.' Catto gulped. It was the first compliment he had ever received from the DDI and he was stunned but at once suspicious that Hardcastle might have an ulterior reason for the blandishment.

'As a reward, Catto,' continued Hardcastle jocularly, 'you can go round to Wilton Street and arrest Kelsey on suspicion of conspiracy to murder.'

'Yes, sir.'

'And take Lipton with you.'

'D'you think Kelsey's really involved, sir?' queried Marriott, once he and Hardcastle were back in the DDI's office.

'Kelsey's done nothing but prevaricate, Marriott. He tipped off Rylance to expect us and then he gave us a false address for Rylance's consulting rooms. And, apart from anything else, plus-fours is a damned funny get-up for a butler to be wearing when he answers the door at half-past ten in the morning. No, Marriott, I don't think Kelsey's a butler at all. There's something rum going on here.'

'D'you think he might have gone to Lancing, sir?'

'Lancing, Marriott? Why should he have gone to Lancing?'

'It's where Kelsey said that Rylance had a cottage and a market garden.'

'Oh, yes, of course he did. But after wasting our time in Harley Street I don't propose going there, Marriott, unless I know that Rylance does own a market garden there.'

'I'll send a telegraph message to West Sussex Constabulary, sir.'

'I was going to suggest that, Marriott. Are you sure that West Sussex Constabulary is the right force? I mean Lancing might come under a borough force. Some of these county constabularies can be very confusing at times.'

'I've made enquiries, sir, and I can assure you that Lancing is definitely part of West Sussex Constabulary, not a borough force. Its headquarters are at Horsham.'

'Why are Lancing's headquarters at Horsham?' Hardcastle managed to conjure up an expression of bewilderment.

'They're not, sir,' said Marriott patiently, convinced that Hardcastle was being deliberately obtuse. 'The Force HQ is at Horsham. Lancing is part of Steyning Division.'

'And where are their headquarters?'

'Steyning, sir.'

'Oh, get on with it.' Hardcastle began to fill his pipe.

Two hours after Hardcastle had sent Catto and Lipton to arrest Roland Kelsey, Catto reported back to the DDI. Suddenly more confident than ever before, he tapped on the DDI's door and stepped into his office.

'The bird appears to have flown, sir.'

'What are you talking about Catto? What bird?'

'Kelsey, sir. He wasn't there. We made enquiries of the neighbours and one of them, a Mrs Pritchard who lives opposite, said that about an hour ago a Rolls-Royce drew up driven by Doctor Rylance. The neighbour knows him by sight although she's never spoken to him. She went on to say that another man – she thought it was Rylance's butler – came out and got into the car. He was carrying a small suitcase. The car then drove away. I asked this neighbour if she'd ever seen a cook but she said she didn't think there was one.'

'Why on earth should you have asked about the cook, Catto? You haven't had a touch of the sun, have you?'

'Sergeant Marriott said that when you and he first interviewed Kelsey, he told you he was married to the cook, sir.'

'So he did, Catto, so he did. Quite slipped me mind for the moment. Very well. Carry on.'

When the message was received at the headquarters of the West Sussex Constabulary, it was passed immediately to the chief constable who had issued an order that any communication from the Metropolitan Police should be shown to him first.

The chief constable initialled the message and directed his clerk to send a copy to the divisional headquarters at Steyning.

The superintendent in charge of the Steyning division initialled the message and directed that a copy be sent to the constable stationed at Lancing.

Police Constable John Dawson had been a member of the West Sussex Constabulary for almost twenty-eight years, and for the last seven of them had been stationed at Lancing. He was, therefore, thoroughly familiar with his bailiwick, and had no need to leave his police house in order to answer the questions posed by Divisional Detective Inspector Hardcastle of the Metropolitan Police.

Within minutes of receiving the message from Steyning, he replied to the effect that no market garden in Lancing or in the surrounding area was owned by anyone called Dr Jack Rylance. Neither did any man of the same name appear on the roll of electors for the area. Police Constable Dawson suggested that if the registration number of Dr Rylance's Rolls-Royce could be provided, a look-out would be kept for the vehicle.

The message was seen by the superintendent at Steyning, who forwarded it to the chief constable. Once the chief constable had approved the contents, he sent for an inspector and instructed him to forward the information, such as it was, to DDI Hardcastle in London.

* * *

Twenty-four hours after the request for information had been sent to the West Sussex Constabulary, Marriott handed the reply to Hardcastle.

'The bugger's run, Marriott,' said Hardcastle.

'Yes, sir. I'll send Lipton across to Spring Gardens to see if the county council can find the number of Rylance's Rolls-Royce in the vehicle register.'

'Unless Kelsey was lying about him owning one, Marriott.'

'Well, sir, as one of Rylance's neighbours claimed to have seen him driving a Rolls-Royce this morning, I think that piece of information might be true.'

'It'd make a bloody change, Marriott,' said Hardcastle gloomily.

It appeared that the neighbour was being truthful. Lipton came back with the information that a Rolls-Royce Silver Ghost was registered with the county council under the name of Dr Jack Rylance with an address in Wilton Street, Westminster.

'These are the details of when it was first registered and the number of the vehicle, sir.' Lipton proffered a piece of paper.

'Give it to Sergeant Marriott and ask him to pass those details to the police at Lancing, Lipton.'

On Thursday, the first of May, Sergeant Glover telephoned Marriott to say that the name of Jack Rylance had been found in army records.

'Don't tell me that we're getting somewhere at last, Marriott,' said Hardcastle, and promptly seized his bowler hat and umbrella. It was a Hardcastle foible that he would not wear his overcoat after the last day of April, whatever the prevailing weather. 'Well, come on, Marriott. We haven't got all day.'

The DDI rapidly descended the stairs and he and Marriott strode up Whitehall towards Horse Guards.

'Good morning, Inspector,' said Glover once the detectives were in the provost office once again.

'I understand that Major Sinclair has some information for me.'

'It's not Major Sinclair, Inspector. Not any more. It's Lieutenant Colonel James Corrigan, Welsh Guards.'

'I know Colonel Corrigan,' said Hardcastle, 'but what happened to the major, Sergeant Glover?'

'I really don't know, Inspector, other than to say his departure was rather sudden. I'll take you in to the colonel.'

Corrigan, immaculate in khaki service dress, was standing behind his desk when Hardcastle and Marriott were shown into his office.

'We meet again, Mr Hardcastle.' Corrigan shook hands with the DDI and with Marriott. 'Sutton's Farm, I think. Number 78 Squadron Royal Air Force at Hornchurch, nearly a year ago, if memory serves me correctly. Please sit down.'

'Congratulations on your promotion, Colonel,' said Hardcastle. 'Major Sinclair moved on quickly, but Sergeant Glover did suggest that this was really a lieutenant colonel's post.'

Corrigan glanced at the door leading to the outer office and, noting that it was firmly shut, leaned forward. 'As a matter of fact, Inspector, Major Sinclair had a misfortune. The Provost Marshal decided to pay an unannounced visit and found Major Sinclair rather the worse for drink. Sinclair wisely decided to resign his commission rather than face a court martial for conduct unbecoming. Not the done thing for a provost officer to be caught half-seas over, so to speak. However, to get down to the business in hand, I have the personal details of Jack Rylance here.'

'I hope it's our man, Colonel.'

'I'm sure it is. From reading the details that Major Sinclair left here, it would be too much of a coincidence for it to be anyone else.' Corrigan donned a pair of half-moon spectacles and opened the file. 'Captain Jack Rylance, an officer in the Royal Engineers,' he began, 'was heavily involved in tunnelling under the Messines-Wytschaete Ridge in 1916 and won a Military Cross. But that was before the accident.'

'What sort of accident, Colonel?'

'There was a fall in one of the tunnels – the tunnel where Rylance and his party were working. Rylance was cut off from the rest of his chaps and trapped, alone in this small, stifling chamber with only thirty thousand pounds of ammonal and a quantity of blasting gelignite to keep him company.'

'Ye Gods!' exclaimed Hardcastle. 'It don't bear thinking about, Colonel.'

'I imagine that Rylance thought his time was up.' Corrigan glanced up from the file. 'Soldiers during the war were concerned not so much with dying,' he said, 'but with the manner of their dying. Or worse, the thought of becoming a helpless, blinded cripple. But, unbeknown to Rylance,' he continued, 'help was at hand in the shape of his sergeant. This chap ordered a couple of "kickers" to grab their shovels and they began tunnelling through the obstruction, determined to get Rylance out. It took thirty hours but eventually the sergeant and his men managed to break through to Rylance. Regrettably, by the time Rylance was found, his nerve had gone completely.'

'I think mine would have done too,' commented Marriott.

'One report,' continued Corrigan, fingering a folio, 'describes him as a gibbering wreck.' He closed the file and looked at Hardcastle. 'I think I would have gone mad in the circumstances, Inspector. Anyway, Rylance was repatriated to Craiglockhart War Hospital that had just been set up in Edinburgh for dealing with the effects of damage to the nervous system brought on by war. He was there for a year's psychiatric treatment before he was invalided out of the army. They did what they could for him, but reading between the lines of this report, I don't think he'll ever be right again.'

'But how can you be sure that this is the Jack Rylance we're seeking, Colonel?' asked Marriott. 'Was there any mention of a scar on the left side of his chin or the fact that his ears had no lobes?'

'No, Sergeant Marriott, there was not, but I have to admit that the army is not as good as you chaps when it comes to including descriptions. And it's possible that the scar was the result of an injury that occurred after his discharge from the army.'

'There must've been more than one Jack Rylance in the army during the war.' Marriott continued to press the matter. 'And our Rylance claimed he was in the Royal Army Medical

Corps and was invalided out after being wounded during the
retreat from Mons. With respect, Colonel, the officer you're
talking about could be another Rylance.'

Corrigan frowned and looked back at his file. 'There was
one other thing that might help,' he said. 'The name of the
NCO who saved Rylance's life was Sergeant Roland Kelsey
and he received the Distinguished Conduct Medal for his
bravery. Does that help in any way?'

'Help, Colonel?' said Hardcastle and laughed. 'It confirms
that you've identified our Jack Rylance.'

'One question, Colonel,' said Marriott. 'It's not really relevant to this matter, but you mentioned "kickers" just now.
Why were they called that?'

'"Kickers" was the name they gave to the sappers, usually
miners in civilian life and often from Durham, who would
lie on their backs and kick their shovels ahead of them to
make tunnels of very small diameter. Hence the name. They
were paid seven shillings a day, as against the infantryman's
shilling a day. Mind you, they earned every penny.'

'All we've got to do now is find Rylance,' said Hardcastle
as he and Marriott left Horse Guards and walked back up
Whitehall to the police station.

'Might I suggest an observation in Wilton Street, sir?'

'What for?' Hardcastle stopped and turned to face his
sergeant. A pedestrian behind Hardcastle cannoned into him,
swore and crossed the broad highway that houses the offices
of government.

'I don't think he's abandoned that house for good, sir.
Surely he's got to come back at some time.'

'It might work, I suppose.' The DDI was always reluctant
to accept a suggestion from a subordinate. 'Find out who
we've got available.'

'Keeler, Lipton, Catto and Wilmot, sir,' said Marriott
promptly.

'What about Wood?'

'DS Wood has got a job running at Inner London Sessions,
sir.' As ever, Marriott knew the duties of all the sergeants and
constables under his command.

'Very well, organize it. And it'll be no good unless it's

round the clock. I daresay they'll have to make an arrangement with a neighbour. From what I remember of Wilton Street, anyone trying to keep observation there would stick out like a sore thumb.' Hardcastle carried on walking but then stopped once more. 'Speak to the West Sussex Constabulary again, Marriott.'

'They've already told us that no one called Rylance owns a cottage or a market garden there, sir.'

'Quite right, Marriott, but in view of what we've just heard from Colonel Corrigan, it crossed my mind that if there is any property in Lancing associated with Rylance, it might be registered in Kelsey's name. It's possible that Kelsey's so loyal to Rylance that he'd even help him commit murder. Or at least cover it up.'

Marriott selected Catto and Keeler for the first spell of observation duty, mainly because Catto had already made the acquaintance of some of Rylance's neighbours. But neither officer was happy at being assigned to a duty that could turn out to be interminable.

'The woman who said she'd seen Rylance drive off in his Rolls-Royce, Catto,' began Marriott. 'Whereabouts in Wilton Street did she live?'

'Immediately opposite, Sergeant.'

'Have a word with her and see if she'd be prepared to let you keep a lookout from her upstairs window.'

'I'll speak to the lady first, Basil,' said Catto. 'We don't want to intimidate her. You wait out here until she agrees. If she doesn't, we'll have to find someone else.' He knocked on the door of the house opposite the Rylance residence.

'Good afternoon, Mrs Pritchard.'

'Hello, Mr Catto. Do you need my help again?' Esther Pritchard was a rather attractive buxom lady of about forty. She was also a great talker, and on Catto's first visit she had spoken of the numerous friends she had and how they often visited each other's houses for tea. She also mentioned that her husband was a member of the Diplomatic Service.

'It's rather an imposition, Mrs Pritchard,' said Catto as he

followed the woman into her drawing room, 'but it would be
very helpful if you could see your way clear to allowing us
to keep observation on Doctor Rylance's house for a while.'

'My goodness!' Esther Pritchard put a hand to her mouth.
'Has Doctor Rylance done something terrible? You hear such
awful things these days. It must be something to do with the
war. And just because he's a doctor doesn't mean he can't
commit a crime, does it? After all, there was that Doctor
Crippen who murdered his wife less than ten years ago and
ran away with his mistress.'

'We certainly want to question him with regard to the death
of a young girl, Mrs Pritchard,' said Catto once she had
stopped talking. 'It doesn't mean that he committed a crime,'
he added cautiously, 'and he might prove to be merely a
witness, or even turn out to be no help at all.' He did not
believe Rylance to be innocent any more than Hardcastle did,
but it did not do to broadcast what the police knew. 'However,
we are hoping he'll be coming back soon.'

'Well, of course you can, Mr Catto. Oh, how deliciously
exciting. Is it just you?'

'Er, no, there are actually two of us. My colleague, Basil
Keeler, is waiting outside.'

'Oh!' Esther Pritchard looked a little disappointed that she
would not have the handsome Henry Catto to herself. 'Do
bring him in, Mr Catto.'

'It would be a case of staying all night, Mrs Pritchard.
Would you mind?' Catto was shrewd enough to add his
requests one by one, thereby lessening the chances of Mrs
Pritchard changing her mind.

'On the contrary, Mr Catto, it would be very comforting
to know that there were two policemen in the house.
Particularly now that my husband is away in Versailles. I shall
have a lot to tell him when he gets home at the weekend.'

'One other question, Mrs Pritchard. Are you connected to
the telephone?'

'Naturally.' Esther Pritchard laughed gaily. 'I think we all
are in Wilton Street.'

That pleased Catto, or more particularly Keeler, who would
be the one who would otherwise have had to run all the way

to the police station if Rylance returned. The Royal Automobile Club had recently started putting telephones in their roadside sentry boxes, but Catto did not know of one anywhere near Wilton Street.

In the event, the observation did not last very long at all.

At just after five o'clock that evening, Police Constable John Dawson was patrolling the streets of Lancing when he saw Rylance's open-topped Rolls-Royce drive past him. It contained two men, each wearing a cloth cap and a muffler. The constable ran to the nearest public house and telephoned headquarters with the information before resuming his patrol. The headquarters of the West Sussex Constabulary relayed this information to Scotland Yard which, in turn, forwarded it to Cannon Row police station. The station officer, unaware of the urgency, placed the message in the CID tray in the front office and carried on drinking his tea.

But well before this information found its way to DDI Hardcastle, Rylance's Rolls-Royce drew to a standstill outside his house.

Catto rushed downstairs and telephoned this momentous news to Sergeant Marriott, who then passed it immediately to Hardcastle.

'I've told Catto that he and Keeler should remain inside Mrs Pritchard's house until assistance arrives, sir. Rylance might be armed and we don't want any heroics.'

'Quite right, Marriott. I would have thought the West Sussex Constabulary might've spotted this distinctive motor car when it was on the move,' said Hardcastle.

When, much later, the DDI was to discover that the Sussex police had done so, and that the information was already in the CID tray of the front office, he sent for the station officer. The sergeant received a dressing down that he was unlikely ever to forget, especially when Hardcastle made mention of the officer's suddenly declining prospects of promotion. As many of the CID officers on A Division could testify, the DDI could be extremely wounding when it came to pointing out a policeman's shortcomings to that individual's senior officer.

That the constable at Lancing had also reported there was

a market garden in the area owned by a Roland Kelsey convinced Hardcastle that Kelsey and Rylance had been engaged in what the law calls a joint enterprise in the matter of Lily Musgrave's murder. But Hardcastle had yet to read that useful piece of information.

TWENTY

B y seven o'clock, Hardcastle had mustered three or four constables from Cannon Row police station to take with him to Wilton Street. But as Wilton Street was within the boundaries of Gerald Road subdivision, a part of B Division, most of the uniformed element came from that station. The duty inspector from Gerald Road took charge of the whole uniformed contingent and was directed by Hardcastle to close Wilton Street at each end.

Hardcastle and Marriott had drawn firearms before leaving the police station, and two of the Gerald Road men were also armed. Detective Constable Cecil Watkins had been instructed to borrow a briefcase and bring it with him, and was told to call at each of the houses opposite Rylance's to warn the occupants to stay indoors and to keep away from the windows. The briefcase was a prop so that Rylance or Kelsey, if either of them looked out of the window, would think that Watkins was a door-to-door salesman.

At twenty-five minutes to eight, Hardcastle and Marriott walked casually along Wilton Street and stopped at Rylance's house. Telling Marriott to keep out of sight until Rylance or Kelsey had opened the door, Hardcastle was about to knock when his grand plan of gently persuading Rylance out of the house was brought to nought.

Suddenly, there was the sound of a single gunshot. A matter of moments later the front door flew open and Rylance ran out into the middle of the street.

'Stand to,' he yelled. 'Stand to, for Christ's sake. Get those men to the parapet, Sergeant.' He had had a revolver in his hand when he left his house but for no apparent reason threw the weapon down and started to run towards Upper Belgrave Street. All the time he was screaming hysterically about another attack. 'The bloody Boche are everywhere. Wake up, you idle bastards. We're under attack, dammit! Stand to. Fix your bayonets. They don't like British cold steel.'

'Get after him, Bodkin!' shouted Hardcastle. 'The rest of you stand still,' he said to the remaining detectives.

Liam Bodkin, one of the Rochester Row detectives, sprinted after Rylance, showing a nice turn of speed for a man his age.

But, as quickly as he had started, Rylance stopped running. He turned and began casually to stroll back towards Hardcastle with his hands in his pockets.

'Hello, Inspector. I was just coming to see you.' Rylance stopped and gazed at his Rolls-Royce. 'That's a nice car,' he said.

'What did you want to see me about, Doctor Rylance?' asked Hardcastle.

'It's Sergeant Kelsey, you see. This German came into the house and, well, I suppose Kelsey's instinct took over and he shot him.'

'Is the German dead, Doctor?'

'Oh, yes, definitely. I know a dead man when I see one.' Rylance carried on walking as though he had not a care in the world.

'Yes, of course. You would, being a doctor.'

'A doctor?' Rylance stopped again and turned to face Hardcastle. 'I'm not a doctor, Inspector. I'm Captain Jack Rylance of the Royal Engineers. We're mining down there, just beyond the parados. Look,' he said, pointing towards Grosvenor Place and Buckingham Palace beyond. 'Just over there.'

'Yes, I can see it now.' Hardcastle continued to agree with everything that Rylance said. 'And I must have made a mistake thinking you were a doctor. But why don't we go somewhere quiet and discuss this business of the Germans, eh?'

'Good idea, Inspector.'

'Bodkin,' said Hardcastle, 'run to the end of the road and

get a cab down here as quick as you can.' He signalled to
Catto. 'Use Mrs Pritchard's telephone, Catto, and call the
station. I want the divisional surgeon to attend the station
immediately. Tell the station officer it's a matter of great
urgency.' Next, he turned to Marriott. 'Take charge here,
Marriott. Make sure that the firearm Rylance abandoned is
sent to Inspector Franklin as soon as possible. Then get
someone to see if Kelsey is dead or alive, because I think he
was the one who was shot. If he is alive, get medical attention. Of course, it's just possible that Rylance surprised a
burglar. Or Kelsey did.'

'Very good, sir.' Marriott moved away to deal with the
tasks Hardcastle had just ordered him to do. But inwardly he
was seething with fury. As a first-class sergeant, he knew
exactly what he had to do and did not need Hardcastle to tell
him.

At that point, a cab drove into Wilton Street from the direction of Grosvenor Place.

Hardcastle opened the door. 'After you, Captain Rylance.'

'Thank you, Inspector. As a matter of interest, where are
we going?'

'I thought it might be as well to get out of the firing line
for a while. A very capable captain has just taken over, along
with the reinforcements.' Despite frequently professing ignorance of military matters, Hardcastle was an avid reader of
the *Daily Mail*, from which he had acquired the basic facts
of how the army was run.

'Thank God for that,' said Rylance and relaxed against the
cushions. He remained silent for the whole of the short trip
to Cannon Row police station.

Despite the presence of a police officer whose four chevrons
denoted that he was a station sergeant, Jack Rylance did not
seem to realize that he was in a police station, even when
Hardcastle escorted him into the barren charge room. Perhaps
in his present imaginative state he believed himself to be at
some sort of military HQ.

The station officer appeared at the door between the front
office and the charge room, a large book and a quantity of
paper in his hand.

'What have you got there, Higgins?'

'A charge sheet and the Occurrence Book, sir.'

'Well, you can take them away again.'

'But if he's not to be charged, sir, I must make an entry in the Occurrence Book to the effect that he has been detained at the station,' responded the station sergeant officiously. 'It's in General Orders.'

'I know it is, Higgins,' snapped Hardcastle, 'and as you are so familiar with General Orders, you may recall that when any officer of the rank of detective inspector or above brings a prisoner into the station, he, and he alone, will decide if and when a charge is to be laid. Or if there is to be an entry in the Occurrence Book or, for that matter, in any other damned book. Now take all that bloody stuff away before you send Captain Rylance into a rage.'

'Yes, sir.'

'Where's the divisional surgeon, Higgins?'

'In the matron's office, sir.'

'Ask him to meet me in here.'

A few moments later Dr Lewis Carpenter strolled into the charge room. He was a bluff, portly, general practitioner with a moustache and was bald, save for a fringe of hair that ran around the back of his head from ear to ear. His surgery was within walking distance and he was always happy to attend the station at any hour of the day or night.

'What have you got, Mr Hardcastle? The sergeant said it was urgent.' Carpenter screwed a monocle into his left eye and peered at the prisoner.

'It is, Doctor.' Hardcastle drew Carpenter away from Rylance, who was now sitting quietly on one of the benches in the charge room, and explained at some length all that was known about the former sapper officer.

Carpenter nodded. 'Not the first case I've heard about, Mr Hardcastle. It's this damnable war, you know. I'm pleased you didn't put him in a cell. That could have triggered all manner of shocking memories and would possibly have turned him violent in an attempt to escape, even to the point of harming himself. What's likely to happen to him?'

'He'll be charged with murder, of course, but his defence

counsel will almost certainly cite the rules in M'Naghten's case.'

'I imagine so.' Carpenter sat down on one of the benches and scribbled a few lines in a notebook. He looked up, a pensive expression on his face, and for a few moments idly tapped his teeth with his pencil. 'I think the best idea would be to transfer him to Springfield Hospital at Wandsworth, Mr Hardcastle. They have the facilities for dealing with this sort of thing and they have adequate secure accommodation, should it be needed.'

'Is that your professional recommendation, Doctor Carpenter?'

'Certainly, and I'll give you that in writing.' Carpenter smiled. 'I know how keen the Metropolitan Police is on having lots of pieces of paper.'

'We'll need to provide a guard until a decision is made about what's to happen next.'

'Yes, of course. They're quite used to that sort of thing at the Springfield. Now, if you'd direct me to a telephone, I'll arrange for an ambulance with some beefy attendants, Mr Hardcastle, just in case Rylance gets excited again. And, no doubt, you'll want to send a couple of your men with him.'

'Excuse me, sir.' Marriott appeared in the doorway of the charge room.

'What is it, Marriott?' asked Hardcastle, steering his sergeant into the front office and positioning himself so that he could keep an eye on Rylance through the window that separated the two rooms.

'It's all quiet in Wilton Street now, sir, and I've dismissed the men. We found Roland Kelsey sitting on the floor in the kitchen, which is at the back of the house on the ground floor of Rylance's house. He'd been shot.'

'Fatal?'

'No, sir. It was a flesh wound in the right thigh but he'd lost quite a lot of blood. I had him conveyed to Charing Cross hospital and Catto and Watkins are with him. I told them to stay there until relieved.'

'What for? Kelsey's not under arrest, is he?'

'I'm afraid he is, sir. He admitted assisting Rylance to

dispose of Lily Musgrave's body at Slade House but denied any part in the killing. So I arrested him for preventing the lawful burial of a body.'

'Common Law misdemeanour,' murmured Hardcastle, 'but it'll depend on the Attorney General. He might decide there is enough evidence to charge Kelsey with being an accessory after the fact. What was Kelsey doing at Slade House that weekend, anyway? It's the first I've heard of it.'

'He introduced himself to the other members of staff as Rylance's butler but told them his name was Randolph Harvey, sir. I think he just wanted to keep an eye on his officer.'

'So he's the missing Randolph Harvey. I wonder why the hell he used a different name, Marriott.' Hardcastle shrugged. 'Oh well, there's no need to worry about it. Right now, we've got more important things to deal with.'

The hearing at Bow Street police court the following day was brief. Hardcastle had asked to see the Chief Metropolitan Magistrate in chambers before the court convened. He explained about Jack Rylance, his war experiences, his stay at Craiglockhart hospital and the events leading up to his appearance today.

'Very well, Mr Hardcastle. We'll make it a very brief hearing.'

Jack Rylance was the first to appear in the dock that Friday morning, much to the annoyance of the previous night's haul of prostitutes who believed their profession gave them the right of being the first to appear. Rylance had been sedated by a resident psychiatrist at Springfield and, far from being overawed, appeared slightly amused by his surroundings.

'You have an application, Inspector?' asked the magistrate as Hardcastle stepped into the witness box.

'I do, Your Worship. I ask for a remand in secure accommodation pending a decision by the Attorney General in this case.'

'You have made the necessary arrangements, I take it.'

'I have, sir.'

'Very well. Remanded to secure accommodation for eight days, but dependent upon the Attorney's decision.'

* * *

It was Monday the twenty-first of July when Jack Rylance appeared in the famous Number One Court at the Old Bailey. He was ushered into the dock and peered around the court with the same amused expression as when he had appeared at Bow Street. His gaze took in the bewigged barristers in front of him and beyond them the impressively massive Palladian arch with its pair of twin columns, and its Royal Arms, all carved in oak. Beneath the Royal Arms was the Sword of Justice, and on each of the high-backed leather chairs were the armorial bearings of the City of London.

The usher appeared and opened the proceedings with the customary proclamation: 'Oyez! Oyez! Oyez! All persons having business before this court of oyer and terminer and general gaol delivery pray draw near. Be upstanding.'

The red-robed judge entered, exchanged bows with counsel and sat down.

'The prisoner will stand,' ordered the clerk of the court.

The two warders took Rylance by the elbows and helped him into a standing position.

'Are you Jack Rylance of Wilton Street, Westminster in the County of London?' asked the clerk.

'Yes.'

'You are charged in that on or about the sixth of April in the year of Our Lord one thousand, nine hundred and nineteen, at Epsom in the County of Surrey, you did murder Lily Musgrave, against the Peace. How say you upon this indictment? Guilty or not guilty?'

For a moment or two Jack Rylance appeared bemused by the proceedings, as though they involved someone else. Eventually, he said, 'Oh, yes. Not guilty, My Lord.'

'You may sit down,' said the clerk of the court.

The Attorney General stood up. 'Gordon Hewart for the Crown, My Lord, assisted by my learned junior, Mr Joshua Stacey. My learned friend, Sir Harry Cork, appears for the defence with his learned junior, Mr John Watts.'

'Thank you, Mr Attorney.'

'This is rather a sad case, My Lord,' Hewart began, and outlined the circumstances of Lily Musgrave's murder and the eventual arrest of Rylance. 'Lily Musgrave led a raffish existence, My Lord, pursuing her own hedonistic wants, regardless of anyone else. On many occasions, she removed her clothing for the delectation of lascivious males of dubious character. Rylance mentioned, when questioned in one of his more lucid moments, My Lord, that Lily had accused him of being the father of her unborn child. Despite disbelieving her, he had shot the girl dead. In fact, Miss Musgrave was not pregnant. There appears to be no rational reason for his actions, nor has he offered one.'

'Thank you, Mr Attorney. Do you propose to call any witnesses for the prosecution?'

'Only Divisional Detective Inspector Hardcastle, My Lord, who will outline the facts of the case, and two witnesses to prove the matter of the firearm.'

In measured tones, Hardcastle gave evidence of finding the body at Epsom before outlining the circumstances surrounding Rylance's behaviour immediately prior to his arrest.

Then came the most telling piece of Hardcastle's testimony. 'After Captain Rylance was escorted to Cannon Row police station, My Lord, I interviewed him at some length. Although he did not dispute having shot a woman, he appeared unaware of Lily Musgrave's identity, claiming that he did not know anyone of that name. He maintained throughout his period in custody that the woman he had shot was a German spy. He did not dispute having buried her, either, even though she was a German, he said. He stated that he had attended many battlefield burials and that he and a sergeant, who he refused to name, had assisted him.'

'Thank you, Inspector,' said the Attorney General.

The judge turned to defence counsel. 'Sir Harry.'

'No questions, My Lord.'

Detective Sergeant Marriott gave evidence next. He testified to receiving the round that had killed Lily Musgrave from Dr Spilsbury and handing it to Detective Inspector Franklin. He also testified to taking possession of the revolver thrown down by Rylance at the time of his arrest and handing that to Franklin.

Franklin appeared next and confirmed that the firearm abandoned by Rylance was the weapon used to kill Lily Musgrave.

Sir Harry Cork had no questions for either witness. 'I do not dispute the police evidence of the circumstances leading up to the death of this unfortunate young woman, My Lord. My submission will be that when Rylance committed this murder, he was of unsound mind and was unaware of what he was doing, or if he did know what he was doing, did not know that it was wrong. I would like to call just the one witness.'

'I take it you intend to cite the Rules in M'Naghten's case, Sir Harry.'

'Indeed, My Lord. I call Doctor William Rivers.'

The man who stepped into the witness box was of medium height and unimpressive appearance, neatly dressed in a three-piece suit. He blinked through a pair of pince-nez and occasionally brushed his moustache while giving evidence.

'You are William Halse Rivers Rivers, a fellow of the Royal College of Physicians and a fellow of the Royal Society?'

'I am, My Lord.'

'Doctor Rivers, please tell the court how you came to be acquainted with the accused Rylance.'

'I was a consultant at Craiglockhart hospital in Edinburgh during the war,' Rivers began. 'Captain Rylance was brought to Craiglockhart towards the end of 1916, shortly after the hospital started accepting patients with forms of mental disorder, mainly neurasthenia.'

'Would you tell the court, Doctor Rivers,' said Cork, 'what, in your professional view, is the state of Rylance's health?'

Dr Rivers launched into a lengthy account of his opinion, and described the treatment that he had recommended. His lucid explanation was such that members of the jury were able to understand it all.

'Can Rylance be restored to normality?' Sir Harry Cork's question could not have been more simply put.

And Rivers's reply was similarly brief. 'No.'

'Would you care to elaborate, Doctor Rivers?'

'His condition can be controlled by medication, but he will require constant supervision in order to ensure that the medication is administered in the correct doses and at the proper times. But to answer your question, his present state is, in my professional view, irreversible.'

'Thank you, Doctor Rivers. Please wait there.'

'Mr Attorney?' The judge glanced at Sir Gordon Hewart.

'I have no questions of this witness, My Lord.'

'You may stand down, Doctor Rivers,' said the judge, 'and thank you for your detailed evidence. It has been of great assistance to the court. Do you have other witnesses, Sir Harry?'

'No, My Lord,' said Cork.

The judge summed up the case in a very few words, before reaching the conclusion. 'This is a case, gentlemen of the jury,' he began, 'where in my view the rules in M'Naghten's case apply. Very simply, it is where the accused may have been sane and rational prior to the act he committed, and indeed sane afterwards. However, he may not have known what he was doing at the time of the commission or, on the other hand, he may well have known what he was doing but did not appreciate that it was wrong. You will go now to the jury room and consider your verdict. You must consider whether the prisoner at the bar is guilty of murder or not guilty. But in this case there is a third option, that he is guilty of murder but insane.'

It took the members of the jury precisely ten minutes to reach their verdict. In reality, each had made up his mind before leaving the jury box.

'Gentlemen of the jury, are you agreed upon your verdict?' asked the clerk of the court.

'We are,' said the foreman, rising to his feet. 'We find the prisoner guilty but insane.'

'And is that the verdict of you all?'

'It is, My Lord.'

'As the Attorney General pointed out in his opening address, this is a very sad case,' said the judge. 'The prisoner in the dock is a war hero, of that there is no doubt. Because he has no visible marks of injury, it does not mean that he has escaped injury. In his case, the harm was caused not to his body, but to his mind. The consequence of being trapped underground for thirty hours, and in danger of death by suffocation or by an imminent explosion, does not bear thinking about. The prisoner will please stand.'

Jack Rylance struggled to his feet, again with the aid of the warders.

'Jack Rylance, you have been found guilty but insane of the murder of Lily Musgrave. I can only sympathize with the condition brought about by your war service that caused you to take the life of this young woman. You will be detained in an institution for the criminally insane at His Majesty's Pleasure. Take him down.'

'Kelsey is up at Bow Street tomorrow morning, Marriott,' said Hardcastle.

'Why Bow Street, sir? The offence was committed in Epsom.'

'Bow Street was ordered by the Attorney General, Marriott. I don't think Sir Gordon trusted a bench of lay magistrates in Epsom to do what he'd recommended. But as you arrested Kelsey, the main testimony will be yours.'

'Is he not to be charged as an accessory after the fact, then, sir?'

'No,' said Hardcastle. 'The Director of Public Prosecutions ruled that there was insufficient evidence so the only charge will be preventing a lawful burial.' He paused to fill his pipe. 'Did we ever find out where Rylance's money came from, Marriott? Enough to buy a Rolls-Royce, a house in Wilton Street and a cottage and market garden in Lancing?'

'Kelsey was of the view that it was family money, sir. Apparently his father, also called Jack, was a lieutenant colonel in the Royal Army Medical Corps and was very well off, having inherited a substantial sum on the death of his father, our man's grandfather. Colonel Rylance was killed at Vlamertinge in 1917.' Marriott knew what was coming next.

'Well, I'm damned,' said Hardcastle. 'That must have been the Jack Rylance that the Royal Army Medical College librarian mentioned. We should have followed that up, Marriott. I'm surprised you didn't suggest it.'

The proceedings before the Chief Magistrate at Bow Street police court were brief. Roland Kelsey pleaded guilty to preventing the lawful burial of Lily Musgrave. Marriott gave evidence of arrest and repeated what Kelsey had said at the time.

'Reading the citation for your Distinguished Conduct Medal, Kelsey,' said the Chief Magistrate, 'there is no doubt that Captain Rylance owed you his life and you were still doing your best for a man you continued to see as your superior officer. Nevertheless, although what you did was misguided, it was still wrong. It is, however, a misdemeanour at Common Law, and I do not think that it merits a greater punishment than a conditional discharge. You are free to go, Kelsey.'

Ex-Sergeant Kelsey drew himself briefly to attention. 'Thank you, sir.' He turned smartly to his right and descended the steps from the dock.

Lightning Source UK Ltd.
Milton Keynes UK
UKHW041919231118
332814UK00001B/7/P